THE

COLLECTED

SOULS

MALLORY SPENCER

Developmental editing by Larissa Melo Pienkowski: https://www.lmpeditorial.com/about

Copyediting by Rebecca Brewer: https://www.brewereditorialservices.com/

Proofreading by Heather Hudec: https://simplyspellboundedits.com

Print format ISBN: 979-8-9988896-0-8

ebook format ISBN: 979-8-9988896-1-5

Publishing house: mountainlightspress.com.

TRIGGER WARNINGS ON FINAL PAGE

For Kate. Whether it was the sibling rivalry or the world I saw you create (who really knows), you inspired me to write.

1

TESS

Fuck Hunter. *Fuck* him. *Me, cheat* on him?

I clench and unclench my fists as I stride down a crowded Court Street, largely unimpeded due to the other pedestrians looking at me askance and jumping out of my way.

I snort to myself. All I could think to retort was a basic "Go to hell!"?

I'm so wrapped up in my rage that I nearly miss the turn onto West Union Street. With a *harrumph*, I pivot and begin searching for Ada's silver Corolla.

Where is she? She said she was parked near Jackie O's.

A fat drop of cold rain strikes my face. I screw up my face in anticipation of a downpour (and maybe a tantrum).

"Teresa! Tess!" The sound of my name in a familiar voice cuts through my haze of anger, and I trace it back to a person with bubblegum-pink braids standing next to a silver car, waving wildly with a broad smile.

Almost instantly my fury begins to ebb. Despite myself, I almost smile.

God, it has been a *long* afternoon. But it is over, and I can move on from it.

Well, it's more than a single afternoon that I need to move on from, but I'd prefer not to dwell on that right now. And seeing Ada's face, I don't even want to simmer on it. I'll simmer when I'm alone, in a few hours.

Ada shrieks and dives into her car as the dark clouds above release their burden all at once.

I yelp and sprint the last few yards to her car and jump into the passenger seat.

"Hellurrr!" My best friend and roommate greets me with a laugh as rain hammers on the roof of the vehicle.

I bring my almost-smile into a full smile as I echo her hearty greeting.

As I relax into the seat, I check that my phone didn't get too wet (it didn't, but it's almost dead). My gaze slides from the battery icon to the lock screen wallpaper.

Hunter, arm around his black labrador, smiles at me from the screen.

Instantly any pleasure at seeing Ada evaporates. I press my lips together and shove the phone deep into my purse.

Rat bastard.

Ada pulls us away from the curb and turns down the Portugal. The Man song that plays barely loud enough to hear over the rain. She glances at me. "Uh-oh."

I scowl at her. "What?"

"Don't talk to me like that; you can't intimidate me," she teases. "But 'uh-oh' as in, 'I know that look and someone got on your bad side.'"

I don't answer.

"Wait, was it Hunter?" The humor vanishes from her voice. "You two were just on a date, right?"

"Yeah," I mutter. "It was Hunter."

"Do you want to talk about it?"

Before I can think of whether I do, a blinding flash of gold light sears my retinas. I screw my eyes shut and hold up my hand to block the light.

"*Agh!*" cries Ada. The car swerves slightly. "God*damn*, that is some lightning! Never seen any so bright."

I blink away the afterimage, but it doesn't appear to be in the shape of lightning—it just seems to me that the whole dang sky lit up at once.

And... I don't hear any thunder.

Maybe the rain is too loud to hear thunder? I bite my lip.

"Are you okay, Tess?" Ada jolts me back to the reality of my life as it stands now.

I close my eyes, rub my forehead with one hand. "I don't wanna talk about it," I say flatly.

"Okay."

We ride without speaking from Athens to Jacksonville, an eternity I fill by taking deep breaths and trying not to implode from Hunter's assholery. My eyes burn (hopefully from the effort of holding off disaster and not from anything else).

"I'm bored with my music," Ada says abruptly. She unplugs the aux cord from her phone and hands it to me without taking her eyes off the road. "Play some of your own."

Her gesture, even so small, makes my throat tighten. *Don't you dare fucking cry, Tess.* "Thanks," I force out. After a few moments of pondering, I settle on George Ezra's *Wanted on Voyage* to soothe my soul. I start with "Over the Creek" and close my eyes, letting the music wash over me and assuage the inflammation of my soul.

It stops raining by the time we reach my parents' home, the blue two-story house I grew up in, fronted with a child's dream of a yard and surrounded by woods.

Without warning, my reality whacks me upside the head the moment Ada puts the car in park; my anger snap-freezes into dread, and I find myself unable to move.

Ada swings her legs out of the car before noticing that I haven't budged. "Are you good to do this? We can go home now if you want."

Hunter's words blare on repeat through my head.

Oh shit, *I can't do this*. My breath hitches.

"Hey," Ada says in a reassuring voice, "just because you've known for a year today, doesn't mean you have to tell them now."

Ada and I had planned this family dinner to tell my parents I'm bi, a year to the day after I had learned about this part of myself.

The same day I'd intended to come out to Hunter.

The same day I *did* come out to Hunter.

"I'm fine," I lie, steeling myself for whatever might come next and climbing out of the car.

"Hi!" I call out as I enter the front door, taking off my shoes.

"We have ar*riiiiived*!" sings Ada from just behind me.

"Hi, Tess!" my mom calls back. Her voice comes from the back of the house.

Ada and I follow her voice to the kitchen, the delicious smell of alfredo sauce strengthening along the way.

My stomach growls. I'd had lunch what seems like a lifetime ago, decades before Hunter had said what he did.

I round the corner into the kitchen and can't help but release a shocked bark of laughter—my parents have draped themselves in white bedsheets. They wave their arms around underneath the cloth, and upon hearing me laugh, they begin to wail in a manner reminiscent of ghosts in old children's cartoons.

"What do you think of our Halloween costumes?" the taller white form moaned.

"Did you...forget to cut eyeholes or what?" I ask. "Can you see anything?"

"Noooooo," the shorter supposed ghost howls. "Your father and I didn't want to ruin perfectly good sheets!"

"Oh my god." I shake my head. "Are these seriously going to be your costumes?"

The taller form throws off the sheet to reveal my father. "Nah," he answers in a normal voice. "We're planning on being Medusa and a petrified victim."

"Oh, nice!" Ada says.

"Thanks," my dad replies. He looks down at his companion. "Are you done playing ghost, Maureen? I'm hungry."

My mother scoffs, tossing off her own sheet. "Didn't you have a late lunch?"

"Yes. What's your point?"

Ada breaks in. "Hey, Asher. How are midterms going for your class?"

My dad beams and commences rambling about the inorganic chemistry class he teaches at the local university, where I had studied nursing for a year before dropping out and working full-time at a local bookstore.

I chew my lip, zoning out of their conversation. Do I even want to tell my parents tonight? Tell them I'm bi, and/or that I broke up with Hunter? I mean, Hunter is pretty freaking likely to come up, considering we'd been dating for three years, and he is (was) a significant reason why I decided to go back to college next year.

We've migrated to the table and begun eating when my mom pulls me back to the plane of existence I typically reside in. "Have you completed your re-enrollment form yet? The early action deadline is next month, right?"

"November 15th," I reply absentmindedly, dragging some pasta around in sauce with a fork. "And no, I haven't."

"Are you ever going to tell us what you want to major in this time?" my dad teases.

My throat tightens. I slowly set down my fork, staring at the blue-and-white-striped placemat. "Women's, Gender, and Sexuality Studies," I whisper.

There's only a heartbeat between my words and any response, but it's long enough for my eyes to burn with tears.

"Honey, that's great!" my mom exclaims. "But what's wrong?"

I swallow without looking up. "Hunter and I broke up."

"Oh, honey," my mom murmurs.

I shake my head frantically. "No. I don't want pity right now. I don't really even want sympathy right now. I don't want to talk about it, I don't want to think about it. Not right now. Please, can we pretend that everything is normal?" My being starts to crack apart.

No one says anything.

Then Ada clears her throat. "*Well*. I have something to admit: I made a *huge* mess out of the kitchen during lunch today when trying to fix stroganoff. I *think* I cleaned it all, but if you find something splattered say, on the kitchen wall, Tess, I hope you can forgive me."

Somehow I make it through the rest of dinner without imploding.

And without telling my parents what I really wanted to tell them. I can't. I just can't.

Ada and I say our goodbyes and drive back toward the apartment in silence, no music to cushion reality or distract from it.

Meanwhile, I try to glue my cracked self back into one piece, so I don't fall apart entirely.

"Do you want to talk about it?" Ada asks about halfway to Athens.

I think back to what he said to me that solidified the need for a break-up. "Yeah, I don't know. I just thought I could trust him. He fooled me for three years." I shrug miserably. "I just—I don't know."

"I'm sorry, Tess."

I shrug again, not wanting to say anything more.

About five minutes away from our apartment, Ada starts patting down her pockets. She swears. "Tess, I think I forgot my flash drive in the library when I was there this morning. Do you mind if we stop by so I can see if it's there?"

"Yeah, sure," I say glumly. When will the glue dry? Will it have a chance, or will I shatter before then?

We soon enough pull up in front of the university library. Ada, parking the car on the edge of the road, turns on the hazard lights and runs inside.

I slouch in my seat and stare at the building after my friend. After a few moments of scanning the façade, something catches my eye.

Something that had never been there before: a red door.

I stare vacantly at it for a while, trying to comprehend its presence. Cardinal red, frame and all, with a brass doorknob, it looks like the entrance to someone's home. But what is it doing there, against the solid brick wall of the library? What is its purpose, considering there is no corresponding door on the inside?

It must be some college student prank.

My eyes drift away but are immediately drawn back when the door opens inward (*into the wall?*) and out spills light and a person. Both collapse onto the sidewalk.

I straighten in alarm. When the person crumpled on the sidewalk doesn't move, I hurriedly unbuckle my seatbelt and exit the car. I run across the empty street to where the warm light, much like midday sunlight, illuminates the motionless body.

Before me lies a rangy, brown-skinned man, perhaps in his mid-to-late-twenties. Blood trickles from his nose and from beneath his rather floppy dark hair.

I check for breath and a pulse as soon as I reach him—both present, both steady.

I remove the bandana holding back my hair and press it against the cut I find along his hairline. Meanwhile, I glance along the length of his body, wondering if he has any identification or emergency contacts on his person.

The only thing I can glean is that he has a vaguely unusual fashion sense: he sports a battered navy jacket, a white sash around his waist, Bangs high tops, and...what looks like a pocket watch hanging from his neck?

I survey my surroundings to see if anyone else is around. No one is here; everyone must be busy partying or studying for midterms; it is a Saturday night in October, after all.

With one hand, I pat my pockets for my phone. I curse when I pull it out to find it dead.

Is there anyone on the other side of the door? Fear rises in my throat when it occurs to me that maybe this man had been hurt by someone on the other side. That fear turns to terror when I see what lies on the other side of the door.

Because it is *not* the inside of the library. Nor is it a brick wall.

There stands before me a cavernous cylindrical room ten stories high and ringed by walkways and doors. Doors of all colors and designs, scores of them. More walkways and even stairs arch across the room, connecting one level to another. Vines and flowers drape over handrails and snake up the wall, fed from above by a bright light almost like the sun's. Directly across the room is a mirror, three feet high and ten feet long. Below that is a console of the same length covered in all sorts of buttons and switches.

I swallow and turn back to the man. Who the fuck *is* he?

As if in response to my thought, he opens his eyes. "Rhys?" He looks up at me but seems unable to focus on my face. "Rhys—where is she?"

I withdraw slowly to avoid startling him into action. My heart hammers in my chest.

With effort, he sits up, swaying slightly. He runs his hand over his face.

The blood and cut vanish. Not smeared, not wiped onto his hand, just gone. Entirely.

I gasp and jump to my feet.

His eyes focus and fall on me. His eyebrows shoot upward. "Teresa?"

"Wh—? H—how do you—?" I can't even choke out *how does this stranger know my fucking name.*

The man stares off into the distance, exhales strongly. His eyebrows knit together before he turns back to me. "Where are we?" His voice is urgent.

"Uh... Athens? Ohio? United States."

Why did I just answer that? I should *probably* be running the fuck away from here.

"What is your national language? What is the most popular book in the world? How is your calendar organized?" He speaks so quickly, and in an accent I don't think I recognize, that for a second I can't understand him. As he reels off the questions, he makes his way to his feet.

"Are you serious? What the fuck?"

"Tell me."

"We don't have a national language, but it's basically English. Probably the Bible, but I'm not sure, and don't ask which version. What was the last question?"

He shoves his hands into his hair. "Deep hells, this is number twenty-six. How is it the twenty-sixth?"

I find this an excellent moment to creep toward the library doors.

I'm halfway there when he snaps his gaze back to me. "Teresa. She will be coming after you next."

"Oh, *hell* no. I am not entertaining *shit*. Goodbye." I hurry to the entrance.

Before I can get more than two feet farther away, a strong hand snaps around my wrist.

I shriek and struggle to free myself.

"I'm sorry," the stranger says. "But I'd rather you not get far away from the ISERE. See, the Collector is coming for you."

I clench my jaw to keep it from trembling as I try to figure out what the word *ahy-sare-ee* is. "Um, do you speak in the third person sometimes? Are *you* this Collector?"

"No, I am the Keeper. The Collector is like bone—signifying death, with white hair, white skin, white dress."

"Y-you're insane."

Am I the insane one? There's no way a man fell out of a door that opened into a brick wall. There's no way a room exists on the other side of said door. There's no way I could have really come across a stranger who knows my name and says such bizarre things.

"It's my turn to ask random questions," I announce. My mind fumbles for a way to break free of his grip. "What year am I in school?"

"How does your school system even work?" At least he's humoring me and not dragging me beyond the door that can't exist?

I jerk my arm. "What's the last book I read?"

"How could I know that?"

"You know my name." Tears of terror spill down my cheeks.

"That is because—" He cuts himself off. "Teresa, I can explain. Just stop trying to run away and we can talk."

I turn my face away. "Will you *please* let me go?" I beg.

Emotions chase each other across the man's—the Keeper's?—face: frustration, sadness, and finally, grief.

I take the chance. I relax my lower arm and in one motion twist it toward the man's thumb and yank it away.

Then I run.

I find Ada at the information desk, leaning on the counter with a bored expression that quickly turns to concern when she sees me.

"Tess. What's wrong?"

"Can we leave ASAP, please? I really want to go home." My throat locks up when I try to tell her that *a stranger who knows my name is out there.*

"Yeah, sure, I'm just waiting on the employee to find the lost and found box. Kind of funny how he can't find the lost and found, right?" She gives me a feeble smile alongside her attempt at a joke, and I know she's trying to cheer me up.

Then she looks over my shoulder, and the feeble smile slides right off her face.

My limbs begin to quake all over again. Is it the Keeper, come to finish me off? Slowly, painfully, I turn.

Smack in the middle of the floor stands a massive, black, opalescent cube, nearly twice my height in all dimensions. It emanates an almost imperceptible hum, one that I think I can *feel* underneath my racing heart.

"What the fuck is that?" Ada whispers.

My mouth goes dry. I find I can't answer, not even with a simple, "I don't know."

A portion of the cube, the size and shape of a door, sinks into the depths of the cube and dissipates into nothingness.

Ada and I stare into the black maw.

A flicker of movement comes from within. Something bone-white emerges from the maw: a floor-length skirt, followed by lightly swaying hands, then the rest of a tall, emotionless woman, everything about her as white and cold as snow.

"The Collector?" I rasp.

As if in response, a crushing weight slams down upon me; the air is pushed from my lungs, my hands and knees are forced to the floor.

The woman drifts toward me. Is she even walking? Her skirt rustles as she moves, but not quite in a way that suggests footsteps beneath. Her unnaturally pale fingers twitch purposefully, each movement leaving a fleeting line of gold in its wake.

I struggle against the weight but am unable to throw it off. My eyes widen as she nears. Still I am paralyzed.

She is fifteen feet away.

Ten feet away.

Five.

A screech sounds from above. In an instant the weight upon me is lifted.

I tumble over, gasping for breath, and look up.

An eagle composed of multicolored streaks of light dives and claws at the Collector, trailing sparks. A globe of golden threads forms, breaks, and reforms around it, but the bird smashes through before the globe can entrap it.

The woman in white snaps her left hand upward. Grasps the eagle by the neck.

The bird dims and dissolves into shadows that fade under the fluorescent lighting of the library.

The Keeper emerges from behind the great cube, his hands enshrined in glowing green light. "Teresa," he snaps without taking his eyes off the Collector. "*Run*."

I stagger to my feet, grab Ada, and obey him. We race toward the back doors of the library. Only when we reach them do I risk a glance over my shoulder to see bright flashes of light.

Ada shoves at the doors so hard that her feet skid across the floor, but the doors do not budge.

"You okay?" I ask as she catches herself.

"No," she mutters. "Something's wrong. Can you help me?" Her beseeching eyes meet mine.

Except they aren't her eyes. They are solid gold. No pupils, no irises, no sclerae. Just an expanse of metallic coldness.

"What's happening to me, Tess?" Her face and voice plead to me. "What's in my head?"

"A-Ada?" I step back.

"Tess, please," she begs. "Help me. Something is *ripping me apart!*" Ada wails and claws at her head. Her wild hands catch at her necklace and snap the chain. She flings the necklace away to continue digging into her skin.

I freeze. Completely and totally, I freeze: my lungs, the blood in my veins, my heart, my intestines, my thoughts.

"It hurts so much!" Ada shrieks.

I scream once, and again as my best friend *crumbles*, her head and shoulders and hands and torso and finally her legs falling off in chunks before dissolving into dust that vanishes into nothing.

2

— • —

THE KEEPER

As Teresa runs away, the Collector gestures; a fiery light streaks toward me.

I stride forward, hands held in front of me as if to catch the light. Magic surges through me and into the air before me. The millisecond before the light reaches me, it strikes an invisible barrier and billows outward to every side, dissipating before finding an edge.

I clap my hands to release a shockwave directed at the Collector.

She only steps back from the force.

I follow the shockwave with two slashes of my hands in quick succession, sending orange bands of light careening in the Collector's direction.

She waves her hands. The orange bands swerve away and swing back toward me.

As I dodge the first, the second clips my left wrist and snaps around it.

My arm goes dead; I can no longer feel the energy of magic flowing through it. I grimace and snap the fingers of my right hand.

The floor beneath the Collector's feet turns gaseous.

She plummets.

I snap my fingers once more to return the floor to its solid state, trapping her in the material of the floor.

This will not slow the Collector for long.

But now I need to find Teresa and bring her back to the ISERE. Which direction did she go?

It is then that I hear a scream. And another.

I sprint toward the source, my left arm heavy from the magic blocker.

I find Teresa by an exit, her round face as white as the Collector's.

When she sees me, she stutters, "A-Ada. She—she—she just—"

Instantly I know what happened. My heart shatters, and I feel like I am falling, falling through the floor and through the earth. *Not again, not this all over again.*

The part of me most desperate to survive scrabbles for the rest of my soul and hauls it upright. *Break apart later, Thane.*

I reach past Teresa and shove at the exit door, pull on it, force magic into it, anything to get it to open.

It stays firm.

I grit my teeth. The Collector's spell, which cut off the building from the outside, strengthened since I fought my way inside. I turn to the dazed woman beside me. "We need to hide."

"This wouldn't have happened if I hadn't gotten out of the car," she murmurs distantly. "What's even happening right now? Am I on drugs?" She holds up her hands and stares at them as if they could give her an answer.

"Teresa," I say as calmly as I can manage. "I am so sorry for what happened, but we need to *run,* to *hide*."

"Where the hell could I go?"

"I can help you. Come with me—we need to buy time so I can fend off the Collector."

Teresa looks at me, a little more grounded. "You weren't lying about her, were you?"

"No, I was not lying. I can protect you, if you let me."

She laughs mirthlessly. "Protect me? From what exactly? This magical bullshit stuff? You know what, sure. I'd like to see you try. While you're at it, make Ada reassemble."

That is a discussion for later. I pull on Teresa's arm and briskly lead her up the stairs.

As we hurry past the fourth-floor landing, the lights go out.

The Collector has fully sealed the building now. Even the electricity is cut off. I wonder about the air.

I slow, holding my hand before me. A sphere of warm white light gathers in my palm, illuminating the stairwell around us. I nudge the light upward and continue forward.

The light bobs along above us.

"Oh my god, this *is* magic, isn't it?" Teresa's voice drips with something like horror.

I can imagine how real this unreal situation must be beginning to feel for her. "Yes, it is," I tell her softly.

We reach the seventh and highest floor of the library, both panting. The light above our heads extinguishes itself, plunging the floor into near-complete darkness. The only light comes from the lampposts outside. Faintly illuminated are the rows upon rows of stacks. Scattered around their bases I can faintly see the occasional desk and armchair.

"Teresa," I murmur. "You need to hide as best you can. If that means going to a lower floor once the Collector gets here—go. Wait a moment." I cup my right hand before me, my left still chained by the magic blocker, and whisper over it. Glowing green, silver, and gold symbols flow from the tips of my long fingers and over my many rings to pool in my palms. When done, I hold out a warm object that resembles a chunk of quartz. "Take it. It is the best I can do at the moment, but as long as it is within a hand's width of you, it can stop the Collector from seeing you. However, you *need* to hide and stay quiet." I do not know her, but it would break me if the Collector took her. *Never again, never again.*

Teresa pulls the object from my fingertips. "Uh..."

I barrel on. "One more thing—can you whistle?"

She shakes her head.

"Here." I remove a ring from my right hand's third finger and hand it to Teresa. "If there is an opportunity for you to leave the building, run. Run to the ISERE—that's the door, the red door—this is the key. Go inside, *shut the door.* You will be safe there. If you lose this or allow the Collector to take it, no key will trust you ever again."

Teresa stares at the key, clearly baffled, but dons it nonetheless.

"*Go!*" I urge.

She runs.

My only reassurance is that there are not nearly as many doors on this floor as there are in the ISERE. After making sure Teresa has disappeared into the dimness, I hurry around the floor, sealing the entrances as best I can. My mind races, but no plan is within reach.

Perhaps my only choice is to distract the Collector long enough for Teresa to escape. I can survive that, can I not? I have so many times before. I did minutes ago.

I find a spot equidistant from both stairwells. There I wait, my fingers dancing from the energy in my veins.

A few minutes later, I sense someone at the barrier atop the front staircase. It will be only moments before the Collector breaks through it.

I search my thoughts to see if a plan is materializing but find none. I grit my teeth.

The barrier atop the stairs shatters.

The Collector, so pale, seems to glow in the dim light, I notice as I peer through the shelves.

I tug a book off a shelf and toss it toward the back stairwell.

She pauses, then glides over to the stairs. Once she sees the book and the intact barrier, she turns in the direction in which Teresa had run.

I slip along after her, thoughts tumbling through my mind without tumbling into place. I watch as the Collector floats off toward Teresa. "Collector!" My voice makes me flinch—so loud in the silence.

Without waiting, I sprint back the way I came, throwing the sound of my footsteps down the front set of stairs. I slide to a stop across from the doorway and duck behind an armchair, my heart pounding.

Behind the chair, I begin forming a spell in my cupped hand.

The Collector whips her head around. Her cold gaze finds me instantly in the darkness.

I release the spell.

She blocks it with an inhumanly quick flick of the arm, deflecting it toward the ceiling, where it explodes.

The lights shatter with it; glass and plastic rain down around us like hail.

Reflexively, I raise my arms above my head to shield myself from the falling debris.

A mistake.

The Collector flashes to an arm's length away from me. I have no time to react before her hands clutch my head.

Under her touch, it is as though teeth tear through my skull and into my brain, into my mind and soul.

My vision goes dark. I lose all connection to my body, all-consumed as I am by the jaws tearing at my soul.

No, no, stop, let me go—

Something is burrowing into my head, clawing at me, ripping me apart. It tears at different parts of me, dredging up thoughts and memories that *I don't want it to touch.*

Please let me help you. Why won't you let me help you? No, believe me, everything will be all right, I'll find a way out—

Eventually the pain and shock subside just enough for me to regain physical sensation but not control; I am on my knees, the hands on my head are now mine, clawing, clawing, clawing, as if I can dig this incorporeal worm out of my mind.

"Stop, please..." The sob tumbles from my mouth without any premeditation or effort. Tears stream down my cheeks alongside my scraping fingernails.

What has happened to the people of the last twenty-five universes will happen to me, I will crumble, I will disintegrate, I will become fragments in the Collector's mind.

I will no longer be, just like everyone I have ever known.

3

— · —

TESS

An explosion rips through the air around me, followed a moment later by a man's scream.

I hunch down farther under the desk and squeeze my eyes tight.

The Collector had passed by me just moments before, and against my instincts to *run, dammit, run,* I wait to make sure she is long gone. For a long time, all I can hear is my breath. Finally, I cautiously push out the chair and wait a few more moments. No one approaches.

Or maybe the Collector is waiting just out of sight. (But then, if that's the case, I'm screwed either way.) So I crawl out from under the desk.

I wince as my hands and knees are pierced with broken glass and plastic. I sweep the debris aside and stand; the detritus is from the burst lights, I realize as I look at my surroundings. I am alone. Shivering at the chill air blowing in from the broken windows, I make my way across the floor, sliding my feet as I go so that the glass and plastic don't crunch underfoot. I stop every few feet to look for signs of life.

Near the top of the front set of stairs, I hear a voice. I freeze and strain to make out who it might be.

"No, please do not take her, not again, not this all over again..."

It sounds like the Keeper. And he sounds like Ada did right before she—

I choke a little at the thought. Shivering violently, I approach the aisle from which the Keeper's voice comes pleading.

There he is, on his knees, fingernails raking down his cheeks.

"Keeper?" I whisper.

He raises his head.

My blood runs cold as our eyes meet. His golden eyes seem to glow in the darkness.

"Teresa," he groans, his voice doleful and pained. "Please run."

I can't even scream. Only a strangled cry issues from my throat. I turn and run for the stairs, but at the top step, something catches my foot and catapults me down, sending the magical quartz flying from my hand.

The next thing I know, I am lying on the landing, in so much pain that my head swims. I sit up but cry out at the sharp pain in my right arm and hip.

I can't do it. I'm dead. The Collector will find me. My downfall was literally a fall down the stairs. What a way to go as a ninety-year-old, let alone a nineteen-year-old.

White fills my vision as the Collector appears in front of me. A light appears to hover above her head.

I wince. "Let's go, bitch," I groan from the floor. "I can still punch with my left."

She doesn't answer.

Hands hook themselves under my armpits from behind and pull me up to eye-level with the Collector, a few inches off the floor. *Who is strong enough to pull me up like this?* I try to see who the hands belong to, but when I look, I cannot see anyone. What, are these hands *ghostly* or *spectral* or something?

But I have to admit, I'm relieved she isn't forcing me to stand on my badly bruised (hopefully not broken) leg.

The Collector cocks her head, her long, fine white hair falling to the side.

"What?" I spit, as if I'm not trembling. "Don't believe me?" *Oh, god, please don't make me crumble to nothing.*

She places a soft hand on my cheek.

I recoil, but her hand stays with my face. "That's about as cold as your frozen, dead heart," I growl.

The Collector purses her lips.

"Do you even *have* a h—" Midsentence, my words are cut off. I hurl silent curses at the unfazed Collector.

Her hand shifts up to my temple. Something like a static shock passes between us, and with it comes the feeling as though my very soul is being cracked open and prodded.

I writhe, but can't break free, can't escape this violation.

Then it stops.

I slump, shuddering, in the grip of the invisible hands.

"Collector," says an entreating voice from the top of the stairs. Unsteady, the Keeper stands there. His eyes are still golden.

I feel the Collector's hand curl into a fist against my face.

As if in response, the Keeper screams. His knees buckle and his hands claw at his head. Abruptly he stops. He straightens and stares at the Collector with steely eyes. Eyes that are clear and green. "Let them go," he demands, his voice strong, his accent changed. *(Australian?)*

The Collector stiffens.

I turn to her and watch her eyes widen.

"Let them go, or I destroy myself," the Keeper decrees. Electricity begins to crackle over his skin. His fingers are crooked.

Something fiery and overwhelming (Rage? More terror?) erupts from an unknown source deep inside me. Next thing I know, my knuckles slam into the Collector's jaw, snapping her head backward.

The invisible hands release me; I cry out when I hit the floor.

Through my haze of pain, I swing my head side to side, searching for the Collector. The light has disappeared, as has she. But I can still see the Keeper's faint silhouette at the top of the steps.

He staggers and crumples forward. He grasps at the handrail, only slowing his fall before he comes to a stop sprawled halfway down to the landing.

"Are—are you—?" I am too pained and befuddled to finish asking if he is okay, or back to normal, or *some*thing, so I just close my mouth and lean back against the wall.

After a time of both of us merely breathing in the dark, the Keeper waves his hand to the steps above him. "There was a tripwire spell up there." His accent has reverted to normal—lilting and rolling like ocean waves.

"You're telling me."

The stairwell lights flicker on. I squint until my eyes adjust.

The Keeper gingerly pushes himself upright and makes his way over to me. He settles next to my feet with a wince. "You are injured." His voice is slower now, devoid of that frantic energy from when he had woken and later urged me to hide.

"No shit," I sigh.

He holds his hand over my knee. "May I?"

"I guess." I don't know what he plans to do, but I'm too tired and overwhelmed to ask.

The Keeper sets his hand on my leg and closes his eyes. A warmth, just like what the quartz emanated, spreads from his hand throughout my body.

Shards of glass and plastic, pushed out by my healing tissues, clink to the floor. The broken bones in my right arm click back into place with only a twinge. All my aches and pains subside, my head clears a bit.

This *must* be magic. I don't know how to feel about that. "Thanks," I say. "You might want to try that on yourself."

As though only just feeling his broken skin, the Keeper touches his face. The scratches from his fingernails turn from red to pink to the brown of his skin.

I wait until he is finished to ask, "Is the Collector gone? Are we still trapped? What even *was* all that?"

The Keeper wearily stands. "I am not certain where the Collector went, but I do believe she will be avoiding us for a short time. We are no longer trapped, and if you come with me, I can explain things." He extends his hand.

I frown up at him. "I won't leave without my friend." Tears spill down my cheeks as I think of what happened. *(No, this is magic, that was just an illusion. Ada is fine, the Keeper can bring her back. This is all magic, right?)* I swipe at my eyes. The moisture of the tears on my face and hands reminds me of the glue holding me together—the glue I think is failing to hold me together.

The Keeper lowers his hand, a despondent expression settling across his face. "Teresa...she is gone."

I shake my head. "No. She isn't." My voice quavers despite my conviction.

He crouches in front of me. "She died, Teresa. The Collector killed her. I...I have seen it happen before. I know how...how it goes." For just a second, his eyes seem hollow. Then the look vanishes.

I shake my head again, screwing my eyes shut and pressing my lips together, but tears spill down my cheeks. When I finally feel like I can speak without sobbing, I tell him, "Prove it."

He hesitates. "I will try." He helps me to my feet, and we head down the stairs. He pries at a glowing orange band on his wrist for two flights of stairs, then begins tapping at the band and muttering under his breath.

I don't know if it's the remaining fog in my head, or my auditory processing disorder, but I can't tell if he's speaking English. Either way, I don't bother to ask.

"Ah!" he exclaims as we pass the second floor. The band breaks off his wrist and dims until it dissolves into shadow, like the eagle in the Collector's grip.

The first floor of the library is empty. The only sound is that of the heat blowing through the air ducts.

I try to call Ada's name, but all that comes out is a croak. My chest tightens until I can barely breathe. "Bring her back," I gasp to the Keeper.

There's the grief on his face again. What is he grieving? There is nothing to grieve, Ada is just hidden, he can bring her back, Ada and I can go back to our lives after this—

The Keeper widens his stance and holds his hands about a foot apart, level with his chest. At first, nothing seems to happen. Then I notice that the veins in his hands have begun to glow bright green, branching away from his right ring finger.

His breathing becomes labored. Sweat beads on his face.

I search for Ada in the vicinity, but she is still nowhere to be found. My heart sinks.

Then out of the corner of my eye, I see motion. I whip around to see a small object fly up from the floor beside the exit and hover, quivering slightly, between the Keeper's glowing hands.

With a gasp, the Keeper drops his hands; the light fades, the object falls to the ground.

As the Keeper leans against a table, panting, I approach the object. A fine gold chain, a pile of charms. A necklace.

I gingerly pick it up and look through the charms.

A sparrow, an emerald in the shape of a teardrop, a mushroom, a tiny compass, a bold letter "A."

Ada's necklace. I can remember when she found the sparrow and mushroom charms, and I had given her the "A." The others had come before we met last year, in our dorm a few days before college started.

The necklace is broken at the clasp.

I hold it to my chest.

"I am sorry, Teresa," the Keeper tells me as he wipes sweat from his brow. "That is all that is left of her."

"She's dead?" My voice is so distant that I can barely hear it.

"Yes." His voice is so gentle that I can hardly bear it.

"What happened to her?" The more time passes, the more real everything is: the feeling of existing in my body, the sense that my world was never what it seemed, the loss of my best friend.

"The Collector happened. She—cuts apart people's souls, keeping the parts she wants and consuming the rest. When the Collector is finished with her victims—Beggars—she breaks apart the bonds between most of their molecules in order to get more energy from them. This...makes them disintegrate entirely."

Dizziness sweeps over me. I catch myself against a table. (God, this can't be real, can it?)

"How do you know that?"

He doesn't answer, just stares morosely at the floor.

"How do you know?" I repeat, pain running under my voice like a river still flows under ice.

"This has happened before," he finally answers, still staring at the floor.

Fury slams into me like a wrecking ball. I want to kill the man who told me my friend is dead, the man who did not bring her back, I want him to have disintegrated too. "Why didn't it happen to you too?" *Why is my friend dead and not you?*

The Keeper gives me an answer I can only see as an excuse. "The Collector was searching for specific information from me, not for pieces of my soul to take. I was not a typical Beggar, though may have progressed to that, given time. But before that could happen, I, ah—was possessed by a person the Collector does not want to destroy, thereby enveloping my soul and forcing the Collector to release me."

I try to cut him apart with my gaze. I don't care about this, I don't care about it, all I care about is Ada.

The Keeper forges on with his explanation. "The Collector victimizes people in two ways: the first way affects the vast majority of people, and ultimately kills them by turning them into Beggars; the second affects very few people—she scours the earth for someone whose entire soul she wants to subsume and incorporate into her own." He pauses. "The difference between the two is that with Beggars, she takes select memories, and with those she subsumes, she augments her own soul." His voice becomes soaked in grief. "The person who possessed me is the last woman whose soul she targeted to be subsumed. Her name is Rhys."

I don't care about this, I don't care about it, all I care about is Ada. But she is gone. "No," I say aloud, as if that will alter reality, stifle the pain welling up inside me. "No, no, *no*." How many times must I say it to stop knowing? The glue holding me together is dissolving. "You're lying to me. Ada's not dead. She can't be. Magic isn't real anyway. I can't—" I gasp for air. "I'm going home. My parents will help. This isn't what I think it is."

"Teresa," he says gently.

"Magic Man." Though quaking, I lift my chin.

"Teresa, this is real. The Collector wants your soul, and she will be back any moment. You cannot go home—you cannot risk her tracking you there and killing your parents too."

"You're *lying to me*! Even if you were telling the truth, I don't give a *damn* whether the Collector comes and does whatever she will to me, but it wouldn't matter if I did, because *you* won't be able to protect me!" My voice has risen to a shout, but I don't care, I don't care, no one else can hear me, and this pain inside me will make me explode if I don't rip it out.

The Keeper looks stricken. He doesn't reply for a moment, but when he does, his voice is calm. "Why do you say that?"

"Why do you *think*, dumbass? You didn't save a single person in this building tonight. You couldn't even save your *own* skin! Your friend Rhys had to save us, and you clearly failed to protect her too!" I wheel around and storm away. He has acted like I was his responsibility all night, and I am *sick* of it. "I am going home. My *parents* will do a better job of keeping me safe than *you* ever could."

"Teresa, wait!"

I pause, albeit reluctantly, but do not turn.

"I doubt you want to risk your parents' safety. Please, come with me, just for a little while, and the Collector will leave your parents alone *so long as you stay away from them*. You will be safe in the ISERE. I will stop the Collector, and then you can go home. You can go home, and forget about me, or hate me for the rest of your life, whatever you want to do."

My legs want to collapse under me. My arms want to wrap around them. My body wants to curl up and die. But my shattered heart wants to see my parents again. "You'll stop the Collector, then I can go home?" I echo weakly.

"Yes." I can barely hear his soft response, but I do hear it.

"I'll go with you, but under the condition you'll *leave me alone*." I don't want this magic, this bullshit, in my life. I just want to see my parents and leave this night behind. Until and when I see them again, I can pretend there is no magic while pretending the Keeper doesn't exist. I'll tell myself Ada died in some mundane way. There will be no need to think about this night ever again.

"As you wish."

"So, Westley. How do you plan on protecting me?"

"Come with me." The Keeper heads off toward the front of the library. He holds out his hand as I follow him. "Key, please."

I had forgotten all about it. Before I return it, I look it over. A smooth gold band, the top third set with two rows of minute square rubies. It had somehow expanded earlier to fit my finger. At this point, I don't even care enough to ask how the hell this is a key.

The cube formerly by the front doors is gone. I never want to see it again. I never want to think about it again.

"Teresa."

I merely grunt in answer.

"What the Collector is doing to Rhys, she wants to do to you."

My mouth goes dry, my steps falter. "What are you talking about?" As if he hadn't just explained.

We pass through the front doors onto a well-lit campus under a cloudy night sky. A few campus security officers stand on the street and sidewalk, looking at the library with bemused expressions as the lights on their cars flash. For whatever reason, they pay us no attention. I dismiss it—it's too much to handle.

The Keeper pays them just as much attention. "The Collector wants to make your soul part of her own. She will do anything to capture you. At the moment, the only reasons you are free are luck and Rhys."

Several responses cycle through my mind. *How would you know, I call bull,* and *I don't care* are the top three. I say none of them.

The Keeper takes my silence as a cue to continue. "Imagine your entire being appropriated by another person. Your memories, your ambitions, anything that is part of *you* becomes part of someone else. Suddenly it wasn't you who drew that picture, it was the Collector. Then imagine being aware of it all, for eternity."

I swallow back nausea.

We stop at the red door.

"Wait," I say. "How do you know she wants me?"

The Keeper winces. "There was another version of you in a different universe that she was going to target, but she died before the Collector could reach her. So she found you, a person that is much the same as the other version."

"Another...universe. Okay then." I feel faint. *Fringe* is real? "You know what? Never mind."

The Keeper turns to the door. "This," he announces, "is the Intra-Space Energy Resource Engine—the ISERE."

I side-eye him, unimpressed with the introduction—more afraid of what lies beyond the door despite the impossibility of it. Or maybe because of that impossibility. "Why exactly do we need a key that is obviously not a key? This thing doesn't even have a keyhole."

"I had hoped you knew that things are not always as they seem." The Keeper twists the ring apart.

Instead of breaking, the ring morphs into a golden key, the head of which is studded with rubies.

The Keeper inserts it into a keyhole that, much like the door itself, simply appeared. He pushes the door inward and steps inside. "Welcome to the ISERE."

The light above gives off a late afternoon/early evening feel, illuminating everything I had viewed before, and then some.

Once inside, I reach out to touch the pink petals of a petunia, its planter hanging from the railing of the first level above the main floor of the atrium. I am surprised to find that it is real. Upon that discovery, I find myself reexamining the greenery.

From what I can tell, vine species appear to vary at each level. Ferns hang widely spaced below each walkway and above the railing of the next level down. Planters filled with a variety of flowers extend from the railings, undisturbed by the vines. The plants are in varying stages of bloom.

I climb the short set of steps up to the first level and gaze along the walkway. This is the only level to not form a complete circle, even including the level set below the main atrium floor. Instead it is blocked by the main entrance at one end and the console at the other. At either end of the walkways are spiral staircases twisting up to the second level. Directly above the console and between the spiral staircases are two matching sets of carved double doors.

I've never seen anything quite like this place. It's beautiful.

I don't like it.

I tear my gaze from my surroundings and watch the Keeper as he crosses the atrium to the console and begins flicking switches and levers.

This man is supposed to be some sort of hero, saving me from the Collector? I must admit, if I had thought up a hero of any kind, I would have imagined someone more impressive, perhaps along the lines of Gandalf or Queen Maeve. Certainly not someone wearing a pocket watch around his *neck*.

"What are you doing?" I call.

"Taking us away from here," he answers. "The Collector would be able to find us if we stay."

"You mean this thing can move?"

"'Travel' is the more appropriate word. Travel with a capital 'T.' But yes, the ISERE can move."

I clutch the railing as the floor begins to vibrate in a pulsing rhythm. I peer through the thick glass of the atrium floor. Deep down in the small intestine of the ISERE, the engine is visible. I watch it work, entranced, until it slows into a leisurely heartbeat that I can hardly sense.

"Magic," I breathe. "Holy shit." I shake myself out of it. *(Forget this shit, right?)* Forget this shit, I concur with myself.

The Keeper turns away from the console and climbs up the stairs to join me. "What do you think?"

"Magic is bullshit."

"That's fair." He gestures for me to follow him and leads me to a white paneled door just down the walkway. "You can stay in this room. I hope you like it."

Apprehensively I open the door. I blink at what I see. Inside are softly lit lavender walls with white wainscoting; bamboo flooring; another white door that I assume leads to a bathroom, a bookshelf beside it; a dresser and pressboard desk against the wall across from the full bed and the door; and a fuchsia, violet, and royal blue bi pride flag on one wall (despite everything, something twists happily in my chest at the sight of this).

It's nice, and it's me. But I burst into tears. "Why is this happening?" I sob. "Why does she even *want* me? Who would want my frigging *soul*?"

I don't even know if I want an answer, but the Keeper gives me one. "I believe it has something to do with personality. All her targets may have important qualities the Collector desires for herself."

I cry harder in response. "'All of'? Do I even want to know what that means?"

"You and Rhys are not the only ones she has targeted for subsumption. Her first was Naida, and she took Naida's body as well..." He trails off.

But...why *me*? I'm only nineteen. My own self isn't exactly one hundred percent concrete yet. I barely know myself well enough to have an idea of what the hell I want to do with my life.

I sniff, tears subsiding for the moment. "I need to be alone. Just...just leave me alone, please."

The Keeper nods. "Teresa, I want you to know that you have my deepest sympathies for the loss of your friend. You are not alone in this."

I stare at him for a few long seconds. Then I close the door in his face.

4

THE KEEPER

Perhaps it is a good thing Teresa shut me out, figuratively and literally. I don't need to care for anyone else only to lose them.

I sigh through my nose and return to the console, against which I lean. The ticking in my mind echoes softly.

What now? Rhys has been captured. My twenty-fifth dimension has been destroyed.

And I still have no idea how to stop the Collector.

I slide to my knees. I drape my arms across the edge of the console and rest my forehead on them.

What now?

Maybe I should just die here. Let the ocean of humanity and salt-water judge me at last.

Before one can reach the afterlife, they must cross an ocean filled with the souls of those they wronged in life; if penance was not paid and forgiveness not found before death, the voyager will be dragged downward into damnation. Or, preferably, a person wrongs as few people as possible throughout life and can cross the ocean safely. In my case, it is far too late for the latter option.

As I kneel there, I notice an odd sensation. But sensation is not quite the right word.

There is a rope in the back of my mind.

I pluck at it, but am reluctant to tug on it, or to see where it leads. Suspicion wells inside me: I suspect it had been a thread before. Before I was a Beggar.

Under the stress of that and the ticking, I shiver.

Do the small parts of souls lose awareness when consumed, or are they separately aware? What should I even hope for?

No, I know. I do not want any of those I loved—love—to have a fragmented consciousness. I do not want them to be aware of the horrible things they have been subjected to.

I, with my intact consciousness, can hardly bear knowing.

I jolt upright as the floor beneath me begins to vibrate at an intensity far above the resting heart rate of the ISERE's engine—the intensity is closer to that of the ISERE Traveling.

My eyes widen and I jump to my feet. "What are you doing?" I shout.

The ISERE, of course, does not directly answer. After a few moments, the vibrations subside. The mirror above the console ripples and becomes a screen visualizing the world outside.

An ocean.

My heart drops into my navel.

Dark gray waves churn before me, their surface speckled by the rain falling from a dark sky.

I retreat, throat tight. It is a struggle to resist the urge to cover my ears and scream.

Did the ISERE bring me to my end? Is this my path to damnation brought into life?

Behind me, the red entrance door swings open with a soft creak, the sound only present to inform me that I need to step outside.

I steel myself and head to the door, where I look down at the threshold. On the other side are rough, warping wooden boards—a pier, I realize, stepping outside and looking ahead at the structure illuminated by lights from shore behind me. I button my jacket against the rain and glare at the ISERE as I close the door.

What is this about? Why did the ISERE bring me here?

I walk along the wharf. Industrial cranes loom overhead. Stacks of shipping containers wall me in as I leave the shoreline.

Shouldn't people be here working? I would have thought that shipping yards had people working at all hours. *Perhaps not.*

The farther I walk, the more I can sense magic at work—lots of it. The energy permeates the air.

Unease presses up against my sternum. My eyebrow itches.

One shipping container catches my eye with a glimmer. Magic, only visible to the eyes of mages, shivers over the container. Disguising something, perhaps.

Could this be why the ISERE brought me here?

I approach and undo the locking spell on the container, which turns out to be pitifully easy to do. Hauling the door open with my own strength is a little less so but is still manageable.

Inside, the shimmer of magic is stronger, jumping over the contents of the container.

I open one of the crates.

At my touch, the spell temporarily undoes itself, revealing dozens of elephant tusks.

I recoil in horror. Fury soon rises in its place. As if killing animals for profit weren't enough, these people were using something so divine as magic to hide their misdeeds! I close my eyes and collect my composure before sparking a flame in my hand. I throw it into the shipping container.

The crates catch fire more easily than they would with non-magical fire and burn more quickly.

I do not wait for the entire container to burn before I move on; I have a feeling the tusks are not the reason I am here.

Soon I come across a few strands of ivy lying across my path. *Odd.* On a whim, I follow them.

Ahead, in the path of the ivy, there lies a mass. As I approach, I see it is a human lying on the ground.

I hurry over.

The man is alive but unconscious. When I try to wake him with a spell, he does not respond. Ivy curls loosely around his limbs.

How long has he been here, if ivy has grown around him?

When I check his pulse again to be sure, my hand brushes against his collar and I see something just below his collarbone. I pull his collar aside to see a blood-red battle sickle branded onto his pale skin.

The hair on the back of my neck prickles. I look up in alarm.

Perched on a nearby stack of shipping containers is a person, crouched but relaxed. Their shoulder-length, dark hair glitters with raindrops. They stand, take a step forward.

I open my mouth to cry out a warning, but instead of falling off the edge, they vanish. I shiver and turn back to the unconscious man.

What to do about him?

I notice lights on in a building up ahead. The ivy is growing toward the same building, which unsettles me, but I cannot just leave the man in the cold rain all night. Perhaps there will be someone there to call for help.

I grab his arm and wrap it around my shoulders to drag him along. The ivy around his limbs trails after us.

A few minutes later, I hear angry voices coming from inside the building. I stop just outside the building's dirty, chipped, white door to listen.

"Do you really not see that there's a pattern?" one male voice cries. "How many times must I spell it out for you?"

"It has nothing to do with the tusk shipments, you fool," a second man growls. "How could it?"

"Well, the ivy certainly seems to want to stop us from working. It grew over the forklift during the lunch break today, and it wrapped around my arm when I tried to pull it off."

"Enough with that crap. It's a damn *plant.*"

My eyebrows knit together as I continue to hover outside the door. Something powerful is at work, something manifesting as ivy.

"I'm telling you, I really think it's the reason everyone's been disappearing," the first man continues. "Hold on—even if you don't believe me, Hosseini and Backman are refusing to come back until the ivy is all gone."

Swearing is followed by sounds like someone rummaging through a drawer.

"A lighter?" says the first man. "Visser, do you really think that will do much?"

The door before me creaks open.

I step back, expecting one of the men to exit, but as the door swings open, I see they both stand halfway across the room—one an old man, carrying a lighter, the younger wearing a rain-soaked denim jacket.

Their mouths are hanging open, eyes fixed on the door, then on me.

"Ah...hello," I say nervously. "*I* did not open the door."

I think we all notice it at the same time: ivy curled around the door handle.

"*Oh,*" the old man, Visser, mumbles.

The ivy releases the handle and falls to the floor. Then it shoots forward and wraps around Visser's leg.

"I *told*—" Before the younger man can finish, the ivy yanks on the old man's leg, pulling him to the floor. The vine hauls on Visser again, and he skids across the floor toward me.

I jump aside as quickly as I can with the man on my shoulders as Visser races out the door past me. I pull the unconscious man into the building and order the other man to call for help before pursuing Visser; I need to know where the ivy is coming from.

I catch up to Visser and the ivy soon. It pulls him toward a warehouse smothered in green foliage. When Visser reaches the building, he simply vanishes into the side of the warehouse. I approach the same wall, but it seems to be entirely solid behind the ivy, with no sign of a door or even a window. I stop to examine the vines themselves.

The leaves are nearly oval with smooth edges and a reddish underside, an unfamiliar species.

When I touch them, I feel a thrumming of magic in my chest. Whoever summoned these vines is powerful.

I sense that this is indeed why I was brought here.

The sound of a man screaming rises behind me. I turn just in time to see the younger man from earlier, in the denim jacket, being dragged by the ivy toward the warehouse.

Something tells me not to harm the ivy. I reach for the man's hand as he slides past, grasping for help. Our hands clasp briefly, but I have no time to do more before he is pulled from my grip and vanishes through the wall.

I try not to be too shaken, too afraid of what the ivy may do to me.

I make my way around the building until I find a door behind the ivy. It is unlocked. I open it to find a thick curtain of vines just inside. Carefully I weave my way through it into the center of the warehouse. It takes a while and leaves me almost dizzy with the feeling of immense magical power. I eventually find myself in a small space, every surface composed of ivy. High above, a single fluorescent light is left uncovered to flicker coldly.

I start when I see that, enmeshed with the ivy itself, there stands a girl. She is perhaps eight years of age, her dark hair woven into the ivy, her pale skin almost blending into her simple white dress. The edges of her form seem to blur into the vines around her.

With her ivory skin and white dress, she chillingly reminds me of the Collector. But this girl's face is round, not oval; a spray of freckles spots her skin, whereas the Collector had bleached Naida's long ago; her eyes are brown, not gray; and most obviously, her hair is far too dark.

"Hello, Thane Rhaz." Paradoxically, the girl's voice is dreamy and serene yet grounded and solemn, a combination rare in adults and unheard of in children aged eight years.

A shiver runs down my spine. "How do you know my name?" Only close friends—or dire enemies—know my name. And with that information they have the power to bend me to their will.

A small smile tugs at her mouth. "I have been observing you for some time. Do not fear how I may use your name, Thane, for I am not here to harm or control you, but only to help you pay your penance."

"'Penance'?" I echo. "What do you mean?"

"Those who have done wrong must pay their penance, Thane."

"Oh." My mouth forms the word, but no sound comes out. "For everything?" I ask, audibly.

For allowing Naida to enter the Tomb and catalyze all this, magically extending my youth and life against the guidance of my mother's culture, practically giving the Collector the ability to control me, dismissing the threat to Rhys. For all the people I failed to save from becoming Beggars.

For never killing the Collector.

"For the wrongs you have committed involving magic." She cocks her head. "Do you really believe you are righting the wrong you committed against Rhys Copeland?"

My blood runs cold. "You know?"

"Yes, I know about the spell."

"I can still save her," I whisper, resting my fingertips on the ring bound to Rhys's soul. My mind goes back to—was that mere hours ago?—when the Collector took Rhys, and I bound Rhys's soul to the ring to stop the subsumption. *Was that when the ticking began? When the thread formed?*

The girl's voice remains calm. "How do you believe you can save her when you only run from your vow as the Keeper?"

I lift my chin, straighten my shoulders. "I do not run from my vow. My title is a reminder of who I was and who I should be: one who keeps his promises, keeps others safe, and keeps the memories of those who are gone. No matter how long you have *observed* me, you have no right to claim that I run from this."

"But you have been running from responsibilities that your oath as the Keeper brings, Thane."

I grit my teeth. "What do you mean?"

"You helped release the Collector all those years ago and have failed to truly attempt to stop her since. All you have done is heal the symptoms of her evil, fleeing death, the final judgment, the pain and guilt of your life, and your oath." All hints of mercy have been stripped from her voice.

Protests wither in my throat. There are no untruths in her words. I have only healed rifts the Collector made, and even the times I faced her, I never tried to deliver a fatal blow. The chilling of my soul at the thought of killing stopped me every time.

I do not even know why the Collector is doing what she is. Or what her plans are.

I bow my head in silent acknowledgment of my sins, my anger drained away.

"Do you know what you have wrought, Thane?" My name twists coming from her mouth. "Did your culture's ideals mean nothing to you when you chose to neglect the world around you?"

I cover my mouth with my fingers and close my eyes.

"Or do you listen to your Crusader half instead of the Veqah?"

"I am not in *halves*. And I am not a Crusader," I retort, my voice muffled.

"You behave like one."

My eyes snap open, my hands fall to my sides, fiery rage surging through me. "I am *not* a Crusader," I repeat in a near growl.

"Then make amends. Pay your penance. Abandon your selfish habits and claim your responsibilities."

My voice comes out small, humbled. "How?"

"Your atonement shall be three-fold: the first is the most obvious—stop the Collector so she may not complete her plans. You must stop her by the next kindling moon, in sixteen days' time."

Kindling moon. That is a term I haven't heard in…decades? Perhaps for over one hundred years, before my universe was destroyed. I do not quite recall what it means, but I try not to let on.

"What will happen then?"

"She will use the power of the kindling moon and the Master Key to the multiverse to condense all dimensions into one, presumably so that she may absorb all the energy from the multiverse at once. You must find the Master Key before she does and stop her from using her

powers at the kindling moon. Secondly, you must use the Key yourself
to heal the multiverse."

This is only part of my penance? Hastily I shove the thought away.
"How do you know this?"

"The Collector performed the first spell that allows the pieces of
the Master Key to be found."

I see. I will have to look more into this Master Key; I remember
little about it. "Why...?" My voice trails off as I recall what I saw
when I accidentally looked into the Collector's mind years ago. *She
wants to be alone with her collection, subsisting off the energy of the
multiverse.* I lick my lips. "What is the rest of my penance?"

She tells me.

My throat is so tight by the time she finishes that I can barely speak.
"How do I do that? I don't—I don't know—"

"Take this." The girl unknits her arm from the ivy and extends her
hand toward me. In her palm sits a broad copper ring with smooth
raised edges and small clockwork cogs knit together around the band.
A violet aura flickers over the ring's surface; I can feel the strength of
the spell it holds from where I stand. "When the first part of your
penance is done, breaking this ring will complete the atonement."

I stare at the ring. "Why? Why this and not...not *any*thing else?"

"Neglect of power is misuse of power, Thane."

"I do not know how to do this." *I am not even sure I can.*

"If you are asking for help...I am not the methods, Thane Rhaz. I
am the consequences."

I have no doubt that she makes for some very real consequences. I
take a steeling breath, slip the ring onto my fourth finger on my left
hand. I feel no different with it on; the weight in my chest formed
before I even set eyes on the ring. I twist it around my finger before

looking back up at the girl. "Do you know anything about the Collector that may help me?"

"Unfortunately, I do not," the girl sighs. "Much about her is well-hidden. She is remarkably powerful. Alas, that is why I have been unable to take her to her penance myself."

"I see. What happens if I fail?"

The girl's gaze lays heavily on me. "You will face a damnation worse than the ocean."

My throat tightens, my stomach churns. I have no time to even think to respond before I find myself on the pier again, facing the IS-ERE under a cloudy pre-dawn sky. Before entering, I hesitate, feeling the ocean call my name, but I unlock the door and step inside.

5

TESS

My fitful sleep is plagued with nightmares. When I wake for the final time, I only have vague recollections of dreams featuring people I know crumbling to nothing.

Still curled up in bed, I unplug and pick up my phone to stare numbly at the screen. A full day has passed since I first entered the ISERE. My only notifications are from NBC News and the Associated Press, spilling headlines I don't bother to read before deleting. I unlock my phone and open the group chat with my parents in the messages app. I hesitate, my thumbs poised over the screen.

What the fuck do I say? Do I pretend everything is all right? Do I tell them the whole truth, or only the part where Ada is gone?

Hot tears well in my eyes.

Ada is gone. I have no one to talk to: no parents, certainly no boyfriend, no platonic friends either. Ada's family will soon notice something is wrong. They will—do—deserve answers, and I don't know if I can give them.

I try to analyze what I feel in this moment—all I feel is pain. Not emanating from a specific point or juncture, just a part of every bit of me.

I can't even summon any rage at Hunter anymore; the loss of our relationship is finally hitting me, and I feel so, so alone.

I sit up and open the blinds from my position on the bed. From here I can see sky, darkening, lit with streaks of red and orange and pink. Upon standing, I view miles and miles of plains and farmland thousands of feet below, lit by a setting sun. Are we hovering above this view? Where is it, anyway?

Wherever I am, it's far from home.

A few tears slide down my cheeks. I wipe them away.

What now? I still want to curl up and block out the world, but that may not be in my best interest.

What can you do to take care of yourself today? Advice my mom always gives me when I don't feel well in some way whispers in my mind.

I take a long, hot shower in the bathroom attached to the bedroom, which is oddly stocked with everything I normally use, brand and all. Even when I peruse the closet and dresser afterward, I find much of the same clothing of the type—and size—I left behind.

Creepy.

But for the moment, I roll with it. What else can I do? Especially since I don't have to scrounge for plus-size clothes elsewhere.

I don black leggings, a black-and-pink flannel over a Barns Courtney T-shirt, and white Converse with black flower designs before Dutch-braiding my hair. I rest Ada's necklace in the pocket of my flannel. On a whim, I also grab my hefty pocketknife and stow it in, well, a pocket.

I only *almost* feel better.

But I need a distraction, and this room doesn't really have any.

Ugh. I might run into the Keeper. But there are so many doors here, maybe I won't, if the doors aren't just for show.

I emerge from the room onto the metal walkway, hugging my elbows.

The atrium is empty.

I peer at my distant self in the mirror above the console to see someone who looks fucking miserable. I look away.

Despite myself I wonder, where is the not-exactly-heroic Keeper? Something about the feeling of my mind settling on him is odd to me—the conflict of associating him at all with...everything...and the seemingly genuine words he spoke before I shut the door in his face.

I make a face to myself and decide to continue with my original plan to find a distraction. On a whim I turn left and climb the staircase by the entrance. The stairs are tight, but not quite as much as I had initially thought. At the top, the first door I face is a robin's egg blue paneled door. I open it.

It leads to a curving corridor lined with widely spaced doors, each unique.

Baffled, I try to figure out the physics, then remember where I am. I shrug to myself, as though indifferent and not unsettled.

The first door to the left is battened and ledged and appears to be made of reclaimed wood. I love it, so I open it.

I gasp at what I see inside. The walls are lined with shelves filled with books of sheet music and countless instruments nestled in their respective cases. I spot every instrument I have ever played, including the clarinet, saxophone, piccolo, and acoustic guitar. I also find instruments I would love to learn, such as the viola and of course, the didgeridoo. On the floor stands a drum set, a baby grand piano, timpani, and other standing instruments.

"Holy shit, you're beautiful," I marvel aloud to the room.

My feet eventually draw me to the piano, where I pull out the bench and sit. I open the lid and experimentally run through a warm-up my dad taught me years ago. (Damn, it's been a long time since one of our lessons.)

My heart aches more than it ever has. I can never tell him the truth about last night. I only hope I can speak to him again, like the Keeper told me will be possible.

Oh, how I want to see Ada again. Just once more. Just to hug her and tell her I love her one more time.

I touch her necklace through the fabric of my flannel before allowing my fingers to float over the piano keys. Then I start to play. I don't choose the song, but thoughts of my best friend pull Bishop Briggs's "High Water" out of my hands and lungs. All the times I had listened to this song, I had thought it would never apply to me one little bit. It had been a consolation that I had no sister to lose.

But I lost my best friend far too soon, and isn't that so similar?

By the end, I am crying too much to continue playing, but it doesn't matter, not with the weight in my chest. I drop my hands to my lap.

Only then do I notice a person in the corner of my eye: the Keeper, leaning against the door frame.

I turn away from him, furiously wiping at the tears that had escaped while I played. Irritation bubbles up in me at the fact that he had intruded on such a personal moment. I screw my eyes shut to stop the tears. (The glue holding me together has still not dried one bit.)

"Did you play all that from memory?" he asks several moments later.

I nod, darting a glance in his direction, but still trying to hide my face, which is surely blotchy. Maybe it shows my fragmented being. "Yes."

"Very impressive."

"Thanks," I mutter.

There is another silence before he asks, "Would you like to talk?"

Actually, I want to forget you exist. "What about?" I ask, voice tight.

"Anything you want to know."

Finally brave enough to face him, I do so. And then I surprise myself. "I suppose I would like to talk."

He unpeels himself from the doorframe. "Come with me."

I push in the bench and close the lid when I stand. As I approach the Keeper, I take in his appearance.

Not too much has changed from the other night. He wears the same loose navy jacket, high top shoes, and white sash, as well as the pocket watch-like device hanging in front of his solar plexus. However, his hair is now neatly combed off to one side, and he wears a pale pink button-down shirt and slim fit khaki chinos. He gives off an air of barely suppressed energy yet is less frenetic than when we met.

My gaydar pings softly. Normally I'd have the urge to smile, but I remind myself that *this isn't a reason to like someone. Remember, he didn't save Ada.*

We walk farther down the hall.

"What would you like to know?" the Keeper asks, hands in his pockets.

"Where do I start?" I shake my head. "I suppose...with you? Who are you? What's your deal?"

He speaks more slowly than he did when we first met but still has a bursting energy suffusing his every action. "I suppose my 'deal' is that I am a magic-user, a mage—"

"I knew it," I mutter resignedly.

The Keeper breaks off, a half-smile twisting the corner of his mouth. "While you correctly deduced that much of the other night was due to magic, I had to resist telling you that your epithet for me is grammatically incorrect."

"Oh, *please*, you pedant. 'Magic' is an adjective, not just a noun."

He shakes his head. "One thing you should know about magic is that it *is* a noun—it is an energy that is all around us, always, everywhere. It can be utilized, certainly, but the only thing that can be described as 'magic' is magic itself, not the person, nor the acts of utilizing it. Regardless, our languages have differences in describing it, mainly because my people understood it and yours do not."

"If you think that's going to stop me from calling you Magic Man, think again." I pause, a hint of horror widening my eyes. "Hold on. 'Understood'?"

"Ah...yes. My people are—are gone in many of the universes I have been through, if they ever existed to begin with."

"Oh." *Why are they gone?* I wince. "So...universes?" I ask after a pause.

"I can explain in a moment."

At the end of the hallway, we reach a dark paneled door, which the Keeper opens with a flourish. Behind it is the most magnificent library I have ever seen or imagined. Vaulted ceilings an atmosphere above, cherry-wood bookshelves leaving no inch of bare wall, interior galleries ringing the walls at various heights. Even the staircases have shelves built into the sides. Massive glass windows appear to look out onto an outdoor garden. Towering open archways lead to vast rooms similar to this one.

"Holy *shit*," I blurt out in awe. "How big *is* this place?" I want to giggle in disbelief. Hunter would probably make some joke about me breaking up with him for this library.

I no longer want to giggle.

"The library?" The Keeper flicks one hand to the side in what I read as an *I don't know* gesture. "It contains every published work on Earth from every universe the ISERE has entered. So it is, to make quite an understatement, sizable."

I turn back to him, eyebrows raised. "And how many universes would that be?"

"This is the twenty-sixth," he answers without hesitation.

I recall him saying something about the number twenty-six when I first met him. "Is this your twenty-sixth as well?"

"Yes."

Judging from what fiction has taught me about alternate dimensions...I can't imagine being so far from home. Traveling around the world to return home within a few weeks I would be fine with, but entire realities away? According to my pop culture references, it wouldn't generally be easy to travel back home.

"Why?"

Pain ripples across his face, to be quickly stilled. "Because of the Collector" is all he says. He avoids my gaze for a moment as he guides me to a table stacked with books, where we sit across from each other.

"What do you mean?"

The Keeper laces his fingers together. "I should probably begin by explaining the basics of the multiverse. The multiverse is an ever-expanding, living construct. Anytime a sentient being makes any sort of decision, a dimension, or universe, splits to form multiple new dimensions, one for each possible choice. For instance, that outfit you chose would result in one dimension, while every other choice, whether it be a different pair of socks or an entirely different outfit, would result in one dimension for every option. This has led to an infinite number of dimensions as each universe continually divides."

I grasp at a thread of understanding. "So a dimension never stops dividing."

"Precisely. Except for one instance—when an interdimensional anomaly occurs."

"And what is...that?"

"Something, usually a magical being, that can harness energy to protect itself from the interdimensional barriers. The being crosses into a dimension that it did not originate from. I am one such anomaly, and the Collector is another. When an anomaly crosses between dimensions, the affected universes stop multiplying so as to prevent the anomaly from spreading."

I feel like the Keeper is my tutor. "So this dimension has stopped dividing."

He nods.

"Will it ever...return to normal?"

The Keeper frowns. "I am not certain. Nothing to this scale has ever occurred before."

His words send a tremor of fear through my body. "'To this scale'?"

"Yes. Normally a small, naturally formed injury in the barriers between dimensions allows something to cross: a minor problem. But the Collector is creating much larger and more numerous rifts that allow many more anomalies through. She uses those rifts to travel between universes herself. Once she successfully crosses into a new dimension, she annihilates the one she just departed." His voice loses all emotion by the end of the last sentence.

Horror gapes in my chest. "Has she done this to...?" I can't even say it.

"Twenty-five dimensions," he says flatly.

"Is mine next?" I whisper, clenching my hands as they begin to shake.

The Keeper looks at his own hands before somberly meeting my gaze. "She will try to destroy it, but I intend to stop the Collector before that happens."

I search his face, desperate to find hope. "How do you plan to do that?"

He winces and scratches his neck. "I—do not know."

"Oh, so we're screwed, then." The thought of what might happen to everyone and everything I have ever known nauseates me.

The Keeper closes his eyes and begins to rub his hands together agitatedly. "I have a place to start. The Collector—she is searching for the Master Key to the multiverse. I have been doing some research today." He gestures at the books on the table. "Not much is known about it, but the Key appears to give its bearer the ability to control the multiverse during a kindling moon; though it may be risky to use, potentially killing the user. The Key exists in five pieces that are accessible only in the month leading up to the kindling moon after specific spells are performed."

"Back up, Magic Man." I grit my teeth in frustration. He's my tutor and I've been skipping class. "Why does this Key even exist? What's a kindling moon?"

"Millenia ago, someone whose identity has been lost constructed the Key, presumably with the purpose of controlling the multiverse. It could not be destroyed, so mages and other beings who wanted to protect the multiverse pulled it into pieces, and hid those pieces separately so they could be guarded by various constructs, creatures, and spells. I suspect the only reason I even have a copy of the book outlining the spells required to access the Key is because of the ISERE.

"As for the kindling moon, that is when the full moon is at its closest point to the earth and a total lunar eclipse occurs concurrently. The event acts as a sort of kindling for powerful spells that could not be achieved at any other time."

I can't keep track of all my questions. "Can you explain a little more? Like, how are these pieces accessed? How do you find them? What is your end goal? Hell, what's the Collector's end goal?"

The Keeper nods. "These pieces are summoned by a spell outlined in this book." He taps an ancient tome bound in black leather, then returns to massaging his hands. "The spellcaster makes the pieces accessible to the current universe they are residing in. Then, further spells can be cast to locate each piece, and the spellcaster can attempt to take each piece one at a time, provided they can skirt the dangers successfully."

I wait for him to continue.

"My end goal is to beat the Collector to each of the pieces so I may use the Key to heal the multiverse. *Her* goal is to collect a satisfactory number of souls and memories so that she may destroy the multiverse at once, absorbing the resulting energy so she can exist alone with her collection forever."

At his last words, I feel like I am both sinking down through the chair and floating up and away—I am escaping my body, the horror his words bring me too much to bear.

"Teresa?" The voice saying my name is so far away.

I don't think I ever want to return to the place I departed.

Without warning, I find myself there again, fully present in my body. "Did you—?" I begin.

The Keeper is leaning across the table, his fingertips resting on the back of my hand. His brow is knit with concern, his eyes searching mine. "I am sorry, Teresa. I should not have told you. This is...too much for most people."

I shake my head. "No, it's—I wanted to know. I think I needed to know."

He doesn't withdraw, so I do.

"I'm fine," I say shortly.

"When was the last time you have eaten?" he asks suddenly.

I tuck a nonexistent flyaway hair behind my ear. "I don't know. Saturday evening, I guess."

"That was a full day ago." The Keeper stands. "Come with me. I will make you something to eat."

I don't want to eat; I don't want him to cook for me. *What can you do to take care of yourself today?* I relent.

He leads me farther into the library, through several more grand rooms.

I find myself reluctant to ask more questions. Except for one. "Do you have a name? Or do you just go by 'the Keeper'?"

"I do have a name. I do not introduce myself with it because names have power. For most people, names are deeply connected to someone's identity, and by extension, their soul. If a mage knows how to do so, they can control someone whose name they know."

My curiosity gets the better of me. "How does that work?"

The Keeper meets my eyes, his gaze intense. "Say your own name. Not glibly, but meaningfully. Do you feel that hum, that ring, however small, when you say it? That sense of connection, of rightness and identity? That is what one searches for in another person when looking to control them. Grip it and wield it." He waves a hand in the air. "However, few people are aware that such a thing is possible, and even fewer can accomplish it."

"Why is that?"

"Magical cultures vary in their methods and uses of magic, and therefore vary in their knowledge of it. Moreover, it is always difficult to control living things with magic; in fact, most mages can only mildly influence them."

I mull that over for a moment. That's kind of cool. Scary, but cool. "Can you do that?"

He tugs his sleeves down over his hands. "I have never tried. To do so would be an abomination."

Abomination—a strong word. "So that's why you go by the Keeper?" I ask. "Why not choose another name?"

He seems to nearly smile. "Thane Rhaz is my name, my identity, and always will be. Calling myself the Keeper is...more a *part* of me. An aspirational version of who Thane can become as well as a reminder of who I have been."

Hm. "So why did you introduce yourself to me as the Keeper? I can't use magic, so can't I call you by your name?"

"Theoretically, you could influence me by saying it, but as a non-mage, you would only be able to do so once. I'd like to spare the option as...as Rhys needed to use it."

Fear flutters in my stomach at his words. "Why did she need to use it?"

The Keeper cringes. "It was when the Collector was taking her. The Collector took control of me by using my name herself. Rhys begged me to help her. So I did the best I could."

You're doing good not to trust him, Tess. He couldn't save Rhys, he couldn't save Ada, he can't save you. The guy doesn't even have the guts to do all he can to stop someone, using their name. I tilt my head, a thought forming under the surface of my mind. I let the thought take its time to form. I ask, "When did you become the Keeper?"

He doesn't answer immediately, and when he does, it sounds like he is choosing his words carefully. His hands are more agitated than ever. "Early on, but years after the Collector first emerged, there was someone I loved. He became a Beggar and died. I had recently found out about the Collector's plans, and I had nothing left to lose, so I decided to devote my life to finding out how to repair the multiverse and prevent her from destroying any more of it. And I became the Keeper."

"Why the 'Keeper'?"

"It is a vow of sorts. I keep promises, keep memories, and try to keep others safe," he says simply.

Eventually we reach what appears to be the main library entrance, a set of large carved wooden doors. The Keeper pushes them open, leading us back into the atrium. Below us and to our right is the console.

As we walk down the spiral staircase and to the level below the main floor, I remark, "Keeper, you didn't really explain how the Collector knew your name."

"Ah, yes." He clears his throat. "When I was your age, my friend Naida and I found what I came to know as the Tomb—the Collector's machine, the large cube. Naida was fascinated by it, as it was really the IDEM, the Inter-Dimensional Expedition Machine, the precursor to the ISERE. The IDEM had disappeared years before, stolen from its murdered creator, Aileth Rawls. The discovery was huge. I could not stop Naida from entering the Tomb. I should have tried harder.

"I am still not certain of precisely how it happened, but the Collector stole Naida's body and subsumed her soul. Over a series of encounters where I failed to properly protect my identity, the Collector made the connection between myself and Naida's memories."

"How many people has she done that to?" I ask in a small voice.

"Used their bodies? Only Naida. The body you see the Collector currently inhabiting is Naida's. Subsumed? A handful, but I am not certain of the number."

I shiver. All those people, trapped, subjugated. And according to the Keeper, I'm next. "Why is she doing all this?"

The Keeper hesitates. "First, allow me to give you some context for how I know. Years ago, I was almost turned into a Beggar. I made a shield that weakened the spell and then I somehow managed to reverse it and see into the Collector's mind. I saw that she wanted to be alone with her collection of souls and memories—that is how she sees it: as a simple collection. She just was not yet prepared or able to try to destroy the multiverse."

'Alone with her collection.' The words send chills racing up and down my spine, but I remain grounded this time. Who would destroy the multiverse to be alone with what they had stolen from others?

I follow the Keeper through a swinging wooden door into an impressive chef's kitchen. Broad granite countertops, top-of-the-line energy efficient appliances, cherry-wood cabinets, a set of stools at the bar of the kitchen island.

Schmancy.

The Keeper offers me a seat at the island, asks me if I have any dietary restrictions. He begins pulling things out of the refrigerator and cabinets, but I do not pay much attention.

Instead I pick at my fingernails, letting the thought from earlier rise to the surface. *He can't save you.* If he couldn't save Rhys, or Ada, or anyone else in the last twenty-five dimensions, how can I expect him to stop the Collector now? Why can't I save myself?

Hm.

I nod to myself. I can use the Keeper to access the pieces of the Key but get them myself.

To pretend I am not thinking dangerous thoughts, I ask what I consider to be an innocuous question: "Where are you from, exactly?"

The Keeper stirs something in a pan as he begins. "I am from a small, isolated island in the northern region of what you might call the Pacific Ocean. My people called it Ayuve Island." He pronounces the name of the island as *ah-YOU-vay*; the way he says it, the word rolls in pitch and emphasis just like an ocean wave. "It was a beautiful place, with rocky beaches bordered by striking cliffs. The trees were old and magnificent, the flowers vibrant. My people lived there in peace for many years, practicing our magic in tandem with the environment.

"Lifetimes before I was born, the Crusaders came. They brought disease and violence and weak, corrupted magic. Their descendants became the Developers, as they 'developed' civilization on the island. They tried to annihilate my culture by either appropriating it or punishing its practice. They would not even allow us to practice magic our natural, direct way, and forced us to use conduit items." He shakes his head. "I speak the Veqah language now but had to learn it in secret as an adolescent. Even now, after speaking it for so many years, I forget a word or proper grammar, and I have no one to ask. So, I have to try to find it in the Crusader language. It is infuriating."

He places a dish of fish cooked with vegetables in front of me. "The blend of Crusader and Veqah should be something I am accustomed to, considering my father was a Developer and my mother Veqah, but it has always been difficult for me to reconcile."

Sympathy twinges in my chest. To be honest, I can hardly believe he told me all that. I had only expected an answer like I would brusquely give: "I'm from southeastern Ohio. You probably haven't heard of the town." And that would be it.

"I can't imagine," I say sincerely.

I look down at the dish he had set before me. "Can I trust you?" I blurt out.

The Keeper smiles, but the expression is filled with something like sadness. "That is for you to decide. I do not lie, and I do what I can to uphold my vow as the Keeper, but...I can only hope that will finally be enough."

6

THE KEEPER

I recall what it was like to lose my universe. It must not happen again.

That day long ago, the sky flashed with blinding gold light. Then the ISERE's sensors picked up a rift that was much bigger than the comparatively small ones that had been popping up across the world. Deafening alarms blared to warn me of the danger. I went to investigate, but I got too close to the rift and was quickly pulled through.

In hindsight, that probably saved me from being noticed by the Collector, as she was still on our home dimension's side.

The ISERE crashed into a hillside in a shower of debris. I was thrown across the atrium and knocked unconscious.

They found me there, the people with skin the color and beauty of the night sky. The ISERE must have known she and I both needed help and so opened her door for them. The people healed my injuries by drawing glyphs upon my skin and helped me out of the wreckage.

Just in time to witness the destruction of my universe.

We could see my dimension through the immense rift, a vast floodplain and a broad river shimmering and warping under the roiling energy.

A dark geometric shape, so small compared to the rift, appeared and hovered within the maw of the tear. Behind it, my world began to dissolve, crumbling away until there was nothing left but nothingness.

I collapsed. It was as though some tie had been severed. Perhaps there *was* a tie; perhaps we are all connected to our own universes, and when that universe is destroyed, something is ripped away from us. All I know is that I have never felt the same since my dimension died.

Teresa should never experience the same thing. Never. No one should.

Teresa, of course, would never go through believing it was a singular, isolated event. So she would not feel the same panic and terror and confusion I did when it all happened again a few years later.

Now, I stay up all night constructing the spell to find the first of the five pieces of the Key. The tome I found on the Key contains information for building the base of the spell, but it appears I must create the rest myself. Luckily, I have the energy and motivation to do it.

The base, I realize after poring over it for about an hour, is meant to be decoded and sung. I try to sing the uncovered words without any sort of accompaniment, but nothing happens. I summon magic into the words in a few different ways, to no avail.

I scribble notes all over the relevant pages of the tome—in the margins, in between the lines.

How do I complete this spell?

How do I complete a song?

Music! I must be a fool; though, I acknowledge to myself, I am no musician.

When I finish tapping out an appropriate rhythm as I sing, it is early morning. Oddly, I have to make a phone call to the location housing the key and schedule an appointment there. After a few minutes of choosing my words carefully and allowing the magic in them to flow over the phone, I am able to schedule one for today.

I direct the ISERE to outside the building where the piece seems to be and head across the atrium toward the entrance. A spark of the familiar admixture of excitement and unease at the prospect of facing an anomaly flares inside me, just like it always has.

A voice stops me just before I open the door. "Hold up! Are you going to find the first piece of the Key?"

I spin on my heel to face Teresa. "Yes. Why?"

"I want to go with you." Steel glints in her eyes, and I also catch a glimpse of cunning.

I raise an eyebrow. Is she thinking of me what I think of myself? "It is too dangerous for you."

It is too dangerous for me, I think.

And yet.

"And it's safe for you to go alone?"

"I can handle myself. I have spent years dealing with magical beings on my own." No untruths spoken.

She crosses her arms with a frown. "Keeper, I don't want to sit around here hoping that the Collector doesn't figure out how to break in here. I want to help stop her."

I believe her. "Do you understand the risks? You could be badly injured, or even killed, not to forget subsumed. I cannot guarantee your safety once you leave the ISERE."

"Come on, Magic Man, it's not like I've forgotten the other night. Do your thing, sprinkle a little protective spell on me, and we're all good to go."

I scrutinize her, considering. I *do* have a protection spell forged into a couple of my rings... "Are you certain?"

Teresa scoffs. "I'm *pretty* certain that I want to stop the person who killed my best friend, yeah. No one deserves her fate."

"Do you need to sign a liability waiver?"

Bemusement scuttles across Teresa's face, followed quickly by re-alization. "Wait, I can come with?"

"Yes. But," I warn, pulling a ring off my left middle finger, "you will need to wear this." I show her the ring, a flat silver-plated band with engraved dandelion seeds drifting across the surface. It was intended to be a supplement to my other protection ring, but I suppose I can simply work on strengthening the spell on that one. "Wait a moment," I say as an idea occurs to me. I remove one of my other rings and place it in my palm with Tess's before whispering a spell over them. It takes a few minutes, but soon enough it is ready to be handed over.

"I'm not marrying you," she says as I hold out her ring.

"Good. This ring contains a spell that makes it virtually impossible for the Collector to find and track you as long as you do not remove it."

She narrows her eyes at me. "'Virtually'?"

"She is quite powerful, Tess. It is difficult to predict what may happen as a result. Even if she does find you, it should shield you from her influence. However, in order to retain potency, this cannot protect you from anything or anyone else; otherwise, the spell would spread too thin. I also just added a spell that would allow us to communicate via our rings in case of emergency."

"Good to know." She slips it on. "Yeah, I feel much safer now."

"I'm glad. Are you prepared to find the Key?"

A young woman emerges from one Dr. Cassius Jaeger's office just as we are about to enter it.

"Dr. Jaeger is brilliant, isn't he?" she remarks to us. Her dark eyes are huge, very nearly popping out of their sockets, as if she is straining to convey that she has just been pleasantly surprised by how brilliant she found this therapist specializing in grief and loss.

"We are new clients," I reply. "I am glad to hear that he has been a help to you."

What help could a guardian of the Master Key be giving to people?

"He's wonderful," she emphasizes. "Everything seems so much less horrible now."

With that, she departs, and Teresa and I step inside.

The waiting room is small, with room for only a receptionist's desk, a few chairs crammed together, and a minuscule stand for magazines. A door on the opposite side leads to what I assume is the therapist's office. Behind the desk is a chipper woman with auburn hair and clear-framed glasses. A nameplate announces her name as Amber.

We exchange pleasantries before I introduce myself. "My name is Damien Rhaz. I have an appointment for one o'clock."

Amber hands me a tablet. "Have a seat and fill out these forms for me, please. Even though this is just a consultation, Dr. Jaeger finds it best to start off with as much information as you are willing to give."

I take the tablet, flashing Amber a grateful smile.

"How can I help you?" she asks Teresa.

"I'm with him."

"She is my emotional support," I tell Amber. "I hope that is acceptable."

Amber cuts her amiable gaze between us. "Of course it is."

We sit, and I get the impression that Teresa is trying quite hard not to read over my shoulder.

"How did you get an appointment so quickly?" Teresa asks, staring intently across the room at a photo hanging on the wall.

I tap at the tablet's screen. "Subtle influence." I murmur, "There is an energy surging behind that door. I can sense it prickling across my skin."

"I'd say that fits the bill of what we're looking for in a therapist."

A few minutes later, I return the tablet to the blandly cheery Amber and return to my seat to wait for Dr. Jaeger to call us back.

Eventually the door to the therapist's office opens, revealing a rather emaciated-looking middle-aged man sporting wire-rimmed glasses and a tie covered in the repeating motif of a rotund orange cat. "Damien?" He ushers us into his office, which is almost palatial compared to the waiting room. A bowl of fruit sits upon the doctor's desk.

We run through introductions as we take our seats, Teresa introducing herself as Dawn, her middle name.

"Nice tie," I comment, not because I like it, but because Jaeger is spending a little too long adjusting it.

A grin spreads across the man's gaunt face. "Thank you. Sometimes I feel I am just as ravenous as Garfield himself." He rests one skinny ankle on his opposite knee.

"So, Damien, what brings you to consider therapy?"

I twist a ring around one finger, suddenly as anxious as though I am truly in therapy. "I lost a friend recently, and…it made me realize that I hadn't recovered from when my parents and sister died several years ago." Twisting my ring turns into scratching my hand.

"What does 'recovered' from their deaths look like to you?"

"Not feeling any guilt. Accepting that there was nothing I could have done. Being able to think about them without feeling overwhelmed." Guilt does burn in my chest—there *was* something I could have done, if only I could go back in time and make different choices.

"Are you feeling guilty and overwhelmed now?"

"I am starting to." My chest is too tight. I take a deep breath and focus on the mission.

"Let's move on, then. If you two don't mind, I'd like to speak to each of you separately for just a few minutes. It will help me get a fuller picture of how this grief has affected you, Damien."

We exchange glances. This request makes me uncomfortable, but I need to work with Jaeger to be able to locate the Key.

"Are you cool with that?" Teresa asks me.

"I suppose so."

"I guess I won't say anything incriminating about you."

"Thanks."

"Dawn, if you could step out for a moment?"

As soon as Teresa closes the door behind her, Jaeger says, "Is there anything off the top of your head that you'd like to talk about now?"

"No." Underneath the feelings he has dredged up, I am impatient to find the Key. Where could he be hiding it?

"Then let's start by going over your personal history, shall we?" Jaeger peruses the tablet in his lap. "I see you were diagnosed with autism and cyclothymic disorder at age twenty-seven."

Truthfully, I had been nearly a century older than that, but I was not about to tell him my real age. "Yes." *Why did I include those diagnoses? To seem more authentic?*

"What has your treatment regimen looked like?"

I stifle a sigh. "Just psychotherapy, but I never meshed well with the therapists, so it did not help much."

"You have never tried medication?"

"No."

"If you like, I can refer you to someone who can prescribe you something."

"No thank you. I have it under control." My voice verges on sharp and hot. *You should not have* told *him, Thane,* I snap at myself. Then, *I am so tired of pretending it's not me.* Then, *You wouldn't even pretend to a fake therapist, Thane?*

He gives me an odd look but says nothing about it. Instead he asks me a couple of other questions before coming to "What is it you would like to get from therapy?"

"Ah…" I stare at his hands. "Better ways to cope with grief."

On his left hand is a silver ring. Instantly I know—can sense—it is part of the Key. My excitement stirs once more.

"I can certainly help with that." He moves his hand out of sight. Did he notice my stare? "If you'd like, we can do a brief exercise that may help before I call Dawn back in; it may help you get a feel for my methods."

"Very well." Anything to remain near the Key and hopefully get closer to it.

"Do you like apples, Damien?"

My brow furrows. "Excuse me?"

"Apples. Do you like them? The exercise involves eating a piece of fruit."

"Oh. Yes."

Jaeger holds the fruit bowl out for me to grab an apple. When I do, he tells me to close my eyes. "Now focus on a good memory with one person you lost. When that memory and its emotions are vivid, take a bite. Focus on the sweetness of both the fruit and the memory."

The memory I choose is one of the few happy ones I have from between my time in the army and when the Collector rose to power: I was with my little sister, Evelyn, who was aged four years, in a field. She had loved the tall grasses and had made us both a loose necklace and bracelet from some long strands. She asked me to weave some into her long hair.

"I can't wait for your hair to grow back, Fay," she said. "I want to braid your hair with it."

Fay. It sounds a little like my name and means butterfly. I had not thought about her calling me Fay for a long time. I miss it.

Before I can think of how I have never allowed my hair to grow very long again and why, I take a bite of the apple. No sooner do I swallow than the feelings of bliss and melancholy are gone.

My eyes snap open. I stare at Jaeger, cold with confusion and the faintest touch of fear.

"That hits the spot," he sighs pleasantly. "Thanks for letting me in."

The apple falls from my hand. I slump in my seat.

"Now, now, don't be so indignant! I do this to all my patients! Well, I only take their *ayuve* with me. But you—" He licks his lips. "—you didn't think I would ever let you leave, with or without the Key?"

Everything goes black.

7

— • —

TESS

I return to the same seat I had occupied earlier.

Amber is nowhere to be found.

I find a *Homes & Gardens* magazine to flip through, wanting to distract myself from the thought that maybe I need to see a therapist for grief and loss. A real therapist, of course. It isn't until I have skimmed the entire thing that I realize how much time has passed. How long was this supposed to take again? The hour-long consultation should be done soon. I shift impatiently.

Amber isn't even back.

I fidget in my seat, rifle through the magazine pile once more, stare vacantly at the photo on the opposite wall that I am pretty sure came with the frame.

Then comes a series of small tapping sounds.

Bored, I look around for the source but see nothing.

(Maybe it's from a neighboring office?)

It comes again. From above.

Slowly, apprehensively, I look upward.

Clinging to the ceiling is a massive spider-like creature. Pincers, a hairy rotund body the size of a pony's, sharply jointed legs. A mostly-human head that looks suspiciously like a certain receptionist.

Amber clacks her pincers and scurries forward a few steps.

"What the f—" My words turn into a shriek as Amber dives. I throw myself out of my chair.

Amber the spider lands where I had been a fraction of a second before in a tangle of furniture and limbs. She hisses in fury and leaps toward me. I kick at her. My foot connects with her chin, barely missing her pincers. I scramble to my feet as she recovers.

She charges.

I jump onto the desk.

Amber nearly collides with it, then lunges at me.

I spring aside and lob a stapler at her face.

It connects (*thank you, years of softball*), disorienting her. She shakes her head.

Before she can even click her pincers again, I scoop up her goose-neck lamp and slam the base down over her skull.

The spider person crumples, motionless.

Triumph flashes inside me, tempered by wariness. Keeping a close eye on her, I hop off the desk. Just to be on the safe side, I overturn the desk to pin her down. I don't feel like making sure she's okay.

"Keeper!" I yell. I pound on the door to Jaeger's office. "Get your skinny butt out here!"

No answer.

I try the doorknob. Locked.

(*Locked?*)

"Keeper?" I lean in to listen. Silence emanates from the other side. I curse under my breath at the chills racing up my spine.

How does one break down a door? I chew my lip. Perhaps with determination. It looks flimsy enough. I take a step back, hesitate, kick the door. It shudders under the impact but doesn't give. I kick at it four more times before it splinters enough for me to fully open it.

"Keeper?" I call as I shove my way inside. To find an empty office. "Keeper?" I repeat, as if he is hidden somewhere in the small room. I nearly step on an apple on the floor as I walk across the office.

What the hell?

I check the window, but it's locked from the inside. So how did they get out?

I turn back to the door. I blink.

It is whole again, closed. As though I had not broken it and opened it just a moment ago.

I swallow. Reach for the knob. Open the door.

On the other side is darkness.

What the *hell*?

Apprehensively, I step through and feel gravity shift just before I am slammed backward into a solid surface. I stand to find myself at one end of an immense table set with a feast.

And when I say immense, I mean set for people thirteen times the size of the average human and stretching into the dimness. Oddly, though, the food is sized for the average human. People—normal-sized, and not spider people—sit in each of the huge chairs. Their eyes are all closed, and they are each translucent.

This magic stuff is...a bit much.

I set off walking down the table, examining each of the people as I pass, able to see only a few at a time due to the dimness of my surroundings. The people are more opaque the farther I go, but never fully so.

The table must be a quarter mile long.

Eventually I hear something: the crack of bones, noisy chewing.

Gross. Wait, I hope those aren't the Keeper's bones—I need his magic.

I move faster, urgency pulsing in my veins, weaving between platters and bowls of food. I slow when the head of the table comes into view.

A skeletal man, tall enough to easily fit the grand chair upon which he sits, leans over his plate, shoveling entire turkeys, whole casseroles, into his gaunt face. The food before him is somehow not running out, despite his best efforts.

Between movements, I spot the tie: a repeating motif of Garfield.

"Hello, Teresa," Jaeger says without looking up from the table.

A chill runs down my spine. How does he know my name—my *first* name? I lift my chin defiantly. "What did you do with my—companion?"

Jaeger gestures to the chair on his left. The Keeper sits there, so small, eyes closed. He is the only opaque form, aside from Jaeger.

I clench my jaw. "What did you do to him?"

"He partook of the feast, which means I am now consuming his *ayuve.*"

I think I recognize the last word—the name of the Keeper's home island?

"Come, Teresa, partake of the feast." Jaeger waves for me to sit in the empty chair to his right.

I cross my arms. "Maybe stop eating *him* first? And tell me what an *ayuve* is."

Jaeger scoops another ham into his mouth before leaning back with a contented sigh. "Fine. I will pause eating *his ayuve.*

"There is no singular word or expression in your language to describe it, but an *ayuve* is the emotional center of the soul in both a magical and spiritual aspect. The people here have allowed me access to theirs so I may take away their pain." He grins with too many teeth. "And then some. But they do not mind." He laughs. "Ah, yes, *ayuve* are excellent fuel for a starving man. Especially Thane's, so volatile and intense."

As my mind races, I examine the food from where I stand. It's not really food at all, I realize, but something else shaped to be like food. Tentatively I reach forward and touch a bunch of grapes. A feeling of bittersweetness diffuses up my arm. Is this food an *ayuve*? While the translucent people are the souls being stolen from?

"So, all these people," I say, "you lure them in through therapy, promising to help with their grief, and instead you just eat part of their soul?"

Jaeger dabs at his mouth with a napkin, a move so dainty for his previous lack of manners. "There is no 'instead' about it, Teresa. They give me permission.

"Come now, come sit with me. Let us talk. I won't eat Thane's *ayuve* so long as we talk." He pats the empty seat beside him.

Can I trust him?

I wend my way through the dishes and pause before the Keeper. "Can he hear me?"

"Oh, I don't know," Jaeger says dismissively around a mouthful of noodles. "His body is here too, unlike the others, so possibly."

I purse my lips. "Hi, Keeper," I say. "I'm here for you." *Mostly the Key, but you know. You too, I guess.* Then I turn and seat myself next to the empty plate at Jaeger's right hand. The plate is at least eighteen feet across.

From here, all I can see is the top half of the Keeper's head.

I watch Jaeger as he continues to devour, both mesmerized and sickened.

Something glints on his finger—a ring. The Key!

Eagerly, I glance at the Keeper. To my disappointment, his eyes are still closed. I recall our rings and shout for him with my mind.

I get no response.

"I can feel your reluctance at calling him a friend," Jaeger says between casseroles. (The variety of flavors cannot be good together.) "I can sense the two of you pulling away from each other while simultaneously drawing closer to the other."

I grunt noncommittally. I *strongly* disagree, but Jaeger isn't exactly a *real* therapist. Or an empath, I'm sure.

He takes a swig of water.

I look to the Keeper once more.

His eyes meet mine.

You're awake! Jaeger must really have stopped eating him. Or, well, part of him. As discreetly as I can, I tap the ring he gave me.

He nods.

Jaeger is too busy stuffing his face to notice. "Teresa, would you consider therapy?"

"Everyone should be in therapy."

"I mean for grief and loss." He grins at me, broth dripping down his chin. "My specialty."

"Hm." I probably shouldn't be honest with a man who eats metaphorical hearts for a living. "No, I think I'm good there."

He chuckles. "We both know that is a lie, Teresa."

My face hardens. "Why do you say that?" I cut a look at the Keeper, suddenly desperate for him to do something. Or signal what I should do.

"I can sense your grief. I could feel it from the waiting room." He takes a sip of wine. "Tell me about that."

Before I can think of an answer, the Keeper leaps onto the table, lightning crackling around his hand. He snaps his hand forward, sending the lightning flying outward.

It wraps around Jaeger's wrists, binding them to the table.

The giant howls and strains against his bonds.

"Get the ring!" the Keeper orders me. He springs onto Jaeger's shoulder, sash in hand, and whips it over Jaeger's eyes like a blindfold.

I grip the ring—it's almost too wide to easily grasp—and yank on it. At the same time, I try not to think of fingers being degloved.

The Keeper whispers into Jaeger's ear.

Jaeger relaxes, slumps into the chair.

It makes it that much easier to pull off the ring. "Keeper, I've got it!"

My voice startles Jaeger out of his stupor; his hand jerks, tearing through his bonds, and slams into my chest, knocking the ring out of my hands as I tumble backward.

I fall off the table. My body slams into a chair, the air flies from my lungs. I try to yell for the Keeper, but I cannot speak, cannot even see him; he is no longer on Jaeger's shoulder.

Jaeger leans forward once more and resumes eating. As though nothing had happened.

Slowly I regain my breath, and when I do, I haul myself back up onto the table.

Where's the Key, *where's the Key*? I fumble for it among the dishes of food.

Jaeger's hand crashes down next to me.

I yelp, but he only grabs a nearby bowl of green beans. My hand collides with something curved and metal. This time I grasp the ring silently, but Jaeger notices.

He howls and before I can react, a massive hand clasps around me.

The ring is knocked from my hands once more and clatters into a bowl of soup.

"Keeper!" I yell. I begin to claw frantically, desperately at Jaeger.

The hand tightens around me, cracking bones and joints.

I wheeze.

The Keeper appears from nowhere, dodging the giant's free hand while holding something in both his own. He rolls aside as one immense arm swings at him. The other fist, with me in it, slams into the table next to him.

The force whips my head around and cracks my neck.

As Jaeger pulls his hand back to strike again, the Keeper bounds onto his wrist and catapults off. In midair, he propels a squash into the gaping maw of the giant.

Jaeger chokes. He drops me.

I fall onto the table with a crack as my ankle snaps with a white-hot fire.

The Keeper lands lightly beside me. He places a hand on my shoulder. The same warmth from the other night spreads throughout my body, and my ankle clicks back into place.

Maybe this magic stuff isn't too bad, if I can always be healed so quickly.

"Where is the Key?" he asks.

"In a dish of soup somewhere."

Frantically we search for it until moments later, I spot the dish and scoop it out.

"Hurry!" the Keeper urges.

I don't need to be told twice. I swear I run a personal record in the four hundred-meter dash as we race along the table, gruesome protracted sounds of choking rising behind us. As we run, the souls around us wake and vanish, the dishes of food disappear.

Jaeger has not caught up with us as we reach the door and dive through.

The Keeper slams the door shut behind us and taps the frame in various places, leaving sparks as he goes.

"Is he dead?" I pant.

"No. I only stopped him from consuming more *ayuve.*" He reopens the door.

I open my mouth to yell, but the door opens onto the mess of a waiting room.

Amber is gone.

I tighten my grip on the ring and smile to myself. Pride sparks in my chest. *I did it! I helped get the piece of the Key!*

As we move into the hall, I remark, "You're an acrobat, then, huh?"

"I am not," he says shortly. "That was from the Crusader army. They put spells on us so we can move like that."

Oh.

My thoughts move to what should be done with the Key. I want to hold onto it, but I suspect the Keeper won't be amenable to that.

Sure enough, he holds out his hands, gesturing at the Key.

I hand it over with a frown.

It shrinks to a more typical size the moment it passes into his grip.

The Keeper is silent and dour as we enter the ISERE. He beelines for the console, where he flicks switches and levers, taking us somewhere far away. As the engine rumbles, he places the piece of the Key in a small compartment of the console. Next he collapses onto the bench nearby. "I do not feel anything," he says, staring at his hands.

My eyebrows knit together as I try to deny the concern nesting in my chest. "What do you mean?"

He shakes his head. "I am...numb. Emotionally. I should have been scared, angry, but was not. I should be worried now over my numbness, but I am not."

Can I be numb too? I shove the thought away and sit next to him. "It's probably just a temporary side effect."

"I would say I hope so, but I do not."

The Keeper soon vanishes behind a pocket door across the atrium from the room I have been staying in.

The moment the door shuts again, I dart toward the console and run my hands over the area where I saw him stow the Key. Minutes pass before I give up, scowling at my reflection in the mirror. "Is it *you*?" I snap at the ISERE. "Are *you* why I can't find it? Some sort of spell or something, so only the friggin' Keeper can access the Key?"

No response.

Figures.

I shoot a look at the door which the Keeper lurks behind and make my way into the room I've been staying in. After locking the door behind me and dragging the bookshelf to block anyone from entering, I stride over to the window and peer outside. A deep breath of relief escapes me upon seeing only a sunset behind jagged, snowy mountains—no Tomb. I slump into the desk chair and pull out Ada's necklace.

What would she be doing right now, if she...were alive? Monday afternoon...she'd be at the gym with me, probably, in between classes and study sessions.

But she's not doing that. Because the Collector killed her.

I clench the chain in my fist.

The Collector killed Ada. The Collector has killed entire universes. The Collector wants to kill the rest.

What if I tried to kill her?

8

—·—

THE KEEPER

I sleep for a few hours. I dream of Adeka, a woman I met in my second dimension, who helped me stop hurting myself. I traced my skin with paint instead of the ink I use today, the way she taught me to. We speak of the Key, words spilling from us that I cannot remember.

I feel better when I wake. For a while, I sit with the memories Adeka brings with her, of me learning to move forward from loss, to find a purpose. Memories of me changing the color of my clothes from the blue of fresh mourning to the white of older grief.

With relief, I notice that the memories bring with them emotion; it seems the generalized lack of feeling resulting from Jaeger has more or less resolved. But when I think back to that memory with my sister, I just feel numb.

To avoid pondering this further, I decide to tackle the spell for the next piece of the Key.

There are six seemingly disparate sections to the spell outlined in the tome, with no notes on how to connect them. After spreading the sections on the table before me—each looking rather like a woven square—I morph my conduit ring into something resembling a crochet hook and stitch the sections together with a fine yarn I form from thin air. Each connection requires several rounds of stitching and unraveling and stitching and unraveling as I puzzle out which kind of spells to use.

As such, the location spell takes longer than the first, but when I am done, I dive immediately into examining the ring that the girl in the ivy gave me. Hours later, I am still tapping the ring and muttering under my breath, unable to decipher the details of the spell it contains.

Books are piled across the library table that I sit hunched over. None of them have been any help, which is unsurprising, considering the spell should not even be possible. Yet here it is, real as pain, and just as discomfiting.

"You never could accept the way things are," remarks a gentle voice from across the table.

I jump to my feet, knocking my chair back. My fingers clench tight around the ring when I see her, hazy and translucent, but most certainly there. "Rhys?" I whisper.

She stands before me, looking much the same as when the Collector took her: short blonde hair, pink blouse, dark jeans, even the locket containing photos of her deceased son. "Yes," she says with a woeful smile. "I'm not sure how I'm doing this, but I know that bloody spell of yours has something to do with it." Her left eyebrow twitches upward disapprovingly.

"Rhys," I repeat, shock flooding my system.

"I can't stay long. The Collector is still furious about the other night, and sooner or later she'll notice that I'm reaching out to you."

I fold my hands over my heart, unable to express my relief over the fact that I still have time. "I am so glad to see you! I have been working on a plan to save you. Thank the oceans it is not too late."

Rhys sighs, her eyes brimming with pain and sorrow. "Keeper... Thane."

I tense, remembering the last time she said my name, but as a non-mage, she would not be able to influence me again.

Pressing her palms together, she continues, "You need to let me go. *Please*, break the spell."

"No." I shake my head vigorously. "No. I can't abandon you." My voice snaps.

"Letting me go is not abandoning me." A tremor runs through her voice. "Do you know what she's doing? It's not just the ticking of whatever clock she lives to. She's taking my memories of my baby and pretending they belong to her." Tears trickle down her pellucid face. "She is pretending *my son* belongs to her. I want to have my boy again. Let me go so I can become part of the Collector, and she can't take my son further away from me."

Anger flashes through me, not directed at Rhys, but to somewhere or someone else, burning. "I can't allow the Collector to take any more!" I can't, I can't, I can't. The losses I have already suffered I know I cannot endure the likes of again.

"Keeper, I am *one* person, and I am already gone!" she cries. "You can't save me, but you can still save Teresa Misner and innumerable others!"

"I can save you! What makes you believe I cannot?" Only after the last word has escaped my mouth do I realize my voice has risen to a furious shout.

Rhys recoils but then raises her chin and straightens her shoulders. Her voice trembles when she speaks. "This is the you that scares me most."

I take a step back, shoulders dropping. "*What*?"

"Don't you know? Keeper, sometimes you..." She swallows, then appears to steel herself. "You get reckless and don't think things through when you're like this."

"Like *what*?" Why won't she *tell me*?

"Forget it! You never listen when like this."

Rhys wrings her hands. "Look, the Collector wants to use you for something. Something big. I don't know what or when, I'm sorry."

"But—"

"I have to go. Just please, take care of yourself. And listen to what I asked."

"Rhys—" In the moment before I can get the words out, all I am aware of is the ticking in my head, louder than ever. "Life awaits." It sounds so feeble, despite both of us knowing what it means.

She gives me a melancholy smile. "You, not me. Now live it."

Then she is gone.

I pace the floor, no longer interested in the copper ring or the spell for the Key. Nearly every possible emotion whirls through me. All the joints in my body grate at Rhys's words. I can't help but flick my hands every few steps; I want to do it more but suppress the urge.

Is there an issue with feeling intensely or reacting quickly? Perhaps I only seem reckless and thoughtless compared to the times I am muted and gloomy. I would take the highs of cyclothymia any day over the alternatives.

A long-forgotten memory comes to mind, stopping me in my tracks. Damien, my Damien, had said something very similar, hadn't he? The context for his assertion has long melted from my memory, but I do recall that he too had been frustrated—no, infuriated—with me. That too had struck me hard, as Damien had been such a gentle person, but I suppose that I had largely evicted the incident from my mind after his death.

The ticking rises in volume until it drowns out everything else. The noise sends an awful itch across my torso. I press my palms against my temples and stumble over to a window. I open it and inhale the lush green air. For just a moment, the songs of chirping birds tamp down on the ticking.

What *is* the ticking? I rub my forehead, try not to scratch it. It had begun after Rhys was abducted, hadn't it? It's so hard to remember. Had it simply been easy enough to ignore until I was a Beggar?

These concerns are interrupted by more of Rhys's words: "*Take care of yourself.*" The sentence is an explicit reminder that I should probably meditate, which I have not done in a while.

I sit near the window and try to take in the present moment: the feelings in my body, the sounds and scents of the library, the thoughts surfacing and submerging in my mind.

The thoughts. They fight to remain at the surface.

Rhys screaming my name. *Tick.* The feeling as a Beggar of people dying in the other library. *Tock.* Damien with golden eyes.

I leap to my feet, a cascade of other thoughts following, each intensifying and spreading the itch. *Misha saying, "Cold. Heartless. Broken." The hospital Damien took me to. My family as Beggars.* I am consumed by the itching. With a sharp inhale that never fulfills its desire to become a sob, I hunch over myself, grinding my knuckles into my scalp. My eyes burn from the pressure building behind them.

This. Must. Stop.

The knife Misha found in my hand flashes before my eyes: entirely black, entirely metal, a blade the length of my hand. Drenched in blood. That knife, I need it.

No, I do not! I berate the thought.

But the itch is only worsening, spreading.

Frantically I search my pockets until I find the felt-tip pen I carry at all times. I shove my sleeves up my arms and bring the tip of the pen to my skin. Lines erupt from the path of the pen, coming together to form flowers and other shapes that smudge as I sweep my hand across my arm again and again. When I complete the outlines, I fill them in until the itch has subsided, whereupon I cap the pen and place my head in my hands. Relief that I managed not to cut again washes over me, floods me.

I am not certain how much time passes before I hear Teresa's voice. "Keeper? Are...you okay?"

I lift my head, a little disoriented. "I don't believe so."

"Do you want to talk about it?" she asks hesitantly.

I tug down my sleeves. "Not here. I don't believe you have seen the garden?"

Still heavy with deep unhappiness yet restless with racing thoughts, I lead her out the front of the library and to the other set of carved wooden doors above the console. I pull the door open for her.

One step through the doorway, she stops. "Is this...?" She turns to me, then back to what lies beyond the door, brow furrowed. "Are we back outside the ISERE?"

I want the urge to smile. "Not at all. This is the ISERE's garden."

"Holy shit." Entranced, she takes a few steps forward on the stone-paved path.

I step in behind her, quietly closing the doors after me. I pause there, closing my eyes and deeply inhaling the scent of nature. It does not do enough to soothe the turmoil within me.

Directly before us is a square pool of water about my height in length on every side, edged by stone troughs overflowing with a variety of flowers native to Ayuve Island. In the center of the pool bubbles a small fountain.

The stone path encircles the pool and branches off on each side. The path to the right wanders off among a grove of trees in full summer foliage. To our left, the path winds through flower beds and rock gardens and over a spring and trickling stream. The two paths converge on the far side of the garden, at which point a branch spirals down through the lower levels.

Teresa turns toward a blue-and-black butterfly as it flutters past her face. She points at it. "How is that in here? Are there other pollinators? Is there a—" She pauses, rolling one hand as if trying to separate the words she wants from the air by winding them around her fingers. "—a whole garden environment's worth of animals and everything in here?"

"Interestingly, yes." My chest is filled with some weight, and I can hardly speak. I gesture to some individual trees visibly harboring birds. "But since this is a space considerably smaller than that many of these organisms require, the garden is loosely connected to my home island. Only small creatures can cross between places though, so no humans or other large organisms can do the same. All organisms here are native to my home, and the ISERE connects to whichever dimension she is in, so harm is mitigated." The weight begins to lift, and I feel a little calmer as I speak, finding a degree of solace in the garden the longer I spend here, as I so often do.

"Wow. Who designed this, do you know?"

"My father designed it. My mother helped him build it."

"They did an incredible job."

I rest my fingers on the Decomis, the device around my neck, and absently rub the inscription on its case.

Teresa moves beyond the fountain, following the path on the far side until it ends at a deck a short distance away.

Old but well-kept metal furniture, including a table, chairs, a pair of sofas, and an ottoman sit neatly arranged upon the deck. Inviting green cushions soften the seats, but I am the only one to have regularly accepted the invitation.

Teresa stops at the railing. When she stiffens, it becomes clear that she has seen the full extent of the garden. After a moment, she whirls on me to find that I am now beside her. "This is *amazing*!"

Below us are three more terraces through which the main path winds. The second and third terraces are organized much like the first, with trees off to our right and the stream running down from the left. The fourth and lowest terrace is mostly taken up by a large oval pond fresh from the grip of winter.

It is odd, this garden. Not simply because of its shape, but because each level cycles through the seasons out of sync with the others, allowing all four to be juxtaposed. Given the time of year it is outside, each season here is just beginning. The top terrace is summer, the second fall, the third winter, the fourth spring.

"How does this work?" Teresa leans out over the railing, her dark hair tumbling over her shoulders. "Do the temperatures vary? Does it ever precipitate? What exactly is the deal with the sun?" Without straightening, she cranes her neck to squint upward.

"That is a simulated sun there, one that reflects the passage of the sun over my island. Each terrace receives the proper amount of light, warmth, and precipitation to remain healthy. It is an enthrallingly complex system."

"Wow." Tess shakes her head, an admiring smile on her face. "Your parents must have been some geniuses."

I touch the Decomis once more. "Yes, they were. My mother in particular, when it came to the garden. As a Veqah, she tended to be more connected to the natural world, magically speaking. The magic of the Crusaders was less nuanced."

Tess watches me tug at the Decomis. "Did your parents meet during this project?"

I shake my head. "They met long before they began building the IS-ERE. No institution on the island wanted to employ a Veqah woman to work on such a prestigious, pioneering project, so my father quit his job and started his own research and engineering facility where he could employ Veqah, including my mother. The two were truly partners in everything."

"Damn. When was this?"

"Hm." I stare out across the garden in thought. "I do not know exactly how long ago, but certainly before I was born, which was one hundred twenty-four years ago."

"One hun—*what?*"

"One hundred twenty-four," I repeat, and tug on my jacket. How does she view magically extending life?

Teresa snorts. "I never would have placed you as being so young."

I place my hand on the railing. The grain of the wood is pleasantly rough against my fingers.

Any agreeable wisp that had arisen upon entering the garden vanishes under the cloud of frustration and anguish surrounding my conversation with Rhys.

Teresa takes notice. Reluctance and hesitancy are audible in her voice when she says, "Why don't we sit down?"

We do, and I spill out everything about Rhys: how we first met when I was repairing an anomaly; how we crossed paths again three years later, after she had had a son and he had died of an illness; how she became my closest friend in decades...

We initially bonded through our grief, but our relationship only strengthened as we came to know each other beyond it.

One time when we were trying to repair a rift being studied by scientists, she and I got into a competition to see who could get a scientist to speak the most jargon so we could learn whether the Decomis translated it, which, as it turns out, it hardly does.

Rhys was creative and thoughtful. Everything she said was thoroughly considered and often insightful.

Of course, that meant she caught on quickly to my ever-shifting moods, and other divergences from the norm I experience. She was the reason I was even diagnosed with cyclothymia and autism.

When I get to explaining what happened when the Collector took Rhys, speaking becomes difficult. "The Collector found us one day when we were both outside the ISERE; I can only assume my protective spells were not adequate, especially considering they did not have an anchor like your ring. Before I was even aware of her presence, she had control of me and my access to magic. She forced me to break down the remnants of my protective spells so she could take Rhys.

"Sometimes I cannot get the image of Rhys begging me to help her as the Collector carried her away out of my mind. But I was helpless. I fought against the Collector, and nearly broke free when Rhys spoke my name, but I still could not save her. All I could do was...tie her soul to a ring in an effort to prevent the Collector from subsuming her."

That spell, and how to break it, was what the Collector was looking for when she turned me into a Beggar.

Teresa tries to disguise her expression, but it is enough.

Ashamed, I stare at my hands, which wring each other without mercy. Does some part of me hope Teresa is ashamed of me too?

"That's…" she tries. "Is it working?"

"Somewhat," I admit. "But…Rhys wants me to cut the spell."

"Does she want it or is the Collector somehow making her want it?"

The birdsong becomes grating to my ears.

I can hardly make myself say it. "I—I think she truly wants it."

"Then do you think you should do it?" Teresa asks abruptly.

The backs of my eyes burn. I feel so, so alone.

I feel terrible: bitterness and agitation and anxiety churn inside me, chipping and wearing at my insides. I hate these moods, this aspect of cyclothymic disorder. They are not quite as common as the highs or lows, but they come. They writhe. They gnaw.

Now I must push through it, for I have delayed finding the second piece of the Key long enough.

The building that evidently houses it is an art museum with a smooth white exterior. Before we enter, I cast a deflection spell over both of us.

"Is this how people don't see the ISERE?" Teresa asks.

I do not want to speak, but I do, for Teresa's sake. "Yes—it deflects attention."

"Then how could I see it the other night?"

"The ISERE can control the deflection spell. She knew you were near, and that the Collector was too, and she wanted you to find the door. To find safety."

"Hm."

As we enter the building, I open the Decomis. I had connected it to the Key-finding spell so I can pinpoint the exact location of the Key.

"I see that is not a watch," Teresa observes, peering over my shoulder at the device.

"A watch?" I force any unfriendliness out of my voice. "Why would this be a watch? No, this is the Decomis, which communicates with the ISERE and can also translate many languages, including those of many magical creatures. I also set it up so it can track items such as each piece of the Key."

We walk up to the third floor and soon find ourselves in a large room, devoid of other people, with three walls that each have paintings. The fourth wall is a mirror, the surface of which appears to be rippling, but only when I look at it from the corner of my eye.

I close the Decomis and approach the mirror.

As I reach out to touch it, a voice from my right warns, "I wouldn't do that if I were you."

Teresa and I both start and search for the source—no one is there. I wave my hand, scanning the area for a hidden person, but find nothing. We exchange glances and turn back to the mirror.

"You figure it's behind the mirror or something?" she asks me.

"One could say that," says a second voice.

I whip around and finally take a closer look at the paintings on the wall.

One painting is of a gray horse in a barn. The one to the right of it is a similar style, but with a different horse, palomino, galloping through a field. They are alive, I notice, as one twitches an ear, and the other's mane and tail ripple slightly.

"Hi!" greets the first horse, the gray one in the barn, when he sees me notice him.

Teresa's jaw drops.

"Hey, don't worry, we're just paintings!" the second horse reassures her.

"Really *cool* paintings," adds the first. "But Kevin's kind of a jerk. He wants to get you killed by convincing you to go through the mirror."

"*Through* the mirror?" I ask.

"Kevin," echoes Teresa.

"Oh, come *on,* Todd," Kevin whines. "Stop making my job harder than it already is."

Todd ignores him. "You two—I strongly advise against going through the mirror. You'll probably die if you do."

"What's on the other side?" Teresa inquires.

"Not sure," chirps Kevin. "But you should *totally* check it out."

"Is the piece of the Key there?" I ask. This is far more irritating than it should be.

"It's not worth it, man," Todd whinnies.

"It's *definitely* worth it," retorts Kevin.

I look between them, annoyed. "I suppose you are two of the Key's guardians of a sort."

"Sure, I guess," Todd says, rather morosely. "*I* am, but I don't see how Kevin would be."

Kevin counters, but I stop listening and turn back to the mirror.

I wave my hand over the mirror; it certainly does seem to be a portal of some kind. I check the Decomis once more to verify that the piece of the Key is on the other side. "Teresa?"

She appears at my shoulder. "Mm-hm?"

Todd and Kevin both fall silent.

"I am going through the mirror. If I am not back in twenty minutes, come for me."

She frowns deeply. "Do you really think we should separate again?"

"This time? Yes."

Teresa purses her lips but concedes. "Fine. Be careful, Magic Man."

I see myself reflected scores of times over. The next room across the other gallery is walled with mirrors, leaving no bare speck of wall to be seen. The ceiling is low and set with bright lights. Reflected in the mirror before me, the entryway behind me shimmers and vanishes.

I turn in time to see another mirror appear in the space I had entered a moment earlier. Uneasy, I turn back to the rest of the room.

A small pedestal stands in the center, where nothing stood before. On it sits a business card and a ring, side by side. A small note sits between the items: *The card will solve your problem. The Key will corrupt you.*

I reach out, but unsurprisingly, my hand collides with an invisible wall before I can get too close. I curl my fingers to summon the items, to no avail—neither object budges. Instead of occupying myself further with the ring and the card, I decide to examine the mirrors.

As I approach one, my reflection shudders and is replaced by another image. My breath catches in my chest. Rhys stands before me in the field where I last saw her in person, smiling at me. My heart constricts. I cannot resist touching the mirror.

I lose all control of my body, feel myself assume familiar positions. Somehow, I know exactly what will happen. Because it happened before.

Sure enough, I feel the magic flowing through my body to form the same spells it did then, spells to break the last of my protective magic, as the Collector takes Rhys away. I cannot fight off the same motions I was forced to carry out not so long ago. Horror floods me again and again with every movement.

After, I collapse onto the ground, trembling.

The ring, I remind myself. *The ring.*

Then I am back in the mirrored room.

I pick myself up off the floor. The card lurks in the back of my mind, but I attempt to summon the ring again. It remains in place—I must have to cycle through the mirrors to obtain the ring.

The sight in the next mirror twists my heart in my chest. The home I shared with Damien for those few years stares back at me. Grief and resignation weighing on me, I touch the mirror and am transported into our home.

Damien stumbles through the front door. His eyes are gold. "Thane," he says. "I am sorry. I did not know he was a Beggar, and I touched him before his eyes turned gold."

He had come to say goodbye.

And he did.

Hardly able to breathe, again I summon an invisible barrier between us so that he cannot touch me, and I know he wants to, one last time, because I want to, one last time. I watch his knees buckle, tears run down his cheeks.

I choke on tears of my own.

"Thane..."

Again I listen to his last words. And watch him crumble to dust.

What must I relive to obtain the ring?

Suddenly I find myself in the mirrored room yet again. Remembering my task seems to bring me back to this room.

Once more, I cannot reach the ring, so I reluctantly turn to the next mirror, hugging myself and rocking slightly side to side as I do.

My heart drops at what I see.

The empty barracks where I had spent a year of my life, where I found myself publicly humiliated and shamed and disgraced, stand on the other side of the glass. The knife sits unsheathed on my bunk.

I touch the mirror with a tremoring hand, dread of what I will experience next constricting my throat.

My skin erupts in the worst, most expansive itch I have ever experienced. *Cold.* My hand reaches for solace, for the knife on the bed. *Heartless.* Unable to wait long enough to roll up my left sleeve, I slice right through it and the skin beneath. *Broken.*

The itch does not subside like it should. I hold back a desperate sob and slice again. And again. Deeply. Blood gushes from the wounds and splatters onto the floor, onto my face. The itch only intensifies.

Finally, I rip off my mutilated sleeve and turn the knife to the side: if my emotions will not escape my skin—

I wedge the blade under my dermis and scrape forward.

The pain, burning oceans, the *pain,* but it clears my head, stops the itching for just one moment—

So I do it again. Cut my skin away in uneven swaths, small at first, then less so.

A sound from the doorway stops me.

Him.

Misha.

"What on the island are you doing?" He approaches, then laughs.

Laughs.

"That is not how you kill yourself." He mimes taking a knife in both hands and driving the blade up under his sternum to pierce his heart.

A calm passes over me. A calm that was never there when this truly occurred. I turn the knife, angle it, stab upward.

The blood gushing from my wound reminds me of the ISERE's door.

Somewhere, I sense my mother smiling—her son is joining her at last.

Somewhere, I smile too.

And then I cry.

I wake up on the cool floor of the mirrored room. Not a sign of blood. The only sign of injury is my scars, barely faded after one hundred five years.

Thinking of what happened, I gag. I lie back against the floor, shuddering.

My eyes catch the pedestal. The card will solve my problems... *No*, I remind myself. *The ring*.

What *did* happen? Why were the mirrors showing me memories, then adding something that never occurred? Is it a way to break me? Make me take the card instead of the ring?

Shakily I stand and, upon trying and failing to reach the ring, move to the next mirror. And see Naida, red hair, freckles, but in the Collector's white dress, sprawled on her back on the floor behind me.

I whip around to find the room still empty, save the pedestal. I face the mirror once more. "Naida?"

She does not move. I am not certain she is even breathing. Then I see the bruises in the shape of hands wrapping around her throat.

"*Naida*!" I pound at the mirror. The moment my hand touches it, everything vanishes. Once more my limbs begin moving against my volition, elbows and knees bending, fingers crooking.

What memory is this?

The atrium of the ISERE forms around me. The Collector, frigid and achromic, faces me from the center of the floor.

Before she can move, my arms do. They flick outward, throwing bands of orange light that snap around the Collector's wrists and drag her backward to slam her into the entrance door.

I recognize the spell as it crackles down my fingers: magic blockers.

My legs carry me over to the Collector. My body pins hers against the door more firmly. My hands fold around her neck. And squeeze.

The Collector only smiles.

I can feel her pulse beneath my palms.

As I choke her, her face reddens, then turns purple. Freckles burst into appearance across her cheeks. Her hair reddens. The gray eyes stay the same.

Naida smiles at me before unconsciousness takes her. Still I choke her, unable to pry myself free.

I scream.

Her pulse flutters to a stop, and only when it is gone for eighteen, nineteen, twenty seconds can I release her.

My first best friend crumples to the floor, freed from the magic blockers and my chokehold.

My breath rips through my throat in horrified gasps. I stare at my hands in shocked disbelief. What did I do, deep hells, what did I *do?* I shove my traitorous fingers in my hair, trying to think.

Naida is already gone, she's been gone, it's just the mirrors, you need to get the card.

The card?

In a blink, I am standing in the mirrored room once again.

I shudder, hug myself, stare at the pedestal. The card...what is it? I need to know. Why did thoughts of it bring me back to this room, just as thoughts of the ring did? Hells, why did I live a moment I have never experienced when the rest were memories, or mostly so?

The card will solve your problem.

Perhaps I can solve everything in a simpler way...

Slowly I walk to the fifth mirror.

In it I see two chalk circles drawn side by side on a concrete floor. A sickle is drawn inside one.

I touch the mirror. I find myself in one of the circles, the one without the sickle. The business card from the pedestal is in my hand. It is blank, except for two blood-red sickles crossed on one side.

I shiver.

My bloody thumb presses the image on the card, and I am shown what happens next. When I emerge from the mirror, I grab the card.

9

TESS

Kevin and Todd don't make great company.

"Oh, I wish he wouldn't have done that," Todd sighs.

"Hey, lady!" Kevin whinnies. "You should go in too! The more, the merrier!"

"In that case, why don't I take you off the wall and huck you through the mirror?" I ask.

"Hm," says Kevin.

"I'd like that," pipes up Todd. "I mean, it's a bad idea, but Kevin could get a taste of his own medicine."

"Aw, man, I thought we were friends."

"Eh...you're definitely the only painting I talk to. I mean, these are the only two people we've spoken to in years. That one lady earlier wouldn't even talk!"

I turn my head so fast that I crack my neck. "What lady?"

"Oh, you know," Kevin neighs. "Tall, white dress, white—well, white *everything*, really."

"When did she go in?" I ask urgently.

"Not long before you got here," Todd informs me.

"Why didn't you say anything before? She could have hurt the Keeper by now!" My hands start shaking, and I clench them into fists in an effort to steady them.

"How were we supposed to know?" Kevin whinnies indignantly.

Without waiting any longer, I step into the mirror. My shoulders are tense, face turned to the side as I half-expect to collide with a real mirror. But thanks to this magic crap, I open my eyes to find myself in a gallery nearly identical to the one I was just in. However, it's like looking at it through broken glass, fractures slicing down and across the room.

Shattered versions of Kevin and Todd hang from the wall.

"You shouldn't have done that," Todd says glumly.

Kevin gives me a horse's grin. "Thanks for coming!"

"Which way do I go?" I ask.

They both gesture to my left, one gloomily and one cheerily.

"Thanks." (*I guess.*) I set off into the next gallery, but instead of a room filled with art, I enter a hexagonal room with mirrors for walls. The brokenness of the other gallery is gone. A new mirror forms behind me once I step inside.

Great. I bite my lip.

The Keeper and the Collector are nowhere to be found.

Stepping farther into the room, I nearly run into a pedestal that I swear hadn't been there a moment ago. On the pedestal is a smaller version of Jaeger's ring and a business card with only two crossed sickles on the up-facing side. I read the note and wonder with a shiver what exactly it means. Solve which problem? Corrupt me how?

I try to pick up the ring, but my hand is stopped several inches away by an unseen force. I should have known it wouldn't be that easy. Rubbing my hand as though touching the invisible barrier had hurt it, I look around the room.

At first, all I see are dozens of versions of myself and the pedestal. I only see from the corner of my eye one of the mirrors change.

Hunter, my ex-boyfriend, sits at a table in a café, wearing the same blue jeans and anime T-shirt that I last saw him in. He gives me the same bemused smile that I last saw on his face.

I breathe his name, my heart aching as I approach the mirror. "You're not really here, are you?" I hate the note of hope in my voice. *Remember what he said, Teresa.* My hand brushes the mirror.

Next thing I know, I'm sitting across from him, clutching my empty mug with one hand and my purse with the other, as if wanting to throw the mug then bolt with my purse.

"Why do you want to study that?" he asks me, puzzled at the major I had just told him was my choice. "I mean, I get you're a woman, but why study being a woman? Or any of those other things?"

"I, uh…" My lips, tongue, jaw all move without my will.

He frowns (frowned?). "What is it?"

"I'm… I'm bi."

His face is expressionless.

I wish I could know what he was thinking, I still want to know how he reached his horrifically erroneous conclusion.

"So you're greedy now? Are you telling me you *have* been cheating on me with Ada?" He gives an incredulous half-laugh.

"What?" The enraged word explodes out of me. People turn their heads, but I ignore them. *"No!* I have *never*—you have *no* reason to believe—" I stop spluttering.

Then, now in complete control, I say something I could only wish I had after the fact: "I can't believe I ever loved you."

The café vanishes. I find myself standing again as the mirrored room reforms around me.

"*Fuck* you," I snap at the room. Too furious to think properly, I grab for the ring. My fingers curl around it. I pocket it and march through the doorway that has spontaneously reopened.

The mirror I passed through initially, shattered on this side, is still exactly where I had come through. (*Did I think it wouldn't be? I think I did.*)

But someone else is reflected in it with me: the Collector.

With a gasp, I whirl around, but she isn't there. She is only in the mirror.

"Hurry!" Todd moans. "The other lady is about to pass back through!"

I dive through and find the Keeper sitting against Kevin and Todd's wall, staring at a card in his hands. "I have the Key. We need to go *now!*" I bark.

He clambers to his feet.

We sprint to the stairs.

A blast rocks the room behind us just as we escape.

The Keeper pauses just long enough to throw a flaming barrier behind us.

I hear it shatter like glass as we reach the ground floor.

The floor beneath us suddenly turns to deep mud. The Keeper and I both nearly fall as we sink. We can barely move forward.

Terror pulses in my veins. *Oh my god, I'm going to lose my soul.*

The Keeper turns and throws a blast of light over his shoulder.

The spell seems to work—we can run again.

I stumble forward out of the grip of the floor. As I catch myself, my hand brushes against my pocket.

My knife.

My knife is there.

The Keeper and I are almost to the lobby.

Despite my fear, I make my decision. And veer away from the entrance.

The Keeper yells my name, but I dive behind a display of pottery and hunch there, panting.

I exchange the piece of the Key for my pocketknife.

A sound from across the gallery makes me jump: a museum patron has collapsed to the floor, clutching his head. I can hear him softly crying.

My heart stops as I comprehend what's happening to him. My hand clenches around my knife.

You're doing this for the people you'll never meet.

I peer around the base of the display case.

Nothing. No one.

Then the Keeper backs into view. His eyes focus on a space just a few yards away from him. His hands float before him, encased in light. His feet glide over the floor. "Teresa!" he yells. "We need to *get out of here!*"

The air around him shimmers.

I see the light fade from his hands as he presses them against his chest.

What is he doing?

It's only when his mouth opens and chest hitches that I realize *he can't breathe.*

Shit—get going, Teresa.

I dive around the other end of the display case and duck behind one a few feet closer to the spot where the Keeper stares—where the Collector must be. I stick my head out and scan for the Collector.

She stands about fifteen yards away from me, her hands held with fingers crooked before her. A focused snarl twists her face.

I snap the blade of my knife open.

Now, Tess.

I dart from display to display. Closer and closer.

The Collector doesn't take her eyes off the suffocating Keeper.

I take a quiet, steeling breath. And sprint toward the Collector. The hand clutching my knife swings toward the center of her back.

And stops.

My whole body halts just as abruptly. I try to throw all my weight behind the blade, but *I. Can't. Move.* I grimace and struggle.

On the other side of the Collector, the Keeper falls to the floor, seemingly unconscious.

And then our adversary turns to face me.

My eyes widen involuntarily as I stare back into her flat gray gaze yet again. My breath quickens as I realize I am *terrified.* Even frozen in place, I begin to tremble.

I have cost myself my own soul.

The Collector reaches for my outstretched hand.

A massive scraping sound comes from my left. A fraction of a second later, a display case slams into the Collector's side.

Her paralyzing grip releases me.

I don't take the time to see the aftermath of the collision—I run.

The Keeper rises from the floor as I pass him. We hurry together out of the museum.

I keep expecting the Collector to appear in our path before we can make it to the ISERE, but she does not.

The Keeper whistles a single note, swinging from low to high, opening the ISERE's door just before we reach it. He slams the door shut behind me and sprints over to the console, pressing buttons and flicking switches to take us away.

Panting, I slap at my pockets to check that I still have the piece of the Key. I sigh with relief as I pull it out. Without warning, my legs become rubbery; I seat myself on a bench so I don't collapse.

My breathing slows the longer I stare at the ring. After several moments, I close my eyes.

The engine calms back into its soft resting rhythm. It's only then I realize how quiet the atrium is.

I crack open an eye to see the Keeper with his back to me, hands planted against the console, head hanging low.

He looks up at me in the mirror without moving his head. "Teresa," he says with pain and exhaustion and a hint of disapproval.

I straighten, opening both my eyes.

"Why did you do that?"

I scoff indignantly. "Excuse me? Why did I try to *kill the Collector?*"

He sighs, straightens, turns to face me. "Why did you put yourself in so much more *danger?*"

"You mean so much more danger than I was already in? Because you evidently couldn't get the Key, so I had to? *Right before* the Collector got it?"

He looks like I just slapped him. "I am sorry," he murmurs. "But I do not believe you want to know the things I saw."

"I'm sure I don't!" I exclaim, just because I can't think of a sufficient retort. "But that's *not the point*! The point is *stopping the Collector, dammit! At all costs!*"

His voice stays low and level when he replies. "You act as if the cost is low."

I blink. "*What?*"

He lowers his gaze but says nothing more.

"I hope the damn business card is worth it," I spit. I throw the ring at his face and stalk away.

In the room of the ISERE that I suppose is my own, I flick through old photos of Ada and messages between us.

Here is a photo of us last Halloween, as Hastur and Ligur from *Good Omens.* Here is the bisexual meme she sent me. Here is the picture I sent of her lying drunk on the sidewalk, and the accompanying replies she sent the next morning telling me of the drunk texts she sent her boyfriend.

I cry and think of the times we snuck chicken nuggets into the movie theater, or when we bought several "weird" Oreo flavors and hosted a party to determine which was the best. (Mint. Strawberry Cheesecake was shortchanged.)

I linger on the memory of me coming out to her, and her telling me she loved me and holding me.

My parents are under threat. I already shut out the Keeper more than once. Who do I have right now?

10

THE KEEPER

When I emerge from the library later that day after working on the spell for the third piece of the Key, I can hear the angry strum of a ukulele and Teresa's irritated voice singing about stabbing someone in the back coming from somewhere up above.

I consider approaching the walkway from which I can see her legs dangling, but I remember our last interaction and decide against it. It is not that I hold a grudge against Teresa—I do not, rather I agree that the Collector should be stopped at all costs—but such a scale of sacrifice is not something I feel I am capable of.

And yet, here I am, having vowed to stop her.

And, for me, the cost is too high—no matter the outcome.

Out of nowhere, an urgently blaring alarm jolts me so badly that I nearly keel over in panic—*this dimension is ending*.

The mirror above the console ripples into a screen and tells me a slightly different story. However, it takes me a few moments to calm down enough to comprehend that.

Teresa races down the set of spiral stairs to my right, ukulele clutched in one hand, face taut with fear. "What's going on?" she calls over the alarm.

Concern tightens my chest. "The ISERE has picked up on an anomaly that urgently needs repaired."

She hurries to my side, just as curious as she is frightened. "What is it?"

"The dimensions on either side of a rift are...pushing through the opening to overlap with each other. I had no idea this was even possible. It is so destabilizing that, theoretically, it should not be. This is only some of what results from the Collector's actions."

Teresa's words from earlier ring through my head: "The point is *stopping the Collector, dammit! At all costs!*"

Her next words startle me with the contrast. "The multiverse has a hernia?"

I close my eyes, not sure how else to react. "I am no doctor, but I suppose you are not entirely wrong."

She claps her hands. "All right, let's go!"

I glance at her. "Whatever you do, avoid touching any interdimensional rifts." I prepare the ISERE for travel to the anomaly.

"Why's that?"

"You are not a surgeon."

The sky at our destination is a weak twilight gray. I button my jacket against a cold wind that smells of the recent rain that has left the ground damp. Before us sprawl grassy hills dotted with small homes and patched with harvested crop fields.

We walk along a paved road, the wind in our faces.

Without warning, dense trees burst into appearance around us, vanish, reappear. After less than a second, the world settles back into autumn farmland, soon enough that I think I imagined it.

I look at Teresa and know she saw it too. Without saying a word, we remain rooted in place with bated breath.

Only moments later, it happens again. One second, the browning grasses sway and dip under the wind. The next, bright-leafed trees tower above undergrowth and leaf mold. The pavement under our feet becomes gravel.

I turn to Teresa again, but she is gone.

"Teresa?" My voice is tinged with anxiety.

She reappears when the original environment flickers back, then vanishes again as the world oscillates back to the forest.

The world settles back into the fields, Teresa at my side once more. Her eyes are as wide as mine.

"That was scary," she comments casually, then clears her throat.

My left shoulder blade itches. "We should probably hold hands, so we don't get separated again," I suggest, holding out my hand.

She narrows her eyes a little.

I begin to lower my hand, but then she takes it with an expression of uncertainty and suspicion.

We continue walking, and as we climb up a hill, the world begins switching again.

"Look." I point across the road to a worn-down white cottage with faded black shutters and loose shingles.

A young woman stands in the driveway, her lips parted slightly as she stares at us. Then like a phantom, she flickers out of sight; trees are painted around us, the cottage's façade brightens, the road turns to gravel under our feet. The trees evaporate, the cottage ages, the woman reappears. Her soft voice is almost lost in the wind. "Are things switching for you too?"

The woman invites us into the living room, which is cozy, though that may only be in comparison to the weather outside. Well-used sofas slouch along the walls, facing a scratched coffee table littered with magazines. The thick carpet underfoot is mottled with various shades of brown, which I doubt was the original pattern or color. Everything is washed in a warm but sallow light.

The woman, who introduced herself as Annette, perches nervously on the edge of an overstuffed armchair as Teresa and I settle onto a sofa. Half of Annette's head is shaved, leaving the rest of her blond locks to flow over one shoulder. She surveys the room with an anxious eye framed with winged eyeliner. "This place, it is not my home. It almost is, but it's a bit like an elderly person lives here instead of us. And outside—" She glances through the window for at least the fourth time since letting us in. "I don't understand it. Farmland instead of forest?" Her accent is markedly different from Teresa's, or Rhys's.

"When did the switching begin?" I ask, trying to emanate calm for Annette's sake.

"Yesterday. It happened twice then but has happened more frequently today. Sometimes my girlfriend would disappear when it happened, like you did on the road."

"Where is your girlfriend now?"

Teresa shoots me a look that I cannot discern from the corner of my eye.

"I don't know," Annette whispers. "She vanished an hour ago, and I haven't seen her since. We were in the dining room." She leads us into the next room, a tight area with a dark dining table and mismatched chairs. A door directly across the room leads to the backyard while the kitchen is off to the left.

"What's her name?" Teresa asks.

"Zazil."

As if in response to Annette, movement in the doorway to the kitchen catches my eye. Nothing substantial, more akin to the flicker of a dust mote floating by and accompanied by a faint whisper: "*Annette!*"

"Zazil?" she cries. "Where are you?" She wheels on Teresa and me. "Do you know what's going on?" Her voice is desperate and frightened.

My voice remains gentle but firm. "Yes, and we can help. Do you know the multiverse theory?" At her bemused face, I continue, "The theory that there are multiple universes, multiple versions of reality?"

Teresa taps my shoulder. "Keeper, she thinks you're crazy," she mutters.

"Oh, so you're *both* in on this?" Annette half turns away, touching her fingertips to her forehead. "And here I was thinking *I* was insane."

"The universes are all thinly layered on top of each other, only one step apart," I persist. "This universe and yours are bleeding into each other. I can reunite you and Zazil in your universe and seal it off."

"Whatever you say. Um, please get out." Annette starts toward the front door, but stops short, eyes widening.

I follow her gaze to glimpse another incorporeal movement.

Teresa follows it into the living room.

I blink in surprise at what I see in the room she enters: the carpet is newer, the furniture too, lighter in color, and arranged differently.

But more importantly, there stands a dark-haired woman that has appeared—or rather, a woman that had been here while we had not.

Teresa rounds on her heel when Annette cries out.

The room flickers once.

I see Teresa reach out and grip Zazil's arm.

The house flickers again, and the two women are gone.

11

—·—

TESS

"Shit." I would say more, but I think that roughly sums up our situation. Then I realize that Zazil has no idea who I am or what is going on, so I fill her in. "Annette's okay," I finish. "She'll stay that way with the Keeper around." I hope my voice projects the confidence I try to throw behind it, especially since I am not so sure how much I believe those words.

"Good." Zazil exhales in cautious relief. She seems to be handling the newfound knowledge of the multiverse well.

We wait in the updated version of the living room for what feels like an apprehensive hour but is likely only minutes. On occasion we catch glimpses of something moving in the living room or dining room, something slightly warping the appearance of objects as it passes by. I am sure it is only the Keeper or Annette, but still unease bubbles up in my chest.

Eventually I decide to start calling for the Keeper, but the moment I do so, the house around us begins to flicker—but not like before. Instead of flitting back and forth between two dimensions, the environment alternates between blinding whiteness and the two universes superimposed upon one another.

The floor beneath one of my feet vanishes entirely. With a startled yelp, I lose my balance.

Zazil grabs my arm before I can fall and hauls me toward her. "We need to get out of this room. Come on!" Without waiting for an answer, she drags me down the hall.

We race into the farthest door and stumble to a halt as the house settles back into what I presume is Zazil's dimension. We stand, clutching each other, in a tidy bedroom with a yellow-and-gray color scheme. The only sound is our breathing until we relax enough to sit on the edge of the bed, still gripping each other's arms.

"So," I say uncertainly, part of my brain focusing a little too much on the fact that Zazil is also queer, and pretty, and holding me. "Nice place you have. Lived here long?"

Zazil gives a nervous giggle. "A few months."

We fall into silence again, mostly because I don't really know how to continue a conversation in this situation.

"You know," Zazil says, "your German is really good. A bit better than mine, at least. I mean, your accent is bad, but your actual pronunciation is g—" She is interrupted by a thin, faint wail behind us.

We whip around to see nothing abnormal.

"Clove is back at it again, it seems," Zazil says.

"What?"

Zazil blushes. "It started out as a joke. This house is old, so odd things happen, and we jokingly attribute them to a ghost named Clove. But in the last few days it seems like there might be an actual ghost in this room."

"How so?"

She shrugs. "Annette and I have heard sounds like what you and I just heard, and a couple of times we saw something there." She points to the back corner of the room.

My gaze follows her finger. At first I see nothing, but upon closer inspection, there seems to be a warping of the air before the dresser. Unlike when we caught a glimpse of Zazil's movement from the other dimension, this oddity seems to be stationary.

I stand and approach the area to stop a couple feet away. Slowly I reach out. My fingers meet slight resistance, then pass through without further event. I look up to see a face grimacing at me, the air condensed to embolden the lines.

With a gasp, I recoil.

A brief moan issues from the apparition.

"There really is something there, isn't there?" Zazil says in a small voice.

I nod mutely. I bite my lip in an effort to quell the horror.

Once more, the flickering begins.

Zazil reaches for my hand, which I take.

As the oscillations between universes slow, someone calls my name from down the hallway.

"Keeper?" My hand rips free of Zazil's as I race toward his voice.

The house flickers back and forth once more.

I emerge into the living room to find it empty. Disappointment and fear wash over me, sending me through the other rooms in search of the Keeper. When I return to the living room, Zazil is there, holding a small piece of paper.

"This was on the floor," she informs me, handing it over.

I must have missed it.

It reads: *The rift is in the basement.*

12

— · —

THE KEEPER

With a twinge of frustration, I find myself back in the dated living room of Teresa's home dimension.

"Was Zazil all right? Did you get her the message?" Annette asks urgently.

"I did not see either of them, but I did hear Teresa. I can only hope that they recovered the note."

"Brilliant," she grumbles. She seems unhappy to have more or less accepted the existence of a multiverse.

I scratch my forehead. "We need to get back to the basement."

The door to said basement is in the hallway. Rickety stairs lead down into a dank, filthy space littered with ancient appliances and cobwebs. The rotting carcass of a mouse sprawls at the bottom of the steps. A few crickets flee our path as we cross the basement to a crevasse raked across the cinderblock wall and ceiling. Tendrils of frayed energy flutter around the edges of the gash. Waves of free energy boil and roll on the far side.

I snap my fingers, carving two broad circles in the floor a safe distance away from the rift. "Annette, stand in one of the circles, please." I make sure she does as I say before turning back to the rift. As I place my hand beside it, the basement begins to flicker between the whiteness and the two dimensions. I need to hurry. I close my eyes and concentrate. I imagine my hand is anchoring me to the wall of Teresa's dimension and her dimension only, sending out tendrils to tether Annette here as well. When I sense the presences of Teresa and Zazil, I reach out to them.

Soon the turmoil subsides, leaving all four of us in the same dimension.

"Keeper!" Teresa's cry sounds more relieved than I believe she would ever want to admit.

"Teresa," I acknowledge, cutting back on my own relief. "Step into that circle. Zazil, step in with Annette. Ensure that your entire body is in the circle, as I am sure none of you would like to have anything cut off. The circles will keep you grounded in your proper dimensions while protecting you from the other as I repair this situation."

"What are you going to do, then? Will you be safe?" Teresa asks.

"Hopefully."

"Are you kidding."

I elect to ignore that remark. After one last look to confirm the others are safely within their boundaries, I turn back to the rift and place my hand over it.

The energy surges over my skin and up my arm. It roils in my abdomen and crackles through my brain.

The power. This amount of energy I have experienced only once before, and it nearly killed me. I can *feel* the instability, the pain of the rift flowing through me.

The ticking pounds in my head.

"Keeper!" Teresa screams from far away. "*Focus!*"

Focus. Her voice echoes through my head.

I cling to it, breathe, and push some of the energy out of my body. I grasp at the folds of energy, struggling to separate them. Sweat rolls down my face, doing nothing to cool my overheating body.

I just might combust. I just might fail.

A hand grips my shoulder.

I open my eyes to see Teresa kneeling at my side. Am I on my knees?

She meets my tired gaze with her steady one. Her lips move, but I can't hear what she says, and can't put in the effort to read her lips.

It doesn't matter.

I find the strength to try again. The universes unfurl beneath my touch, layering properly on top of each other. With further effort, I tug the edges of the rift closed and weave the loose tendrils of energy together, pulling in nearby free-flowing energy to fill in any empty spaces.

I fall back onto the floor.

Annette and Zazil are gone, Teresa still at my side.

"You shouldn't have left the circle," I mumble.

"You shouldn't try everything alone," she retorts.

Some part of me desires to relax into her shoulder and close my eyes. Instead, I climb to my feet. "We should be going."

"There's something I want you to see in the bedroom first. It won't take long."

The bedroom is just as aged as the rest of the house, and once we round the bed, I see why. An elderly white man, likely in his nineties, is crumpled on the floor beside the bed.

Teresa gives a soft gasp.

"He must have been caught between the dimensions as they pushed past each other," I murmur as I examine him.

"He's dead, isn't he?"

Solemnly I nod.

Together, we lift the man's body and lay him on the white bed-spread.

"We can't just leave him here," Teresa says.

"No, we cannot. After we leave, I will call the authorities to request a welfare check. Hopefully someone will find him before long." On our way out, I pocket a piece of mail with the man's name and address. I leave the front door unlocked.

The walk back to the ISERE seems so much longer than it was before.

13

TESS

We sit in the music room, side by side on the piano bench.

I try to put together Bishop Briggs's "I TRIED" a measure at a time, having never played it before on the piano.

Neither of us speaks for a long time; in the wordlessness, the song becomes more coherent and flowing.

"How are you doing?" the Keeper asks.

I pause, mildly surprised, and look at him askance. "What?"

"You have been through a lot the past couple of days. How are you doing?"

"Oh." I ponder how to answer. I mean, I'm not doing great, that's for sure. There's still a chasm yawning inside me, where the love and presence of Ada used to exist. But I don't really want to mention that. It's...weirdly intimate to admit. I'm also scared shitless about the safety of my parents, and obviously my soul, the latter of which I would never admit aloud. But at the same time, I've been feeling this pull, this drive to leave the ISERE and stop the Collector, and it's stronger than my sense of self-preservation. And the exhilaration that's come with success? Well. "I..." I begin. "It's complicated." How much do I tell him? I still haven't told a soul about what Hunter said, and oh, how I want to divulge that memory to *some*one. "But I'm surviving. So far."

He nods. "Grief alone is a series of complex experiences, so I understand. And I am sure you are feeling all sorts of other emotions as well."

"Spot on. Are you Cassius Jaeger?"

He twists a ring around a finger. "I have lost everyone I have ever known, Teresa. Many times over."

His words strike me like a sucker punch. I'd known that was the case but turns out I didn't really...*understand* it until he verbalized it so directly. I swallow, hard, and focus on playing the music.

"Will you tell me if things become too much?" he asks.

I contemplate the possibility. "Maybe." I turn back to the piano. Then something occurs to me. "What about you? What will you do if things become too much for you?"

He gazes down at the keys. "I am...not certain," he answers finally.

I'm here, I think. Should I say it? "You are not alone," I whisper to him.

Please don't shut me out like I did you, I find myself hoping.

He looks at me and gives me a melancholy smile. "Thank you, Teresa."

I shift to a different song by Bishop Briggs, "SOMEONE ELSE." It fits my mood a little more than the previous song.

I don't want to sing, but I wish the Keeper could hear the words.

I find myself doomscrolling not long after that conversation with the Keeper. And there sure is a lot of doom to scroll through.

People dissolving into dust. Yet more with fates unknown. Rifts appearing all over the world.

To put it mildly, news outlets are making bank trying to keep everyone updated on the deterioration of our universe.

A text notification from my dad appears at the top of my screen: "*Hey, I just wanted to say I love you.*"

His words twist my heart into a knot—which is likely not good for an organ already broken and precariously held together. I close my eyes against the pain and tension and try to take some deep breaths. I don't think I have the strength to respond. And I don't think I can stand to keep seeing his messages.

So, I mute him.

And I hate myself for it. But I hate the Collector more for even putting me in this position.

I slump further into my pillows, despairing.

Will it really take three more dangerous missions to have a chance at stopping the Collector? Shouldn't there be a better, maybe closer-to-foolproof, way?

I think back to everything the Keeper has told me about magic and sit up abruptly when I recall his words on the power of names.

Could he stop the Collector by using her name? Does he even *know* her name? Or is he too busy being scared of becoming an 'abomination' to take the smoothest route?

14

— · —

The Keeper

I 've pulled a chair from the deck in the ISERE's garden nearer to the stand of trees on the upper level, sketchbook propped on my leg and a box of colored pencils from which I struggle to select the best choice set next to me.

The sketch I craft is an attempt at a more impressionistic style than I normally use, and I fight the urge to erase and redraw the same aspect over and over again; I am unaccustomed to stylizing my work or using colors more vibrant than what I observe. Perhaps I should have tried a different subject for this drawing—the light trickling through the layers of leaves fades and shifts too quickly for my slower drawing pace, and of course my darkening surroundings are an additional challenge. It is possible that I subconsciously chose this subject at this time of day to dissuade myself from putting more effort into impressionism in the future.

Behind me, the doors to the garden open with a *click* of the turning handle, and a soft foot steps onto the pavestones.

I pause.

"Keeper?"

"Hello again, Teresa," I acknowledge without turning. I return my pencil to paper but only hold it in place.

How will this interaction proceed? Are we going to return to fury and spat words and pain, or are we going to continue on the path that appears to be wending through mutually acknowledged burdens?

Teresa appears next to me. Her words sound tense and planned, and unusually diplomatic. "I would like to know next steps for our little quest."

"Third piece after rest," is all I say, as I am too busy reading into her tone and choice of words to say more.

I can feel the weight of her desire to say something more. To give the appearance of not sensing it, I exchange the pencil in my hand for a different, random one.

Teresa's voice shifts to something lighter and unexpected. "That color doesn't match the rest of the drawing. Is that deliberate?"

"What?" Startled, I raise my head. Our gazes lock, and I feel I am staring into a bright light, but I don't know how to look away.

"Mahogany. It's a little dark compared to the rest of the colors you've been using. The contrast could be an interesting choice, though, I think."

Finally I have a good enough reason to break eye contact. I turn back to my hands. Sure enough, the pencil I currently hold is mahogany. In the corner of the paper I have been sketching on, I begin doodling a pair of round brown eyes. Eyes much like Teresa's.

I glance back at her. "Would you mind if I drew your—?" I stop myself midsentence, realizing how ridiculous my request would be.

She narrows her eyes. "Draw my what?"

"Your friend. Ada."

She looks taken aback. "Why? I mean, you never met her; why would you want to draw her?"

"For you," I say. "I know you likely have photographs, but I thought that perhaps drawings would..." I trail off, uncertain of how to explain.

"Oh." Teresa blinks. Her voice thickens. "That would be very...sweet."

"Oh," I echo, setting my sketchbook and pencils aside without fully looking at her. "That reminds me—I was wanting to take you somewhere if you were up for it, but when we were talking earlier, the time was not quite right."

"Is it perhaps somewhere we can learn the Collector's name?"

Why on the island would she ask that? "No, I think you will enjoy this." I stand. "Come along?"

She snorts and follows me out of the garden.

A few minutes later, we step out onto the edge of a crowd of people, none of whom seem to notice our sudden appearance as they lounge or stand or pick their way through the throng. We stand at the top of a gentle slope covered in turf. Sprawling at the base of the slope is a stage, upon which venue staff work with the lights gazing down upon them. A warm breeze drifts through the crowd, reminding me of our latitude.

Teresa turns to me, a hesitant, surprised smile spreading across her face. "A concert?"

I smile back. "Wait until you see who is performing."

She opens her mouth to say something, but before she can, the band walks on stage. The lights dim and the name of the band appears on screens around the stage.

"*Magic Man*?" Her smile becomes pleased. "You bastard!" She glances at me thoughtfully. "And I may only halfway mean that in the way you think."

I smile again. "Did you really give me that sobriquet because of the band?"

"Call it fortuity."

I laugh.

As the music begins, quiet bliss spreads across Teresa's round face, and she begins swaying to the music.

I relax a little, too, even though under the music I can still hear the ticking and feel the rope in my mind. I wonder if the Collector will find us. But the ISERE is untraceable, and Tess and I have spells on us to protect us from the Collector.

Besides, life awaits.

Several songs in, the music bleeds into a solo piano that is played with a hint of melancholy—not the raw grief with which I have heard Teresa play, but with bittersweet loss. The melody shifts and the lyrics begin, but the feeling is much the same.

The sound is a shadow of what I have felt before.

For Teresa, however, it must be what casts the shadow. Partway through the song I see tears glimmering on her cheeks. "Ada loved this song," she says from far away. "She was the one who—who introduced me to—" Here she gasps, cutting off a sob.

I wordlessly place a hand on her shoulder, conjure some tissues for her.

She nods her thanks, wiping at her tears. When they subside, she reaches up and pats my hand. "Thanks for this, Magic Man," she says. "And you can call me Tess."

15

— · —

TESS

I run the chain of Ada's necklace through my fingers, back and forth, back and forth.

I miss her singsong voice.

I wish I had a photo of Hunter to burn.

Those two thoughts are not entirely unrelated: Hunter had only been a strained sort of civil with Ada. Now I know why.

The asshole had thought we'd been fucking, as if two people can't love each other without that.

Grief swells inside me, tests the halfway-mended cracks in my heart—and it's not just for Ada, I realize.

The grief is for Hunter as well. I miss him, or at least the person I thought he was.

Because he wasn't always so awful. When I had his attention, I *had* it. He wouldn't be occupied by anything else. And he liked to listen to me play music, and he'd tell me every joke he'd heard just to make me laugh. He...made me happy.

Of course, what I loved in him wasn't all about how he served me. His morals were absolute, as far as I had known—for example, he believed in bodily autonomy and medical care for *everyone*, not only people he liked and agreed with on these issues. He volunteered in a handful of local organizations. He was studying pre-law, with a goal of becoming an environmental lawyer.

All that considered, how could he have still believed such an awful thing about me? Who was Hunter, really?

Deep below, something shifts. It feels and sounds like the ISERE is Traveling.

Forgetting what I was thinking, I anxiously pocket Ada's necklace.

Is the Keeper trying to find a piece of the Key without letting me in on it?

I emerge into the atrium to see the Keeper approaching the console.

"What is going on?" he asks no one in particular.

The screen-that-is-usually-a-mirror above the console flashes blue.

I join the Keeper at the console as the screen flickers to a view of a flat expanse of desert freckled with sagebrush. In the center, a slab of pale rock protrudes from the desert floor at a precarious angle.

A woman with ebony skin and dirty robes of red-and-white linen kneels beneath the stone, straining to keep it from toppling to the ground.

The Keeper whistles. "An Aivar in human form. What is she doing?" He zooms in to peer closer at the base of the rock, where something that looks suspiciously like a hole in the universe roils. "Ohhhh," he exhales. "She is holding open a rift leading to an island dimension, isn't she? Something important is on the other side."

I stare at him for a moment. "What are these words you speak?"

"Aivar: a child and protector of the multiverse, born from a collapsed island dimension. Island dimension: a fragment of a universe. A defect, if you will. Island dimensions are inherently unstable. They do not divide. Eventually they collapse, creating the Aivar."

"Wha—" My eyes widen. "First of all, is the ISERE an island dimension? Is it going to collapse on us?"

He shakes his head, not looking away from the screen. "The ISERE is what is known as a pocket dimension—a stabilized island dimension."

"Okay... Secondly, what is going on?"

The Keeper whips around to stride toward the entrance. "Someone—I believe I know who—appears to be trapping the Aivar, the protectors of the multiverse. This explains why I have not encountered them for some time," he adds, as if to himself. He clears his throat upon opening the door. "I need to free this Aivar. The ISERE brought us here so we can find support in our quest to stop the Collector."

"Oh. Okay. I'm in."

He frowns at me. "Firstly, no. If you, as a non-mage, so much as touch that rift, you will burn into nothing."

"I won't touch the rift, then."

"No. Secondly, the Collector may be waiting for us to save the Aivar."

"I'm coming."

Furiously he points to the inside of the ISERE.

"Come, come." I stride past him. And immediately wince at the blinding sunlight. "Oof. I need sunglasses."

Resignedly, the Keeper reaches into a pocket and flicks out a pair of sunglasses with round pink frames.

Pleased, I pluck them from his fingertips. "Saving folks in style."

He pulls out a similar pair for himself, but with green frames instead of pink.

"Fabulous," I inform him.

"Are you taking this seriously?" he asks.

"I take the preservation of eyesight very seriously, yes."

We hurry across sandy earth as mountains loom over us from a distance that seems a few minutes' walk, but I know would take hours to cross by foot.

The imprisoned Aivar wearily raises her head. A faint spark of relief flares in her dark eyes but is quickly smothered by exhaustion. "Thane Rhaz," she rasps.

The Keeper's steps falter.

"Failing guardian of the multiverse...save my kin. There are...others...in there. Aivar." Her gaze drifts downward to the rift.

My companion waves his hand over the tear. "It seems my suspicions were correct: it leads to an island dimension that will collapse either when the stone closes it, or at any moment."

I nod, steeling myself. "Then I'll help her hold it open until we free the other Aivar or find another way to hold it open."

The Keeper scowls. "Once more: no. Choosing the first option may kill or severely incapacitate you, and on top of that, only a living being can hold this open."

"Okay, I guess I'm playing Atlas with my new buddy while you save the other Aivar." Without another word, I take my place next to the Aivar.

"Why do you use so many names I *do not recognize* when you ignore me?" His words seem to be more directed to the rift, because he doesn't wait for an answer before jumping in.

16

---·---

THE KEEPER

Untethered energy crackles across my skin as I pass through the rift.

My legs buckle beneath me once I strike the ground, my knees colliding with a soft surface. Moss. I stand, taking in my dim surroundings and tucking my sunglasses back into a pocket.

Fog shrouds everything beyond the range of a few steps—all I can see is the carpet of moss underfoot. Moisture collects on my skin and clothes, chilling me as I turn on the spot.

The rift is a dark stain angled in the air at shoulder height. It will be difficult to see from a distance, so I summon a fountain of green sparks and rest it just above the ground, where it pops and shines despite having no evident source.

I straighten. The ticking in my mind is conspicuously loud in the eerie silence. "Aivar?" I call into the stillness, my voice muffled by the fog and the moss.

"Rhaz!" someone calls faintly from somewhere off to my left.

I set off in that direction, watching my steps.

"Thane!" More urgency this time.

The tone worries me. I pick up my pace.

"Help!"

Faster, faster, until I am racing through the fog.

Where are you?

The earth collapses beneath my foot.

With a cry, I twist and scrabble for a grip. Magic surges into me and out of my hands, enabling me to grasp the earth beneath the moss with enough strength to stop my fall. I pull myself back onto solid ground, panting.

I look ahead to see—nothing. Looking carefully, I see that even the fog blends into something less substantial.

Nothingness.

I had nearly fallen off the edge of this island dimension.

I shudder and turn away.

The Aivar calls for me again, this time ahead and to my right.

I follow the sound more cautiously this time, but my muscles itch with agitation to *move faster.*

"Thane?"

My pace inadvertently quickens.

This time I sense the ground dipping before it drops away. I skid to a stop so quickly that I fall backward. My feet dangle over empty air. I crawl back before standing.

It seems that something is trying to make me step right off the edge of this island dimension. A shivering itch passes over me at the realization.

I take a deep breath and tap into the magic around me. My exhale is amplified into a strong breeze that blows the fog out to the edges of the island.

In the center stand three black Aivar, all in human form. They stand in a tight circle, facing each other and staring at the sky, frozen like statues.

I step up to one of the Aivar to begin freeing them, but before I can touch them, the rope in the back of my mind tautens and Tess's voice tears through my mind. I am yanked backward. My body spasms.

Suddenly I understand why the ticking is so loud.

17

TESS

Dear lord, am I a fool.

My muscles seem to be tearing, my joints fused together under the weight of this stone.

"Stay strong, Teresa," the Aivar groans.

I'm trying! My silent retort will have to suffice, because the fire in my every cell keeps my jaws glued shut.

Seconds, or perhaps hours, after undertaking this death wish, the ground begins to rumble. Dust and loose rock fragments fall around us.

I pry my eyes open enough to see a swath of air near the ISERE shimmering intensely, but not from heat. Something is appearing in that spot, something composed of small black squares fading into existence to amalgamate into the sides of a massive black box.

Oh, shit. My heart drops.

"Teresa," the Aivar says, "I need you to hold this on your own. Can you do that?"

No. No, I can't. "Yes," I whisper. I brace myself.

I thought the pain couldn't worsen, but I was wrong. So wrong. The heat of agony fogs my mind.

Through the crack in my eyelids, I can see a section of the Tomb's nearest wall sink inward. A ghostly form emerges from the doorway.

Oh, *shit*.

The thought of the Collector getting close to me once more makes me tremble worse than I already was.

Where the hell is the Keeper? If I can call for him, could he hear me? Can I even yell?

"Keeper!" My voice comes out as more of a choke than a word.

A few yards away, the Aivar has transformed into a black dog the size of a Ford F-250. She barrels toward the Collector with a roar, the earth cracking beneath her every step. Then the Aivar vanishes. Less than a racing heartbeat later, she reappears behind the Collector, jaws poised to snap.

The Collector whips around, hands aflame, and strikes her in the head.

The Aivar is thrown across the desert floor before coming to a stop several yards away. There she lies, unmoving.

Terror grips me. I squeeze my eyes shut and pour all my available focus into screaming with my voice and mind.

"*Keeper*!"

18

THE KEEPER

My head feels like a hammer struck it. My chest is tight with fear.

I need to get out before the Collector can shut me in. But I need to free the Aivar. I need to protect Tess. But I do not know if I can do it alone.

I clutch my head with one hand and place the other on the shoulder of the nearest Aivar. I test the bonds.

The spell is like a complicated knot that I must carefully unwind.

Hurrying, I nearly botch the unwinding. But after far too long, I smooth out the string of the spell. "The Collector is here," I pant as soon as the newly freed Aivar can move. "Go. Protect Teresa Misner. I will free your kin."

The Aivar, recovering quickly, bounds away into the returning fog.

The spell binding the next Aivar is also like a knot, but of a different kind. I struggle with it, then take a deep breath and try to tackle it more calmly.

My eyes snap open the second I unwind a very particular part of the spell.

No. No, no, no.

This is not an Aivar.

This is a construct posing as an Aivar.

The flesh under my hand turns into cold and unyielding granite.

I back away slowly as gold glazes over its eyes. I risk a glance at the other supposed Aivar to see it is also now a mobile statue with eyes of metal.

Empty gazes follow me, necks grind, left arms grate as they rise.

I find it probable that the statues can move much faster than this, and that they will stop me before I can reach the rift.

I lick my lips. "What are you? Are you animated carvings? Living beings?" If they have any amount of sentience, hopefully they are listening and not focusing on my hands. "It's got to be a bit boring, hasn't it? Just staring up at the fog, waiting for either this place to collapse or a rather unfriendly visitor to arrive?" I throw my hands out to either side, flinging emerald orbs along their path.

The orbs each shoot directly toward a statue. Each sculpture shatters upon contact.

I do not stay to watch. I run.

To my relief, the flare I set still scintillates beneath the rift. I jump through and tumble onto the hard desert ground. My skin stings and burns in the warm, dry air. I push myself to my knees to see a black panther battling the Collector while a massive dog climbs to its paws a distance away.

My heart hammers in my chest. My thoughts tear apart in my mind—seal the rift, fight the Collector. There cannot be time to do both. There is not even time to hesitate! I grit my teeth as I waver between the rift and the battle.

Next to me, Tess labors alone to hold the rift open, sweat pouring down her red face.

The torn thoughts in my mind piece back together.

"Tess," I say urgently, leaning close to meet her pained gaze. "Can you keep this open for a few more minutes? Please." *Trust me.*

Resignation flashes across her face. "I'll try."

"Thank you." Before I stand, I brush my fingers across her cheek; hopefully the sparks of energy in my fingertips are enough. "Stay brave." I jump to my feet and stride forward. I reach into the swirling energy around me and feel the magic flood my veins. An ecstasy fills me along with the magic. My blood pulses and glows with power. A thrill courses through me.

"Collector!" I bellow.

The woman meets my gaze. A hollow smile flickers across her lips.

"You miscalculated."

Chains erupt from the air around the Collector and dive for her limbs. Before they even touch her, they dissolve into dust.

I twist my hands in the air; the earth twists around the Collector's feet to trap her.

The two Aivar bite down on her arms. All three vanish and reappear just outside the rift.

I extend my hands and yank one back as if tearing a piece of paper. The rift widens in synchronicity with my movement.

The dog swats the Collector in the head, knocking her into the rift.

At the last moment, the Collector's hand snakes out and grasps Tess's ankle.

"*No!*" I do not know whose voice it is, I only know its desperation.

I lunge forward as Tess slips. I grip her arms and haul her toward me.

In the moment before the rock can crash down and Tess's leg can be dragged into the rift, the panther Aivar snaps his jaws shut on the arm holding Tess.

I stagger back when Tess is released, but not fast enough—I can see it, the stone is going to collapse on her. I close my eyes so I don't have to watch.

Teeth sink into the back of my jacket and drag us backward.

Just as Tess is clear of the rock, it slams down upon the panther Aivar, whose jaws are still embedded in the Collector's arm on the other side.

Tess and I collapse onto the ground, the dog-shaped Aivar towering over us.

"He is dead." Her voice is saturated with grief. "No one can survive being sliced in two by an interdimensional barrier, not even Aivar."

I close my eyes against the blinding sky and feel my energy begin to ebb away. Horror yawns distantly inside me.

I had hoped that the Aivar could help us defeat the Collector. But she came so close to success and only lost because she was so outnumbered. She had, in fact, won a victory by killing one of the few Aivar in existence.

I open my eyes and sit up as Tess shifts next to me with a small moan.

She lies almost lifeless on her side, eyes closed. Her sunglasses are gone.

I rest my hand against her cheek. "Tess?" I whisper.

"A few more minutes, and she would have died," growls the Aivar, snuffling at Tess's hair.

Once again, I dip into the magic within and around me. This time, the energy is gentle and pleasantly warm, already knowing it is to be used for healing.

Tess, though still weak, stirs as the magic flows throughout her damaged body.

I pull her against me, burying my face in her neck. *Thank the ancestors you are okay.* If I had lost her, the guilt might have broken me.

"Hey," she croaks.

For some reason, a weak, relieved laugh bubbles out of me. I pull away just enough to kiss her forehead. "You courageous, strong, foolish woman."

She shakily returns my smile. "You weirdo." She closes her eyes to open them again a moment later, searching. "Are the Aivar okay?"

"One is," I murmur. "Thanks to you."

Tess's relieved, weary gaze flickers over to me. Her brow furrows in concern. "You're hurt."

"Me?" Her words seem to remind my body to feel pain: my skin smarts from the superficial burns I sustained from crossing the rift, and the back of my shoulder throbs from the Aivar's teeth grazing my skin. "Ah. Well, my injuries are hardly serious. Can you stand?"

She winces. "Maybe." Her legs buckle under her weight even as I support her.

In the end, the Aivar suggests that Tess lie on the back of the dog-shaped beast so we can get her to bed. The Aivar shrinks down to the size of a hefty wolf.

I stare apprehensively at the Tomb as we approach the ISERE. "The Collector is not gone, is she?" Does the ticking emanate from the Collector or the Tomb? I can still hear it...

"She is not," the Aivar replies grimly. "I sense that she is still alive, and I am sure she will escape before the island dimension collapses."

"I recall reading about the hypothesis of a spell that could accelerate the collapse of an island dimension..." I trail off, trying to remember the details.

The Aivar sighs. "That is all it is—a hypothesis. Even if it were possible, the amount of energy needed would drain the surrounding dimensions of all energy."

Disappointment and despair well up inside me. I try not to dwell on it.

Tess is already asleep by the time we reach her bedroom. I doubt she heard any of the conversation.

I settle her onto the bed, tug off her shoes, and draw up a blanket that had been folded at the foot of the bed. Reluctant to leave just yet, I sit on the edge of the mattress, my back against the wall.

Without waking, Tess drapes her arm over my leg and presses her forehead against my thigh.

My heart twists in my chest. Gently I brush flyaway hairs from her face. "She reminds me of Naida."

Strong-willed, curious, intense, loyal.

Naida was a Developer by blood, but while her parents drank themselves to oblivion down the road, she spent as much time with me as a sibling would have. By the time we were old enough to comprehend the issues of race employed on the island, we were inseparable. Until she stepped into the Tomb.

The memory replays for me as though I might forget. Naida and I, both Tess's age, were wandering through the woods as if we were twelve again. That is how Naida wanted it, *us*, to be—back to before I was haunted by sharp objects or Misha's eyes. I almost felt at ease that day. But the feeling ended when we came across what I would come to know as the Tomb, forbidding even when partially obscured by vines and branches.

I had wanted to believe the way Naida did about our finding the Inter-Dimensional Expedition Machine being an incredible discovery, but every part of me down to my toenails told me that *we* were the *machine's* discovery.

As it turned out, Naida was the discovery.

Her awe evident in every movement, my friend rested her fingertips upon the Tomb's smooth surface. "Thane, come here! This is it—it's alive!"

I can never recall my response, only that part of one wall sank in and disappeared to reveal an entrance.

Naida, ever inquisitive, simply had to ignore every warning composed against entering unknown magical spaces. She grinned at me over her shoulder as I protested and stepped into the Tomb.

Then the door shut behind her.

I screamed for her and ran toward the Tomb. The moment my hand contacted the wall, an unseen force flung me backward and rendered me unconscious. When I woke, the Tomb was gone, Naida with it.

The Aivar's low voice cuts through the memory before it can continue. "Certain things fall easiest when brought down by the same tools that built them."

I frown at her, slow to process her words as I shake off the memory.

"A Veqah proverb, referring to the circular passage of time. You know this. I was not removing it from the original context."

"I am sure you were not." I rub my face. Why must my thoughts have slowed down so much? Perhaps I would understand if I could only think as quickly and clearly as earlier. "But Teresa is not Naida."

The Aivar blinks slowly. "I never said she was. But to the Collector, they are both merely tools, Thane."

I lean my head back against the wall.

Would Teresa accept all of me, the way Naida did? Naida didn't know the names of my disorders, but she recognized my differences and loved me for them. What if I were to tell Tess about my diagnoses?

"So this is the one the Collector wants," the Aivar remarks softly. "You have a habit of surrounding yourself with the women she desires."

"Mm." I say nothing more for several moments. "Has she trapped all your kin? Or killed them?"

A pause. "I cannot sense the last of my kin. From our birth, we are eternally connected, but now it seems we are not. He has not been killed—I would feel that—but the connection is missing. I suppose trapping us is easier than killing us."

"Under certain circumstances," I reply, thinking of the death of the other Aivar who the Collector had trapped.

Another pause. "I need to find the other. There is only one more of us. But any number could help in the fight against the Collector."

The Aivar vanishes, leaving me alone with my slowing thoughts and ebbing energy.

19

TESS

I sense only comfort, the way one feels when in bed after strenuous exercise. I ache, but pleasantly.

I wake in the bedroom of the ISERE that I suppose is my own.

Although there is just enough light to see everything in my room, it takes me a moment to make sense of what's there. Across the bed from me someone slumps over the pile of pillows arranged at the head of the bed.

I blink and peer closer.

The Keeper? He looks so different from yesterday, when his veins glowed as he fought the Collector. He seems about ready to fall off the bed but doesn't so much as twitch when I carefully crawl off.

My muscles are not happy with yesterday's exertion—turns out the pleasant ache was only pleasant because I wasn't moving. I yearn to burrow back into bed and retrieve that sense of comfort I felt when asleep.

Instead, I take a wonderfully refreshing shower, and when I return to the bedroom, the Keeper is gone. (Hopefully I didn't wake him; I had tried to be quiet.) I try to French braid my hair, but every muscle involved protests intensely. With much bitching, I settle for leaving my hair down, held back by a lavender headband. Then I head out to check on the Keeper.

It is dim and quiet in the atrium, giving off an early morning feel. Small warm lights indicate the sides of the stairs. I cross the space, approaching the door almost directly across from mine that belongs to the Keeper. I knock on the pocket door and bounce on my heels until the door slides open.

The Keeper's hair is damp and lays flat against his scalp and forehead, which is furrowed over drooping eyelids.

"Hey, Magic Man, how you feeling?"

He closes his eyes briefly as he sighs, "Every muscle associated with my spine aches."

"I bet. I thought only cats could sleep in positions that awkward."

He welcomes me into his room. "Only cats should. How do you feel?"

"Sore as well." I step into his room and take a good look around; this is the first time I have seen it. "Nice room."

On the right is an alcove with a raised floor, where his mattress rests below a broad window. The only other furniture is a simple desk, a chair, and an armoire. Ferns hang from the corners of the ceiling above a polished stone floor. The entire far wall is layered with pages and pages of drawings.

The Keeper taps his index finger against his upper lip while I look around, solemn and thoughtful as he eyes me.

Unsure of what else to do once I've taken in the room, I return his stare.

"You exceeded all possible expectations yesterday. I am proud of you."

"Um, thanks." My cheeks burn. I break eye contact and wander over to the far wall. I am totally unprepared for what I see—the artwork knocks the breath from my lungs.

Some drawings are graphite, some ink, some grayscale, some color. Portraits mostly, a few landscapes, all in a far more realistic style than his drawing from the other night.

The Keeper drifts across the room to join me. "When I was young, I believed I would never forget the faces of the people I loved," he says wistfully. He rests his fingertips on one of the only photographs on the wall, depicting four people in sepia tone: a teenage boy I recognize as a young Thane (his hair is long, but it is most certainly him); a baby in the arms of a slight, glasses-wearing woman with wavy hair down to her waist and her chin raised in confidence; and a tall, barrel-chested, broad-shouldered man with shoulder-length dark hair swept back from his face. Thane and the woman I assume to be his mother are both wearing sashes around their waists. "All I have to remember their faces by is a photograph and my art. Even then, I worry about how accurate the drawings are, or whether I may lose them."

A wayward tear courses its way down my cheek. I've been trying so hard not to break down that I hadn't even thought about forgetting Ada's face. Until now. "You can't even draw everything about them," I murmur. No art would be able to capture the feeling of Ada's presence, the knowledge of all that she was.

"You are right."

I shift my gaze to the drawings near the photograph of his immediate family. These are portraits as well, though calling them such is not entirely accurate: the people drawn have no faces. Their graphite bodies and even hair are intact, if lightly rubbed to a blur, but the faces lack any substantial definition. Faint blurred lines delineate the vague shape of a jaw or a nose or an eye, leaving the mind to fill in the person that should be there. Or not fill in.

"Is this how you remember some people?"

"In a way, yes, sometimes. The more time that passes, the more difficult it is to recall whenever I am not looking at my drawings." He leans in front of me to point out color portraits on the other side of the photo of his family.

I inhale sharply as my eyes fall upon them. Dare I believe these are not photographs? They remind me of the work of Paul Söderberg or Pedro Lopes.

There is a side portrait of a woman with freckles, an aquiline nose, and a blond pixie cut that shows her pondering something in her lap, the shadows across her face more perfect than reality.

"This is Rhys," he says, gesturing, "and this is Damien."

My eyes fall upon the portrait of a man with skin a few shades darker than the Keeper's and long black braids who half-grins, half-laughs at something beyond my shoulder. I have the strangest urge to stroke his face, to see if the stubble is as coarse as it looks, to know if his lashes are really that soft.

"Wow," I breathe. "This is incredible. Are you self-taught?"

"Mostly. I have occasionally had lessons and the like, but I have had decades to work on technique."

I shake my head. "Don't be so modest. I mean, a lot of these must be from a long time ago, right?"

"I suppose so. All the drawings of my family are from my adolescence."

"Come on. Brag a little." I nudge him.

He smiles sadly. "Perhaps another day."

"Well, if we aren't going to work on your pride, what are we going to do? Look for the third piece of the Key?"

The Keeper purses his lips. "Actually..." he begins but stops.

My brow furrows at his hesitation. What is he thinking? Is he trying to kick me off the mission to stop the Collector?

"I have been thinking," he says slowly, "and I believe that you should no longer leave the ISERE."

"God*dammit*," I huff. "Listen, you've *needed* me. You're probably going to need me again. Strengthen the spell on my ring if you want, but I'm helping you get the rest of the Key whether you like it or not." It then occurs to me that he could probably put a spell on me so I couldn't go with him. Would he do that? It would certainly put a wrinkle in my plan to exploit him and his magic.

He rubs his forehead. "This is just so dangerous, Tess, especially for you."

"I am aware." *He's just concerned, Tess. Don't be an ass to him.* I try to inject a little sympathy into my tone when I add, "But I'm not alone, and I'm not stupid. Besides, this is important." To lighten him up a little, I add, "I can still sign a liability waiver if you want, though."

The Keeper scrunches up his face in a scowl of uncertainty. "I...will not commit to anything at this moment. For now, I have something to take care of."

"Without me? Are you going to tell me, or leave it a mystery? It's not dangerous, is it?"

"It is not. I will simply be...making an agreement." Resignation swells in his voice.

His words give me pause. "What...kind of agreement?"

He does not answer but instead pulls a business card out of his pocket.

I exhale sharply when I recognize the blood-red sickles on the face.

The Keeper turns away from me and leaves his room for the console without saying another word.

I pursue.

He clips the card to the console, flicks two switches before answering. "This agreement, though unsavory, could end things."

"'End things'? How?"

His eyes meet mine in the mirrored screen. His lips are pressed into a thin line, brow fused into a rigid line above a hard gaze. "By killing the Collector."

20

THE KEEPER

The ceiling of the abandoned airplane hangar arches high above me. Sand from the desert outside coats the entire floor, piling up in the corners.

Swallowing back a sick feeling, I sweep my arm aside to clear away the sand around me.

The stability of the universe is much more precarious than I had previously thought. The 'hernia,' as Tess called it, demonstrated that the effects of the Collector's actions are endangering life even when she is not actively ending a universe.

This agreement is more crucial than ever.

I take a deep breath and crouch to draw two circles side by side with a piece of chalk onto the concrete floor. In one circle I draw a sickle. I stand in the other, exchanging the chalk for the business card. I reach into another pocket with my opposite hand and pull out a needle. For a moment, I hesitate. Steel myself.

It's not a blade.

I prick my thumb deeply enough to draw blood and smear the deep red drop across the print on the card.

Upon contact, the summoning words flow from the card into my hand, up my arm and neck, and into my mind. Magic courses upward with the spell, intermixing and spilling effortlessly from my lips.

"Exorcist, ruler of dimensions, lord of souls, I humbly petition your presence. Grant me this request so that we may enter a contract together. In asking this, I vow to pay a fit price for your visit and services."

Before I finish speaking, the world around me dims and blurs; it makes me feel as if I should be growing lightheaded and faint, but my mind and body remain steady, firm. The last words exit my throat. I flick the card into the other circle, where it catches fire and flutters downward, spewing far more smoke than it should. Smoke billows outward, completely filling the space before me.

I step backward in my circle, but the thickening smoke appears to strike an invisible wall—the edge of the circle. Its outward path obstructed, the smoke swells upward to a point not far above my head. There the opaque column pauses before finally breaking past its upper barrier to roll out and dissipate. The smoke skirts the edges of my circle.

In the center of the other circle now stands the person I saw in the shipping yard. Hair the color of tar sweeps down to his shoulders. His clothes—trousers, a tunic belted at the waist, and a bandana wrapped over the lower half of his face—are the color of smoke. Gleaming war sickles dangle from his lithe white hands. He gives off an aura of powerful magic.

The Exorcist's eyes, deep-set and the color of frost, crinkle into a smile. "Hello, Thane Rhaz. Charmed to finally make your acquaintance." His voice is low, gravelly, provocative.

My brow crinkles into a frown. "Likewise. Though I must say, you could have come and said hello much sooner."

The Exorcist slowly shakes his head, his intense gaze uncomfortably refusing to leave mine. "I cannot initiate contact." He hangs his sickles from his belt. "Why did you call me, Rhaz?"

I lift my chin. "What exactly is it that you do?"

With a sigh through his nose, the Exorcist prowls the edge of his cage. "It is quite simple," he drawls. "I make deals. I slice human souls free of their corporeal bodies, send the souls to my own realm, and..." Here his eyes slide back to mine with a sly, self-satisfied look. "...I hunt them."

The last three words send chills ricocheting up and down my spine, but that is not my primary concern. "After you separate the soul from the body, can it be restored?"

The Exorcist gives a fluid shrug. "Theoretically, I suppose. I have certainly never attempted it, and neither has anyone else." He cocks his head. "Are you really intending to try?"

I flatly return his gaze. "I am always interested in theory."

The Exorcist chuckles.

"Explain to me your 'realm.'"

"There is not much to explain." He pulls one sickle from his belt and twirls it in his fingers as if it is a twig. "I inspired the idea that led to your little machine, but instead of stabilizing an island dimension, I created my own dimension: one that I can enter and exit at will, at any location. More fantastically, a dimension that can harbor unanchored souls in a semi-corporeal form for as long as I desire. This permits me to hunt them and wear them down, chase by chase. Some are even more fun to hunt than others..." Still swinging his sickle between his fingers, the Exorcist begins to sing. "*Today'll be the day, I believe it when I say, things'll start to go my way...*"

"Who did you inspire?"

The Exorcist breaks off mid-song, turns slowly back to me. "What was that?"

I repeat my question.

"Aileth Rawls of course." The creator of the IDEM. "Who else?"

"The Collector, perhaps?"

"The Collector effectively destroyed Aileth, so what does it matter?"

"What do you mean?"

"I mean what I said, Rhaz," he answers impatiently. "Get on with why you called for me."

Sick unease pools in my abdomen. Clearly the Collector had killed Aileth Rawls, but something about what he said unsettles me. I flex my hands. "I—I want to make a deal with you."

The Exorcist rolls his hand at me, encouraging me to continue.

I swallow. After I say this, there will be no going back. "I want you to exorcise a soul for me. The Collector's."

The Exorcist chuckles again, long and low, as he returns the sickle to his belt. "I cannot help you there. I do not execute contracts against my own clients."

I close my eyes, as if that will be enough to dispel the despair that wells up inside me at his words. "Who does she want you to kill?"

"That is confidential."

"What is she offering you?"

"The contract is still in the works. Besides, why should it matter?"

"Because the Collector wants to destroy the entire multiverse."

The Exorcist rolls his neck, evidently indifferent. "Do you really believe that I would leave myself with nothing, especially while my clients cannot break their contracts?"

I do not answer.

He crosses his arms. "Are we done, Rhaz?"

I hesitate. "I suppose we are."

"Excellent." He lifts his chin, hair sliding back over his shoulders. "Then all that is left is the consultation fee."

"What is your price?"

The Exorcist looks me up and down, thoughtfully tapping a forefinger against the upper edge of his bandana. He then speaks so quickly that I know he was trying to pretend he hadn't had his eye on it for a good while. "The sash."

My answer comes out just as fast. "No. You are not Veqah."

His eyes narrow in apparent irritation. The next request is longer in coming but is just as firm. "One ring."

My lips part in the beginning of an automatic refusal, but I stop myself before a sound comes out.

The Exorcist lets his hands fall to his sides, leans forward conspiratorially. "Do you value your humanity, Thane Rhaz?" he whispers.

I find myself mirroring his posture and volume. "Of course."

He winks. "Some of us don't." He leans in closer—so close that I can see his clothes are not flat gray but appear to be woven from the very smoke he had appeared from. "You are still young."

I start at the sound of his deep sniff.

"I can smell it," he whispers hoarsely. His eyes glint with excitement. "But I can also smell the rot of magic and inhumanity setting in."

I am frozen as the blood drains from my face.

The glint in the Exorcist's eye sparks into a flame. "You are letting the magic consume you, Rhaz. Do you know why humans cannot be immortal? Because in time, we *stop being human*. The magic burns your soul into an ashy, rotting carcass and there is *no* coming *back* from it." At that he giggles, glee lighting up what little of his face I can see, arcing like lightning down throughout the rest of his body. He straightens, hands against the barrier, giggling uncontrollably.

Suddenly, silence.

"The ring." His voice is cool again.

I look down at my hands. Eight rings, four of which are linked to my immortality. Which one? I remove the ring from my right middle finger and reach across the chalk lines to drop it into the Exorcist's upturned palm.

His fingers curl over it and he raises his hand to his nose to sniff again, this time with eyes blissfully closed. "Sentiment, power, time, life..." he murmurs. "Better than the sash."

A moment later, the Exorcist vanishes, taking the chalked circles with him, but leaving me hopeless and wondering what it would have cost had I been able to seal a contract.

21

—·—

TESS

I've been sitting in the atrium for two hours—waiting for the Keeper to emerge from wherever he disappeared to after he returned from his trip to make an agreement with the owner of the business card—when he finally reappears.

As he descends the spiral staircase from the library, I call out, "You never told me how the agreement went." I can't help but allow hope to seep into my voice.

He appears to be struggling to meet my expectant gaze, even as he reaches the main floor.

My heart sinks. "Shit."

"Yes," is his only response.

I close my eyes, my shoulders slumping. *Shit.* Judging from the pit forming in my stomach, I had let my hopes get far too high; I should have known things wouldn't turn out to be so easy. "What now?"

The Keeper pulls a lever on the console, still not looking at me. "Now I search for the next piece of the Key."

I scowl. "Not '*we*'?"

"No."

My expression does not lighten as I lift my chin and straighten my shoulders. "You know I'm going with you whether you like it or not."

He finally looks into my eyes, his face impassive. "Is that so?"

"Of *course*. You really think you can accomplish any of this on your *own*?" I nearly wince at the venom in my voice. But I stand firm.

The Keeper's expression shifts slightly.

What I see makes me waver. I clench my jaw to stop myself from apologizing.

And I can feel I'm going to regret that.

We stare at each other in silence for a long time; he must be waiting for me to speak, while I fight against a growing swell of some unidentified emotion.

My breath becomes shallow and rapid under the weight of what I see in the Keeper's face. A massive pressure blooms in my chest.

Is it...guilt?

"Keeper—" I finally say. And everything spills out after that one word. "You're not capable, Keeper, not alone. I'm sorry, but I can't trust you to stop the Collector—I never could. From the moment you told me about her capturing Rhys, I knew I had to use you to get to the Key and use it myself."

The following silence is smothering.

The Keeper breaks it by taking a deep, slow breath. "Is there anything else for you to admit?"

I shake my head. I've begun to tremble, whether it be from the release of admission, or terror of his coming response.

"Then I suppose I should admit something as well: I do not want this to be the truth, because I want you to stay safe in the ISERE—but I need you with me. You are correct that I am not capable of stopping the Collector alone; out of the two of us, it is not I who will be able to make the call to...plunge the knife, so to speak."

"I *do* have one more thing to admit," I blurt out.

He raises his eyebrows inquiringly.

"I've never once thought that making that call—nor even plunging the knife—would make someone an abomination. So, you need to stop that from holding you back."

The Keeper turns away. His voice is calm but firm when he says, "Only one out of two for today, I'm afraid."

I don't know what I expected, considering one piece of the Key was in an office building and the other was in a museum, but I am somehow a little surprised that the search for this segment has brought us to an outdated apartment building.

While the Decomis leads us to the fourth floor, I can't help shooting glances at the Keeper. I don't know what I'm looking for, but I kind of want to shake him and shriek something about how utilizing all your available tools to stop the destroyer of twenty-five universes could *not* make you an 'abomination.'

The Keeper knocks on the door of one of the apartments.

A small boy of East Asian descent, perhaps seven years old, answers.

"Hello. I am the Keeper, and this is Dawn. Is there an adult home?"

The boy looks at us curiously. "Why?"

The Keeper smiles. "We would like to know if they have noticed any strange developments recently."

"You don't need an adult for that. There's a new monster under my bed."

The boy, named Jun, leads us to his bedroom and points to the space under his bed. "It came a few days ago. Mommy and Daddy don't believe me. They don't see it when they look."

"Where are your mommy and daddy?" I ask.

"They're at work."

The Keeper kneels to peer under the bed. "You are right, Jun. There is something under the bed." He straightens and meets the boy's eye. "But you are perfectly safe as long as you do not join it under the bed, understand? Dawn and I can take care of it and make it go away. How does that sound?"

Jun beams. "You can really do that?"

"We certainly can." The Keeper waves me over. "Come look."

I kneel next to him. "It looks a bit like the rift in the basement and the one to the island dimension," I remark as I squint into the dimness. A faint roar reaches my ears.

"That is precisely what it is. My presumption is that it leads to a pocket dimension where the piece of the Key resides."

"Why can Jun see it and not his parents?"

"Children have a higher affinity for magic. Adults like you need spells to help them see these things."

"Does that mean it would be difficult for me to learn magic?"

"It means it would be impossible for you to survive it."

"Darn." I feel a twinge of disappointment. How cool would it be to learn magic? (Despite how much bullshit it brings with it.)

"Jun, why don't you go sit in the living room while we take care of the monster?" the Keeper suggests.

Jun frowns. "You won't hurt it, will you? It hasn't hurt anyone."

The Keeper smiles again. "We will not harm it. We will just have it move somewhere it will not scare anyone else."

Jun nods solemnly. "Good." He marches out of the room.

"Is it safe for me to cross through this rift?" I ask, recalling the Keeper had said something about beings needing to protect themselves when crossing interdimensional barriers.

"Hm." The Keeper waves his hand before the rift. "Since this is a pocket dimension and not an island dimension, I believe you will likely be fine. However, just to be safe, if you will allow me to place a spell on you that will conduct the energy around you…"

"Um, sure."

He taps the top of my head with two fingers.

I feel a curtain of warmth unfurl over my skin from head to toe.

"Are you ready?" he asks.

"Sure."

We move aside the bed and plunge into the rift.

The other side is pitch black until the Keeper forms a light in his palm and nudges it up above our heads. We find ourselves in an old brick tunnel.

The Keeper peers closely at the Decomis. "This way."

We walk perhaps a hundred yards, the light bobbing along with us, before we reach a fork in the tunnel.

"Hm," the Keeper says.

"What does the Decomis say?"

He checks and shows me. "It says nothing about a maze or labyrinth."

Sure enough, there is a signal a distance away from ours, but no visible path toward it.

"Do you want to go left?" he asks.

"Why not."

Perhaps a quarter mile down the tunnel, we hit a dead end. Without saying a word, we turn and head back the way we came so we can go down the right tunnel, which turns out to be winding and long.

I find myself thinking about the boy we had just met. How he found a monster under his bed but still didn't want to hurt it. Jun reminds me of the Keeper. I find my frustration at the man softening the more I consider this. "Hey, Keeper, can I ask you something?"

"Only after we decide which way to turn," he replies as we come upon another fork, this one with three choices. "Middle?"

"Middle," I concur. I pause. "It's kind of a personal question."

"Ask."

"Did you ever want kids?"

To my surprise, he laughs, but with only a hint of mirth. "I am sorry," he says, "but it is almost amusing."

"Sorry. You don't have to explain." I suppose he's been asked a lot and had to explain about as many times.

"Do not apologize. I can explain. It is simply...complicated." He exhales, pauses, then continues, "If I did decide to have children, I would want at least one person alongside me to raise them. But there are...circumstances...factoring into why that is not, and has not been, a possibility. Firstly, I was an absolute mess when I was younger. In my third dimension, I met my love Damien and began to heal. Then he was killed. I went years—I do not recall exactly how many, but more than you need to know—traveling the worlds, refusing to stay in one place for too long after he died. I had already lost so many people, and I was afraid to bond with anyone else. Until I met Rhys." His next sentence is a near whisper. "Then I lost her too."

"I'm sorry. I can't even imagine." I feel a surge of sympathy.

"Secondly," he struggles on at a normal volume, "I have never...experienced...the feelings required for such a partnership or for, ah, having biological children."

"Oh, so does that mean you're aroace or something?" I blurt out.

He stops walking. "What?"

"You know, aroace. Aromantic and asexual?"

He turns to me, his face inscrutable. "No, I don't know."

"Oh. *Oh.*" This was probably not the time to bring this up. "Well, aromantic basically means you feel little to no romantic attraction. Asexual means you feel little to no sexual attraction."

The Keeper begins to shake, just enough to notice. "What?" he says faintly. "So never experiencing romantic or sexual feelings... means...?"

Welp. We've gotten this far; I might as well go all the way with this explanation. "I guess—simply put, sexual attraction is like...when you look at someone and want to have sex with them."

The Keeper looks horrified. "*People feel that*?" he whispers.

I would laugh if he weren't so serious. "Uh, yes. Most people feel sexual attraction."

When he doesn't seem to recover from the shock of what he's heard, I frown in concern. "Keeper?"

"I—" He covers his mouth with one hand. "I am not broken."

Oh, honey. "No, you're not," I affirm as gently as I can. "That must be horrible to have felt that you were."

Still dazed, he nods distantly. He looks at the light above our heads.

(He may not have *been* broken...but I believe I may have just broken him. Crap.)

After a few long moments, he seems to climb out of his thoughts and shut them away. "Okay," he murmurs. "Enough of that for now."

I scrutinize him for further vulnerability, but he turns away and continues down the tunnel before I can find any.

We continue in silence for a few more minutes. Eventually tree roots begin breaking through the bricks, dangling down or clinging to the walls.

I realize as we wend our way deeper into the roots just how dank the tunnel smells, and how tired my eyes are from straining to see what the darkness beyond the Keeper's light may be hiding. More concerned with that discomfort as well as where the Keeper's mind may be, I don't pay the roots much attention until my shoulder brushes up against one. Before I can even think to react, a root whips around my upper arm. I gasp. Another root wraps itself around my neck. I rip myself free to see that a few feet away, the Keeper is under attack as well.

He tears himself free from the roots, and upon seeing that I am not bound either, takes off running.

I am hot on his heels, my heart already racing.

As we run, roots snag at us. Two grab me at the same time: one spears the hood of my jacket and another grips my right ankle. I'm yanked so hard that I don't even have time to get my hands out to break my fall. My face slams into the ground, and everything goes black.

When I wake, my vision sways. I think I am hanging upside down? It's too hard to tell—it's getting darker, and besides, my head hurts so much that I am sure if I move at all, it will hurt even more. My feet are stuck in something, and that something is creeping up my legs. My mind is too dazed and jumbled for me to fight it. So I just hang there, blood adding pressure to my throbbing head, waiting for what will happen to happen.

Someone comes into view. (*The Keeper?*) It is difficult to tell be-tween the bobbing light and my unsteady vision. He unleashes a bright flash of light that nauseates me with its intensity.

Whatever grips my feet releases me; I plummet to the ground in a shower of dirt. The moment before I strike the brick, my fall slows, and I touch down softly.

All I can do in response is groan and clutch my head.

The Keeper places his hand on my forehead. Warmth, painlessness, and steadiness spread from his touch.

I relax. "Thanks."

He helps me to my feet. "Let's hurry before the roots are no longer stunned."

We run until the roots are far behind us.

"How do you feel?" he asks.

"Fine now, thanks," I reply, touching the part of my head that had hit the ground and feeling nothing of note. *How are you?* I fail to say the words.

We encounter another fork, followed by a dead end, and fork after fork after dead end.

God, I'm thirsty. Is there a spell for that?

Eventually we come to an ancient door, wooden and unvarnished.

The Keeper waves his hand before it, but seems to find nothing harmful, because he opens it.

On the other side is a small, dim room, at the center of which is a wooden table that matches the door. Upon the table sit five skeleton keys in a line and a piece of parchment. Across from us is another door.

The Keeper picks up the parchment and reads aloud to me.

"*Through the near door is safety, through the far door danger. Both doors are now locked. To find the key to either door, this riddle will help: The key in the middle is not one you want, nor is the one to its immediate right; these present danger. The key taking you to safety has peril on either side and does not touch the key to the far door. Hazards lie on either end.*"

"So, it's the third and fourth keys we can ignore?"

"It seems so." He holds out the parchment so I can read it too. "The key to the door we just came through cannot be keys one or five."

"That one must be number two then, right? Though we don't want that key—we want the key to the far door, so it could be either three or four..."

"I believe you are overthinking it. I suspect it must be number two."

"Okay. Going off that then, 'Safety does not touch the key to the far door' means the key to the far door must be five."

"I agree."

"How sure are we on this?"

The Keeper flicks a hand to one side.

"Do you want to try the fifth key, or do you want me to?" (I would rather not.)

"I suppose I will." He picks it up and pauses, as if expecting to immediately burst into flames, but nothing happens. He carries the key to the door and inserts it. When he turns it and twists the doorknob, the door opens with a *click* and swings inward.

We exchange glances and step through the door. The Keeper summons more lights to illuminate a cavernous room scattered with boulders from the ceiling, which is pitted with holes. Not another living thing is in sight.

"What are we supposed to do now?" I ask.

No sooner do I begin speaking than something in the corner of my eye moves. A giant lizard-like creature the size of a semi-truck skitters from the left wall to the far end of the ceiling. When it stops, it blends so well into the ceiling so I can no longer see it.

I look at the Keeper, who stares off in the direction of the creature with an expression of awe.

"It is beautiful," he murmurs. "I hope we do not have to kill it to get the ring."

"You saw the ring?"

"I saw something hanging from the creature's neck."

"What's our game plan, then?"

The Keeper bites his lip. "Let me try talking to it."

I let him. Am I testing him, to see if he'll make the necessary call? I try to shake off that thought.

Cautiously he weaves his way among the debris in the direction we last saw the creature move in. As he climbs onto a boulder, the creature reappears where we last saw it, racing toward the middle of the room. It has a long tail coiled up near its hind legs. There it stops and vanishes.

The Keeper turns toward where it must be perched, perhaps listening. "Hello," he calls.

The creature flickers into sight once more, takes a few steps away from the Keeper before stopping and disappearing again.

"We are not here to hurt you," the Keeper continues. "I am fairly certain you can understand me." He lifts the Decomis, as though to demonstrate why. "Again, we do not want to harm you. But someone is coming who will likely hurt you, and we can help protect you. All we want from you is your piece of the Key."

As soon as the Keeper mentions the Key, the creature reappears. Its long tail whips out and strikes him in the chest, sending him flying across the room.

He smashes into the wall and crumples to the ground.

"Keeper!" I cry. I race toward him, fear tightening my chest.

He lies motionless on his side, his legs crumpled beneath him. Is he alive?

Then I see his chest hitch as he tries to find his breath, hear him groan.

"Keeper." I gingerly place one hand on his shoulder. "Can you hear me?"

"Yes," he gasps.

"Where are you hurt?"

He doesn't answer until his breathing is mostly normal. "Don't know—I'm numb."

My heart sinks. He might have a spinal injury. "Can you heal yourself?"

"I—don't know." His voice is frightened.

I take one of his hands in both of mine. Shove down my worry. "Try. I believe in you."

He closes his eyes and takes a deep breath. His hand grows warmer. As I watch his face, I notice his blood vessels begin to glow green, just like his hands when he tried to bring back Ada, and when he fought the Collector last.

Soon the color subsides and his eyes open. "I think I am healed," he mumbles.

I feel a trickle of relief. "Are you ready to move?"

He hesitates, but nods.

I help him sit up, then after a moment of testing, stand.

He squeezes my hand before releasing it. "Did you see where the creature went?"

"No." I'd been too concerned with the Keeper to notice.

Without saying a word, he climbs onto a nearby boulder. At the top, he holds out his hands, one above the other. He begins making strange gestures and movements with the upper hand, from which a glittery golden substance falls into the upturned palm of the other. He stops after a minute or so, lowering his upper hand. Next, he raises his upturned hand to his chin and blows the glitter across the room.

The glitter travels much farther than it should, covering every surface before the Keeper. It even covers the creature, clinging to the far wall.

The creature races around the room, but the glitter sticks to it no matter how fast it goes or how hard it shakes itself.

Sympathy rises inside me.

Eventually it settles on the far wall, eyeing us with great wariness.

The Keeper maintains his distance. "Someone else is coming for the Key," he warns. "Someone who will have no qualms about hurting you. If you give us the Key, we can prevent her from reaching you. We do not want you to come to harm."

The creature shakes itself again, releases a plaintive squawk.

"I see," the Keeper replies. "Give me just a moment." He raises one hand and gestures some more.

All the glitter in the room disappears at once, and I can no longer see the creature.

"Do you believe me? At least partly?"

The creature climbs onto the floor and stops.

"Thank you. I swear on the ocean that my friend and I will not harm you. We only want the ring hanging from your neck."

The creature creeps forward.

I bite my lip, hoping it will not hurt the Keeper again.

The Keeper holds his hands out, as if to show he is not a threat.

Slowly the creature approaches, the ring glinting from the rope around its neck. Only now do I get a good look at it: vermillion and jade feathers adorn its powerful body, and cautious, yellow eyes peer out over a beak-like mouth.

I inhale in awe.

When the creature reaches the Keeper, the ring settles into the Keeper's outstretched left hand. The rope dissolves, and the creature wastes no time racing away.

"Do you want me to free you from the room?" the Keeper asks.

The beast turns toward him and blinks.

The Keeper must take this as an affirmative response, because he sends a blast of violet light toward the ceiling.

The structure explodes, sending rubble raining down upon us.

I shield myself and curse the Keeper, but nothing strikes me. Apprehensively I look up to see a shimmering dome over the Keeper, the creature, and myself, shielding all three of us from the debris, which bounces and rolls off the dome.

Light trickles, then floods into the room as the ceiling crumbles, then collapses.

The Keeper lets the dome fade away after the last pieces fall.

The beast doesn't hesitate before escaping its prison, shimmying up the walls and over the jagged edges of what was once a ceiling.

The Keeper climbs down from the boulder. His face is sweaty, and he looks shaky.

"Are you okay?"

"I simply used a lot of strenuous magic in a short span of time. I am fine." He doesn't look fine, but I guess I have to believe him, at least a little.

We head back through the door we entered through, grab the second skeleton key, and return to the labyrinth. The Decomis leads us back to the rift with no trouble, though the Keeper struggles to maintain a steady pace. (We dodge the roots with relative ease this time.) When we cross back through the rift, it closes behind us.

The Keeper and I return Jun's bed to its proper spot and say our goodbyes to the boy, who had waited patiently in the living room the entire time. Then we return to the ISERE.

I follow the Keeper to his bedroom; he looks ready to collapse at any moment. I ensure he makes it into bed and turn to leave, but he stops me.

"Tess," he mumbles, "will you stay with me?"

I hesitate.

"Please. Just for a little while."

So, I climb into the Keeper's bed and hold his hand as he falls asleep.

22

THE KEEPER

I lie in a hospital bed. Paralyzed. The drug they have given me suppresses the overwhelming magic surging inside me, but it also renders me unable to move. On top of that, I am restrained. Bound to the bed by my wrists and ankles. Or is it the lizard creature that paralyzed me? Oh, it doesn't matter. I cannot move either way.

I am utterly helpless.

The faceless nurses enter my room and grab me. Examine my scars roughly. Their fingers are covered in rings.

I try to fight, try to protest, but I cannot move.

I am utterly helpless.

Tears spill down my cheeks as my limbs and even my stomach and chest are scrutinized without my consent. I want to scream for the person who saved me, but I cannot remember their name.

My arm jerks. I can move! Relief and joy flood me.

The hands all over me are heedless of my motion; they continue pawing at me, threatening to drag me through the bed and into the ocean.

I muster all my strength and will and shove at the nearest person.

Suddenly I am back in my bedroom in the ISERE.

Tess is on the floor next to my bed, stunned.

"Did I shove you?" I ask, my mind muddled with bewilderment.

"Yeah. You were having a nightmare and then you just—" She mimes pushing something away.

"I am sorry. I thought..." I shake my head. "I am sorry."

"It's fine. Am I allowed back up on the bed?"

"Yes. Please come back up."

She does.

We rest our backs against the wall.

I lean my head against it, wanting to lean it on Tess's shoulder but not knowing how she will take it, especially considering I just thrust her off the bed. "I thought I was paralyzed again," I try to explain without explaining too much. "People were grabbing me, and I could not fight them. It was a nightmare I have lived, and I was so afraid to be back."

"That must have been scary."

"It was."

"Do you mind if I ask what happened?"

"Have I ever told you about Damien?"

"Not past a mention or two."

A warm fondness mixed with melancholy suffuses me as I think of him. "When I was crossing from my second to my third dimension, I was thrown from the ISERE. My body absorbed more energy from the interdimensional barrier than it could take; I was burning up inside and out. Damien found me in that state and did what he could before taking me to a hospital. It was an abysmal hospital, but it was specifically for Veqah. While I was there, they did not siphon away the remaining excess energy. Instead, they gave me a drug that suppressed my body's access to magic. But the drug had a side effect: paralysis." Here I pause, trying not to give too much away. I am not yet prepared for that conversation. "The staff did not treat me well while I was there; that was the nightmare."

One day, a nurse had come in to change my bandages. Early on, she took notice of something on my arm. When she shot me a furtive look filled with horror and disgust, I knew she had seen my self-harm scars.

My heart sank.

She called in another nurse, and together they examined my arm in detail. Soon they moved on to my other arm, then my legs, and then my torso.

Shame welled up inside me, tears pricked at my eyes. Those people were scrutinizing one of the most horrific aspects of my life. Without my consent. While I could not move, could not protest.

Then Damien came. He stopped in the doorway, clearly puzzled. "What are you doing?"

The other nurses began to explain, but the moment it was clear they were not concerned with my burns, Damien cut them off. "Finish changing his bandages, then *leave*," he ordered. "Those scars are none of your business."

To my immense relief, they averted their eyes, listened.

When they were gone, Damien came to me and placed his hand on my cheek. "I will get you out of here, love," he promised. "Everything will be all right."

I continue telling Tess about my time with Damien. "So Damien took me to his home, where he and his grandmother again saved my life and helped me recuperate. We...became very close." My face burns as I remember that I had already referred to him as 'my love.' "We grew to love each other, and I stayed with him until he became a Beggar." I fall silent, not sure what else to say.

"Tell me more about him."

"He was so kind and loving and understanding. He was gentle and sweet and passionate, especially about his patients. He was a nurse, you see. A good one. He didn't judge me for my past or my moods. He helped me become my best self." I close my eyes.

"It sounds like you really loved him."

"I did." I still do. I miss him every day.

It may be important to note that the Veqah had several words for love, one for each type of love. There was universal love (*hape*); the love of a caregiver (*enfe*); familial love (*manne*); romantic love (*kane*); platonic love (*ade*); self-love (*daie*); committed love (*pire*); passionate love (*flore*); obsessive love (*irne*); and a kind of love that is related to both platonic and romantic love, but is beyond either (*ame*). This last kind may be best described as 'queerplatonic.'

In the hospital, Damien used the word for universal love.

Damien stands on the beach next to a small boat.

I smile. "You waited for me."

He had even built a boat for us to cross the ocean together.

"I've missed you," he says.

We are on the boat, in the middle of the ocean. The boat moves forward on its own, no need for an engine or for rowing.

A girl aged about eight years, her hair and skin the same shade as mine, sits next to me. "You are not allowed here, Fay," she reminds me sternly. She pulls a ring out of the ivy wrapped around her body and places it on my finger.

It wraps around my wrist instead, and my arms and legs become bound.

I scream for Damien.

I wake with his name on my lips. His image fades from my mind as I shake off the sleep for good. There was something I wanted to tell him, wasn't there?

At this moment, I recall what I had learned about myself not long ago. A feeling—no, many feelings—intermix inside me: joy, bemusement, relief, others that I cannot identify.

I am aromantic and asexual. I am a person who does not experience romantic or sexual attraction. I am.

I am not broken. I am not wrong. I am not missing anything vital. I am not.

It is, to say the least, an odd sensation, to finally know these things. To have descriptors for myself that are neutral, or possibly even positive, instead of negative and painful.

This reminds me of when I realized the term 'autistic' applied to me. Life is different for me than it is for most people—I've known that my entire existence—but that does not mean that I am in need of repair. I am in need of understanding. And knowing the correct terminology can aid in reaching that understanding.

I turn to Tess, who still sleeps beside me.

Because of her, my world has shifted around me, expanded. I had always known there was something everyone else knew that I was not understanding, and as it turns out, that was—in part—sexual attraction.

Again I wonder how she would react to the other parts of me for which I have words.

The feelings swirling inside me start to churn the more I consider them and what brought them on—churn like the ocean. I rub my face as I attempt to stay afloat. Eventually I manage to find a piece of driftwood to cling to, at least for the moment.

I climb out of bed, careful not to disturb Tess. I run my thumbs against the insides of my other fingers a few times. Sensing the many rings reminds me of the Key. I still need to complete the spell for the fourth piece. I sigh, not wanting to do so.

Instead, I shower until I can no longer keep the most recent dream and the thoughts it carries out of my mind. The piece of driftwood ceases to be enough. So I step outside of the ISERE onto a deserted rocky beach.

Waves roll in under a clear pre-dawn sky. The low tide creeps closer.

I find a spot that is only mildly uncomfortable and sit there, arms propped on my knees. For a time, I close my eyes, listening to the thunder and the *hush*ing of the waves after they break. The sounds soothe me like my mother did when I was a child; indeed, the spreading of the waves across the beach sounds like her telling me *ssshhh*.

Perhaps that is what the waves are doing: hushing me, pacifying me. I can almost hear the ocean call my name, can certainly feel some tug that urges me toward the water.

But for now, I simply sit, thinking, feeling, waiting. I imagine a boat like the one in my dream, Damien next to it. Not for the first time, I wonder if anyone does get a boat to cross the ocean to the afterlife.

Do the unequivocally good find a boat on the beach, or at least the supplies to build one? The better the person, the better the boat they find?

I know I will have to swim. I know I will not be able to swim far before the hands of those I have wronged through my neglect grip me tight. Even with my penance, I am not so sure my journey will be long.

My penance.

The copper ring.

Ruminating on this makes me want to drown my entirety in the ocean if only to drown my thoughts.

The truest reason I do not arrives at just the right moment.

"Keeper?" Her voice opens my eyes for me, turns my head.

"Hello, Teresa."

She stands outside the ISERE in jeans and a maroon sweater pulled over a flannel. Her posture speaks of uncertainty and nerves, as if she feels she has walked in on something private.

I suppose she has, in a way, but I do not mind.

I invite her to sit next to me. As she does, I realize dawn has recently passed. The water is much closer now.

"What are you thinking about?"

"Heavy things." I stop twisting a ring to toss a rock across the narrowing beach. "The ocean was very important to my people, and not simply because it surrounded us and nourished us. It plays a role in many of our beliefs, perhaps most notably those about death." I toss another rock. "We must cross an ocean when we die to make it to paradise. The problem is every person's ocean contains parts of the souls of everyone they wronged and were not forgiven by. The people in the ocean try to pull you down into damnation. If there are too many people, you drown."

Tess is quiet for a while. "Just parts of their souls."

I nod. "Grudges fragment our souls. Forgiveness keeps us intact." I do not know what happens if one were to not forgive but simply let go.

"Do you believe it?" Her voice is not judgmental or skeptical, simply curious.

"Yes." A rock falls from my hands. I drop the pieces and take a steadying breath. "I am afraid of death, Tess." I keep my eyes to the offing. "I have done so much wrong in my life. No one is alive to forgive me. I cannot even forgive myself." I decide not to tell her about the nightmares I have of being dragged down, only to find the hands are my own.

"Most of those people that died didn't even know you, Keeper. How can they begrudge you?" Her voice is gentle, but her words pierce my heart nonetheless.

Fury at her ignorance burns in my chest. "That does not *matter*, Tess, don't you see?" I snap. "So long as they hold a grudge, their soul will still find that of the person or people who wronged them. It does not matter if they begrudge the universe, it is still *my fault.*"

Tess flinches at my tone.

Instantly I regret speaking to her in such a way. "I am sorry."

"Apology accepted. It's just—I was thinking it's really the Collector's fault. Maybe you and I have a responsibility to stop her because we know how to, but that doesn't mean you are responsible for the wrongs she has chosen to commit." She pauses. "And that means you aren't—and will never be—an abomination, Keeper."

My shoulders slump. "I do not know. I have not seen it that way." Isn't it still my fault that I never learned how to stop her until it was my penance to do so? Until I was threatened with a damnation even worse than the one I imagine daily?

But...? Could...?

No.

Yet now there is doubt, planted in my mind, my soul.

This is the second time she has opened my worldview in as many days, I realize with a spinning mind. I clear my throat. "Tess, about yesterday..."

She knows what I mean. "You don't have to explain. It's wild to have your self-perception change like that."

I tug at my sleeve. "It is a little more complicated than you might think. I would—I would like to explain why. I will not go into details, but I need to warn you that part of it may be...unpleasant to hear."

"Okay."

I take a deep breath. "At age eighteen, I was conscripted into the army and placed in an all-Veqah unit." I stop there, suddenly unsure if I should continue. Am I prepared for the consequences of saying these words aloud?

My back itches, just between the shoulder blades.

"I, ah... One day, my peers were trying to convince me to...see a woman. They had picked up on my lack of...not interest, per se, but desire. See, these things—romance, sex—were frequently at the forefront of my mind so I could analyze what I said for innuendo and try to glean why everyone else was obsessed with the concepts; I had no desire to participate, but it was in my interest to understand them.

"They said many things: 'You won't know if you don't try it,' 'You just haven't met the right person,' 'Only the broken feel nothing,' and so on." I could list every phrase I remember of those that they had all thrown at me time and again, and the list still would be far from complete. "They ended up locking me in a room with a woman who was...interested in pursuing me."

Tess gasps.

"Nothing of much consequence occurred then, but..." I spread my hands. I decide against telling her that two days later, I had a breakdown and tried to cut off my own skin. That one fellow conscript, Misha, had found me in the act and dragged me in front of the unit to put my wounds and scars on display. That I was dishonorably discharged and returned home to a family who did not understand why I no longer wanted to wear my own skin.

"Keeper, that's horrible. I'm so sorry."

I flick a hand to one side.

"Thank you for trusting me enough to tell me."

I nod, unable to say anything more. Tears threaten. I had stopped telling anyone because so many of those I had told before let me know that I was a problem to be solved, that the soldiers were right about me, that the woman could have cured or repaired me.

"Do you want a hug?"

"Yes," I whisper.

Tess wraps her arms around me, and I lean into her, finally allowing tears to trickle down my face.

I close my eyes, comforted by her touch. I do not want to leave her embrace.

Tess does not leave my side as I work on locating the fourth piece of the Key. She watches as glyphs spill from my fingertips and into the Decomis, as I hum to maintain the spell.

After hours, I emerge from my state of concentration.

Tess waves.

I wave back.

"Rhaz," states a low, gravelly voice from behind me.

I jump. The dog-shaped Aivar stands there, her fur as shaggy as before, her ears pricked upright. She is still the size of a brawny wolf and is just as intimidating. "Hello," I say as I try to calm my heart.

"I have located another of my kin," she announces, "but I need your help freeing him."

I open my mouth to volunteer but hesitate. Surely, we should get the next piece of the Key first? I decide perhaps a protector of the multiverse has her priorities in order. "All right."

I direct the ISERE to an old forest whose deciduous leaves are in the middle of changing into vibrant orange, red, and yellow. The evergreens stand proudly with their constant color.

The Aivar leads us without a visible path, stopping to sniff the air every now and then. The farther we walk, the more her tail wags, but I have my doubts that her excitement is of a positive kind.

"Not complaining or anything, but why did you—uh, park?—the ISERE so far away?" Tess asks.

"It was difficult to pinpoint the exact location of this Aivar's prison using the ISERE. In this case, it is much simpler to bypass magical means of illusion by walking," I explain.

"Okay, makes sense. But, out of curiosity, *is* there a way to magically pop over to wherever you want to go if you know the destination?"

My face burns from something other than exertion. "Some can. I never could learn it."

To be entirely truthful, the Veqah had never learned how to Travel. On our island, small and isolated as it was, Traveling was not necessary. When the Crusaders came, bringing the Traveling magic with them, they originally forbade Veqah from learning it, lest my people escape. So we were never taught. Unless we were in the military.

I was never able to grasp the skill, no matter how hard I tried.

Another thing Misha tormented me for.

I scratch my chin.

Somewhere up ahead, a bellow tears through the trees.

The Aivar bounds forward, leaving Tess and me to jog after her.

The trees thin ahead of us, and then I can see it: a massive bear, three times the size of the largest grizzly and entirely black, stands in a clearing. Gouges in the earth and shattered trees evidence its fight against the coils of golden chains gripping each of its legs.

I slow to a stop, awe pooling in my stomach with a hint of fear. This Aivar is enraged, and despite its bindings, incredibly dangerous.

The unbound Aivar trots forward. She yips as if to signify her friendly presence.

The bear Aivar's head snaps up. In a half-growl, half-roar, it bares its long fangs at us. "Stay back!"

"We came to free you," Tess reassures it.

"You!" he snaps at her. "You are in danger. And *you*!" He whips his gaze to me.

"Yes, yes, I already reminded him that he is a failing guardian of the multiverse," the dog Aivar chimes in, leaning in to sniff at her kinfolk's chains. "Now calm down so we can free you. The Collector may be here any moment."

I approach and kneel next to the nearest chain. Apprehensive, I place my hands on the cool metal.

Instantly a cavern widens inside me, gaping, pulling all of me in and then some, leaving only the hollow despair of nothingness. Deep hells, this is all that I am. An empty, infinite pit. A vacuum devoid of humanity.

With a cry, I recoil. A moment later I become aware of the Aivar thrashing against the chains, which whip alarmingly close to my head.

"Hey, hey, it's just the chains; it'll be okay." Tess stands by the bear's head, her hands buried in the ebony fur, soothing. "He's not trying to hurt you. It's just the chains."

It's just the chains. But I cannot do it, I cannot bear that void inside me; I have already languished in it for too much of my life. It terrifies me as much as the ocean does.

Gradually the Aivar calms like I wish I could.

"Keeper," whispers Tess. "Try again. I'll do my best to keep him calm for you." She nods to the dog Aivar. "You help the Keeper."

I meet gazes with the freed Aivar, silently beseeching her to do as Tess asked. *I cannot do this alone.* I had not even begun to figure out the spell of this chain.

The dog Aivar morphs into a woman, wearing red-and-white robes just as she was when we met. She guides my trembling hands back to the chain.

The pain returns in full force, but I focus on Tess saying "*It's just the chains*" to anchor me and use the woman Aivar's power to endure. Eventually I find the spell must be undone using a conduit—in my case, my first ring. The remaining chains cause the Aivar and me various forms of pain, and each require a different method of magic to undo the spell (after the conduit, the methods are words, gestures, and symbols).

Under different circumstances, I would find it fascinating, as the vast majority of people learn one method as a child and are never able to learn another.

When I am done, the bear Aivar extricates himself from the loosened chains while I remain slumped on my knees, quivering. I feel hollow, drained, and pray for it to pass. I always knew that this empty feeling—this state of being—would return; it always did, but the knowledge was juxtaposed with terrified denial.

Tess's voice penetrates the haze of my mind. "You made it."

I look up to see her still stroking the bear's neck.

He pulls away to gaze down at her. "You must find safety. The Collector will have sensed my chains breaking."

I force myself to my feet. "He is right, Teresa. We must go." Is my voice as hollow as it feels? As I feel? Because of this hollowness, saltwater spills into every bit of my being, drowning me, threatening to take me.

Tess notices the wrongness of my current state. "Keeper? We should get you back to the ISERE."

I try to shake out the water. "I need to obtain the next piece of the Key."

"We can talk about this back at the ISERE," Tess says firmly, taking me by the arm.

I am grateful for her support, and for the two Aivar flanking us as I stumble back to the ISERE. My head clears a little along the way, surrounded by the rustle of nature as I am. Once I unlock the door, I break free from Tess and hurry to the console. I open the Decomis and translate the coordinates on its screen to the buttons and switches and levers of the console.

"Keeper, are you in the right mind to face another guardian of the Key?" Tess asks.

I wave her off. Something in my abdomen signals that I made the wrong decision to free the Aivar first.

The mirror above the console ripples, stills.

My horrified face stares back at me, far too able to comprehend that I still gaze upon a mirror, not a screen picturing the site of the next piece of the Key.

Tess leans forward to look me in the face. "What's wrong?"

"She has it," I croak.

23

TESS

The Keeper slumps down to the floor and drops his head into his hands. He groans something unintelligible.

I look over my shoulder at the pair of Aivar.

They are solemn. No, grim. They are grim.

My heart sinks.

This is much more serious than I had initially thought, isn't it? We can't just be happy that the Collector doesn't have three of the pieces?

I kneel next to the Keeper. "Are you okay?"

"Nnnnooo," he mutters, the word painfully drawn out. His chest hitches. "Ohhhh, deep hells. Ohhhh, burning oceans. I'm damned. I'm damned!"

What is he talking about? I mouth to the Aivar. "What do you mean?" I ask the Keeper.

He shakes his head. "I can't fulfill my penance. I'm damned to a fate worse than the depths of the ocean."

"'Penance'?" I echo. Fear makes me tremble. "Keeper, you're scaring me."

He gasps and bolts upright, hands dropping to his knees. His wild gaze darts around to finally land on me.

I fall back onto my behind. "Okay, now you're *really* scaring me."

The Keeper pulls in a deep breath. His turmoil seems to subside just a little. "I met an entity who incites people to right the magical wrongs they have committed. If the incited do not fulfill their penance and right their wrongs...well, I can't say I know what happens to others, but I shall face a fate worse than the damnation those in the ocean can give."

The agnostic in me wants to laugh. Is this entity playing as a god?

The Keeper must see the skepticism on my face. "Magic is... Oh, how do I explain this to someone who didn't grow up knowing this? Magic has many manifestations. This entity is one. She—magic—does not want to be used to the detriment of the multiverse or those who reside in it. But magic is an energy that does not have control over how magical beings utilize it. I am doing an awful job explaining this. Does it make sense regardless?"

I wrap my arms around my knees, thinking. "Magic's just exerting what control it can by getting people to try to undo the bad things they've done using magic?"

The Keeper waggles his head from side to side. "Eh. Not a bad understanding."

I still think this entity is playing as a god. "What's the penance you're supposed to pay?"

He closes his eyes. "I have to stop the Collector, heal the multiverse, and—" He opens his eyes to stare at the ceiling high above.

"And?" I prompt.

"And...nothing."

"No wonder you don't usually lie. You're *terrible* at it."

The Keeper's expression reminds me of a deer caught in the head-lights.

I sigh. I won't press it.

The Keeper retreats back into his hands.

I gesture at the Aivar, who for some reason are still watching. *Go!* I mouth. When they vanish, I turn back to the Keeper. "We can work something out."

His voice comes out muffled. "What could we possibly work out?"

"I don't know. I just don't think it's time to give up on how your fate will turn. I mean, we can still get the last piece ourselves, and then we can find a way to trick the Collector into giving up the fourth piece or something."

"I don't know if she *can* be tricked, Tess."

"We can work something out," I repeat. I fight back tears, telling myself that my succumbing to fear of the Keeper's future would not be helpful. "We can work something out."

24

— · —

THE KEEPER

I t is difficult to breathe, to focus on constructing the spell for the final piece of the Key. Somehow, I persevere. Somehow, I complete the spell.

When done, I search for Tess. The first place I look is her bedroom, from which I hear a melancholy song emanate as I approach. The words, something about being another's safe and sound, clarify once I raise my hand to knock.

I hesitate.

It is then that Tess opens the door. "I could see your shadow under the door. You're not sneaky."

"I wasn't trying to be. Tess," I say, lowering my hand as slowly as I speak, "do you feel safe with me?"

She looks surprised. "Yeah. I mean, of course I still feel like I'm in danger when dangerous things happen, but I feel safe around you. I don't believe you would let me come to harm. Sorry, rambling a little. Yes. I feel safe with you."

As I look down at her, I see such innocence and trust and naivete in her eyes, as though she truly has the deepest faith in my ability to keep her safe. Perhaps not to stop the Collector, but to keep Tess safe. I am seized with the desire to protect those qualities in her at all costs, to defend her more completely than she could know, for to know would mean she would lose them.

She pushes her braid behind her shoulder. "Why do you ask?"

I work my jaw, trying to piece together the words.

Tess narrows her eyes, seeming to suspect my reason. "Do *you* feel safe with *me*?"

This jolts me out of my line of thought. "Of course."

"You shouldn't. If I could catch the Collector off guard with my punch, I could knock the daylights out of you," she deadpans. She tilts her head. "Is that what you came here for?"

I want you to be *safe, not just* feel *safe.*

"No. I finished the spell. We should retrieve the final piece of the Key immediately."

'We'? Was that what I meant to say?

Tess smiles that steely, cunning smile.

25

— • —

TESS

We turn up outside a Walmart, the parking lot of which is oddly empty. My first thought is that it is closed, but what Walmart is closed in the middle of the day?

The Keeper and I approach the entrance with some trepidation (well, I suppose he may not be as nervous as me—he walks with confidence).

The doors slide open to admit us.

I don't know why it surprises me, but the inside looks like a normal Walmart, just silent and devoid of humanity.

"Stay close to me, and stay quiet," the Keeper murmurs. Maybe he is nervous.

I nod and follow him through the personal care and then the garden sections.

As we approach the sporting goods section, the Keeper seems to notice something, for he signals me to wait. He creeps around the end of the aisle. "Hello!" he exclaims. "How are you today?"

The only response is a grunt and a thud.

The Keeper does not come back into view.

My heart leaps into my throat. Against every fiber of my being, I quietly retreat down the aisle. I sneak a few aisles over and back to the same end where the Keeper disappeared, and peer around a corner to try and catch a glimpse of him.

At first, I don't see him. A huge fire pit, much larger than what would be sold, sits in the middle of the walkway, a disproportionately small fire crackling inside. A petite woman stokes it, singing to herself. Her tidy bun faces me, so I am not too worried about being seen.

A moment later, I do see him. He is propped upright on the other side of the fire pit, his arms behind his back and his legs pinioned together by blazing orange bands.

Shit.

I withdraw behind the shelf, chewing my lip. I need a distraction to get the woman away from the Keeper. An idea percolating in my brain, I head for the toy section. Rather quickly, I find exactly what I want: an RC car.

"Dammit. No batteries," I mutter. Hold on. I'm in a superstore devoid of employees. I can steal whatever I want no problem! I nearly smack my forehead. I take the car and its remote control and walk back to the front of the store where I had seen batteries on the way in. After putting in the proper batteries, I play with the car to get a feel for how to work it. A few minutes later, I head back toward the woman and the Keeper.

I set the car to one side of the fire pit and sneak over to the other side. My hands clench the control. I force my grip to relax and direct the car toward me.

The whine of the engine hopefully draws the woman's attention as it passes her. I drive it down the next aisle and when it pops out my end, I steer it away from me and duck behind the shelf as it speeds away and slams into another several yards away.

I hear footsteps follow the RC car, and then a few moments later walk back in the direction it had come from. As quietly as I can I hurry over to the Keeper.

He stiffens when he sees me. "Go away!" he whispers urgently.

I ignore him and look over his bonds. Can I undo magical bindings? I'm afraid to touch them.

"You cannot free me," he whispers. "And I cannot free myself; these are magic blockers. You have to convince her to free me."

"How?"

"I don't know! Now go, but hurry, because she wants to *cook* me!"

My heart stutters, but I obey him, heading back to the front of the store. What do I do, what do I do? How do I communicate with someone without being seen? It's not like I have magic to make me invisible. A megaphone would lead her to me, I'm sure... My eyes fall upon the phones at the checkout counters.

I set one of the walkie-talkies next to the phone, with the button pressed to page, and make my way across the store. I find a hiding place in view of the fire pit (which now contains a blazing bonfire), but close enough that I should be able to hear the woman speak.

I see a glittering chain around her neck, which I assume holds the piece of the Key.

"Hi there," I say in a low voice into the walkie-talkie in my hand. My voice comes again a moment later over the speaker system.

The woman jumps, whips her blond head around.

"I hear you want to cook that guy you have tied up there."

"Uh...that is true." Her loud voice carries just well enough that I can hear it from where I hide.

"I totally get it. Mages are delicious."

"You've tried them?" Her head swivels as she continues to look for me. She seems reluctant to leave her meal behind.

"Hell yeah. They're a delicacy." I pause. "The thing is, you're going about it all wrong."

"How's *that*?" Now I've piqued her irritation.

Crap. I bite my lip.

"The magic blockers. You see, when magic infuses the flesh, it really brings out that umami flavor." (I don't even know what umami means.)

"Mages tend to be sweet..."

"Exactly. You really want that blend of sweet and umami. It's even better than you might think."

"Who are you?" Her hand wanders to the chain around her neck.

"Someone who wants you to get the best out of your next meal." (I curse myself. I don't want her to *kill* the Keeper.) I add, "You also want to cook your mage alive. It enhances the texture."

Even from my hiding place, I can see the Keeper's eyes widen.

The woman's voice becomes more suspicious. "Are you only doing this because you want a share?"

"No, don't worry. I merely want what's best for your tastebuds, then I'll be on my way."

"Then what are you doing here?"

"I wanted to look over your battery selection. Which is excellent, by the way. I really needed some nine-volt batteries."

A hint of pride enters her voice. "Our battery selection is better than the Menards."

"Menards *sucks*," I reply just to butter her up a little. (They don't really suck, not when they have discounted Renaissance Faire tickets for sale.)

"I'm glad you realize that. If you'd like, you can join me for a bit of this mage. The fire is just ready for me to begin cooking."

"I would love that." But I hesitate. Is this a trap? It couldn't be this easy to get close to the ring, could it? I decide to grab a baseball bat and stash it nearby just in case; the Keeper may prefer nonviolence, but when it comes to life or death, I have no qualms.

When I emerge from the shelves and finally meet the woman face-to-face, she looks disappointed. "You're not a mage."

"No, I just eat them. I'm Dawn, by the way."

"Maggie." She gestures to the Keeper, who immediately keels over, unconscious.

I suppress a gasp.

"We don't want him getting away when I undo the magic blockers," she explains as she does just that.

"Good idea," I force myself to say. Shit. I should have seen this coming. What now?

Wait—I reach for what the Keeper mentioned: I reach for that hum, that ring, that sense of connection to her name. I try to grip it and wield it. "Maggie," I intone, "wake him up."

Her tone is icy when she speaks. "Excuse me?" Her frigid gaze makes me take a step back.

My heart sinks. I should have known it wouldn't work on a guardian of the Key. But I try again anyway. "Wake him up, Maggie. It's more fun when they're conscious."

"Did you just try to use my name against me?" she hisses.

I swallow, inch back. "No."

"You *did*!" Her jaw unhinges, revealing rows upon rows of jagged teeth. "Get over here so I can eat you!"

"Okay." I dart for the hidden baseball bat. My hand has barely closed around it when something grips my ankle and drags me back toward Maggie. I twist to see a thick rope wrapped around my leg, taut and drawing me closer to danger. When I am within striking distance of Maggie, I swing the bat as hard as I can.

It glances off her leg.

She howls but doesn't fall; the rope stays tight as it pulls.

I swing again.

This time the bat connects with a satisfying *thunk*, sending Maggie crumpling to the floor.

The rope around my ankle loosens enough for me to scramble free.

I stand over Maggie, bat poised to strike once more. "Wake. Him. Up," I snarl.

"Fine!" She waves her hand.

I don't take my eyes off her. "Keeper?"

As if in response, ropes form from nothing and snake around Maggie's limbs.

She writhes in a vain attempt to free herself.

The Keeper appears at my shoulder. "The Key?"

"Around her neck." As he bends, I warn, "Watch her teeth."

A blue haze settles over Maggie, freezing her in position.

The Keeper removes the ring from the chain around Maggie's neck and straightens.

Almost immediately the ground beneath our feet quakes. Products tumble off shelves, and I nearly topple into the Keeper.

He steadies me, and without a word, we run for the exit.

The earth shudders harder the closer we get to the doors. A light smashes to the floor beside us. The Keeper stumbles and nearly falls.

An immense crash sounds behind us as we reach the front doors. I risk looking to see the center of the ceiling collapsed behind us. I get an eyeful of grit for my trouble.

I race blindly out the door and come to a halt many steps away, coughing from the dust.

The tremors beneath us begin to subside.

"I have dirt in my eyes," I tell the Keeper. "I can't see anything."

He touches my temple. A spark passes from his fingertips, through my skin, and to my eyes, clearing them.

I blink the tears from my eyes. "Thanks. What about Maggie?"

He waves a hand. "She isn't a living being, merely a powerful construct."

I nod. "What about you?"

He stares at me.

For a moment, I worry I've pissed him off, but even worse, he begins to cry.

In the middle of an empty Walmart parking lot, dust billowing around us, I hold the Keeper as he sobs.

26

— • —

THE KEEPER

I stand in the open doorway of the ISERE, gazing down at an enormous swath of flat grassland.

Up this high, the air should be thin and cold, but the ISERE's doorway provides a buffer against that.

What it does not provide a buffer against is my thoughts.

What would it be like to fall? To simply let go...

Naida and I, when we were young, climbed trees together. Tall, tall trees, high, high up. I would perch in the branches and imagine pushing myself off. Sometimes I thought the only reason I never did was because there were branches in the way: I wanted to fall, not collide.

Sometimes, as I am doing now, I still sit or stand in the doorway of the ISERE far, far above the earth and ponder falling from there. However, the ISERE would stop my descent.

My mind moves, inexorably, to the ocean. Last night I had another nightmare wherein the hands clutching and dragging me were covered in rings. Eight still, not the seven I have now since my meeting with the Exorcist. One each on every finger of my left hand except the middle, and on the right hand, one on my first and middle fingers, and two on my third. The ringed hands were attached to scarred arms. My own face loomed above those arms, glowering at me as I fought. Some bared their teeth.

Then I drowned. I stopped breathing in reality, too, and woke from it.

A voice stirs me from my reverie. Low, gravelly, almost flirtatious. "Hello, Thane Rhaz."

I freeze. My heart skips a beat.

No. No, it cannot be.

Agonized, I turn.

The Exorcist stands in the center of the atrium, bathed in light. I can see the self-satisfied smile in his eyes. "We are going to have so much fun." He lunges.

When I wake, I see nothing at first. Just feel. I sit slumped in a hard metal chair. No pain. My body seems intact but trembles.

I blink several times until my vision comes into focus. The light is dim, but I can see clearly: trees tower overhead, shielding me from even a glimpse of the sky. I wipe sweat out of my eyes and turn to my more immediate surroundings: a card table amongst the ruins of a small shack.

"Go fish."

"Oh, please, you hafta be lyin'!"

I turn my head to see three white men: two across from me, one on my left.

"The only time I lie is in Bullshit, Randall, you should know that," the first man growls, though 'mountain' is a better descriptor than 'man.' His bald head gleams like polished stone, his muscles bulge like rocks in a full bag. He lacks his left forearm.

"Well, you got any sevens then, George?" The second man, Randall, is sinewy, tough-looking, covered in scars. The biggest slashes his neck open, but no blood drips out—the wound is entirely dry.

"Randall, it's not your turn anymore," the third man scolds in a slow voice. "You just went, so it's mine." His eyelids sag. This man is much older than the others, but he has a hardened, dangerous look to him nonetheless.

"Fine, fine," grumbles Randall.

"Got any sevens, Randall?" drones the third man.

Randall spews curses and hands over two.

"Oh, shut it," the third man says dully.

"What is going on?" I finally ask.

George the mountain answers. "We're playing Go Fish while we wait for the Exorcist to hunt us again. Maybe we'll die this time."

It is only then that I remember the scene in the atrium: the Exorcist swinging his sickles, slicing me open—

I put a hand over my eyes.

"Don't worry, fella, gettin' cut don't hurt too bad."

"Yeah, it does," Randall protests. "My neck *still* hurts!"

George hushes him. "We don't wanna make him more scared."

"It doesn't matter," I tell them.

And it doesn't. I am dead, or as good as. Anything is better than the ocean. My heart lifts. What comes after this? Oblivion? Oblivion is far better than damnation...

"How does it not matter?" exclaims Randall.

"I think he just wants us to shut up," suggests the old man.

"Are there other people here?" I ask.

The old man shrugs. "Somewhere. They don't like playing cards with us. They'd rather hide, as if that does anything."

I stand. My legs tremor beneath me.

As if in response, the other men tense.

"He's back," George breathes.

"He's coming," growls the old man.

"*Run*," Randall says.

All three scramble off in different directions, leaving their hands scattered across the table.

Instinctively, I run too. I know the Exorcist will be coming for me. Most of me does not mind, but a strong part of me still screams for self-preservation.

The ground beneath the trees is bare dirt, quiet underfoot. I see nothing else moving around me in the forest.

I meet the edge of the woods. Before me is a grassy field with a hill in the center. Atop the hill is a cold, forbidding castle. The Exorcist's home.

I retreat back into the trees and sprint in a direction different from the way I came. The trees here are more widely spaced but older, their crowns thick, allowing little light. I slow.

What now?

"*Thane...*" The whisper rattles through the trees.

I jump, stop myself from running. I look around.

The Exorcist is perched in a tree off to my right, one hand against the sturdy trunk, the other draped across his knee. He makes me think of an insane owl. "Are you ready to have some fun?" Without waiting for a response, he drops to the ground, landing in a crouch. He pulls his sickles from his belt.

He vanishes.

I duck.

Blades slice the air above my head.

I spin and kick the Exorcist back.

He recovers quickly, sickles poised. His eyes gleam. "Oh, this is going to be better than I expected." He slices at my feet.

I jump away.

The Exorcist surges forward.

I dodge his blows, entirely on the defensive. My back strikes a tree.

The Exorcist's eyes spark with glee. His blades scissor together toward my midsection.

And stop.

My hands grip the Exorcist's, holding them still. It takes all my might. Sweat rolls down my temple. Slowly, slowly, I force the blades away from me.

His pale eyes widen. "H-how?" he grunts.

Suddenly the rope in the back of my mind tightens and yanks me to the ground.

The sickles cleave through empty air where I had been less than a second before.

The rope reifies, wrapping around me, binding my arms to my sides, my legs to each other; it snakes around me until I am encased, only my head free.

The Exorcist screams in frustration. "Collector! I only want to play!"

The ropes begin dragging me backward. Toward the Collector.

I struggle against my bonds, to no avail. I freeze when I see the Exorcist raise a sickle above his head.

"Get your soul out of my realm, Collector!" he howls. And swings downward.

I flinch.

The ropes around me fall away, sliced clean through.

The Exorcist is thrown back from the force of the magic freed by the cut ropes and sprawls on the ground, moaning.

I stand and run alongside the ropes. Toward the one who doesn't want me dead.

The Collector.

27

TESS

I sit listening to Bastille's *Wild World* album, trying to resist the urge to intrude on the Keeper's precious space he requested, trying to resist thinking about how the Collector still wants my soul, trying to resist pondering my universe's impending demise.

I sink back into the pillows on my bed and half-heartedly mouth the words to "Winter of Our Youth."

So, basically, I am alone.

Then someone touches me.

I shriek and shoot upright.

In my bedroom stands a person—or, well, an apparition; she is tall, thin, blonde, and familiar.

"Rhys?" I gasp, my heart pounding. *What? WHAT?*

"Hello, Teresa." Her face is grim. "Thane needs your help." She speaks with an Australian accent. It *is* Rhys.

I scramble to turn off my music. "Where is he? What happened?"

"He is in the atrium."

I dash out my bedroom door, Rhys on my heels.

"His soul has been severed from his body by an entity called the Exorcist—who has chased Thane into the Collector's soul. Now Thane is being chased by both of them. You need to find him and bring him back to his body."

The Keeper lies listlessly beside the ISERE's open door. The dog-shaped Aivar stands over him, sniffing at his chest.

I check the Keeper's breathing and pulse; both are steady. I turn to Rhys, shaking. "How do I do that?"

"I will guide you," growls the Aivar.

My hand brushes against the Keeper's shirt collar, pushing it down to reveal a mark on his skin. Frowning, I pull his collar down farther to see a blood-red sickle tattooed over his collarbone. Dread thumps in my chest.

"Teresa, the Exorcist wants to kill him," Rhys says urgently. "I don't know what will happen if he breaks one of his own contracts, but it can't be good for anyone. You need to hurry." She looks over her shoulder. "I need to go. I'll try to slow down the Collector, who wants to trap Thane—" She vanishes.

The Aivar steps to the other side of the Keeper. "Teresa, are you ready?"

"No." I swallow. "Let's go."

I reach out and touch the Aivar's scruff. Her presence comforts me.

I don't know how we got here, or where exactly we are. We stand in a small dark room, perhaps ten feet by ten feet. An empty black throne sits against one obsidian wall. There are no doors to be found.

The Aivar leads me to the wall on the throne's left-hand side. "Just step through the wall, Teresa. Trust me."

I bite my lip, step with her into the wall.

We emerge into a parlor straight from the early 1800s. The furniture has been shoved back against the walls to clear a space in the center of the room, where someone has chalked two circles next to each other. An unfamiliar woman enters the room, her chin lifted regally, her long blonde hair flowing over her shoulders and back. A business card is in one hand, a needle in the other. As if we are not present, she continues forward and steps into one of the circles. Next, she pricks the pad of her thumb with the needle and smears it onto the card. "Exorcist, ruler of dimensions, lord of souls, I humbly petition your presence. Grant me this request so that we may enter a contract together. In asking this, I vow to pay a fit price for your visit and services," she intones in an accent much like the Keeper's. She tosses the card into the other circle, where it spits smoke that fills the column inside the circle.

When the smoke dissipates, a man in gray clothes with sickles hanging from his belt stands there.

The woman wastes no time introducing herself. "My name is Aileth Rawls. I want you to teach me what you know about creating a realm that can hold souls."

The Exorcist tilts his head back. "Interesting," he drawls. "No one has ever done their research quite like you have."

Aileth says nothing. (Where have I heard that name before?)

"What will you offer for it?"

"My mother's soul and five years of servitude, to be done with as you please."

"Your mother? Boring. No. I want to make it interesting."

Aileth's eyes flash.

"No, it will cost you more for me to teach you all of that. I want your father's soul and twelve years of servitude."

Aileth hesitates, but caves. "Very well."

"What is this?" I ask the Aivar.

"A memory. The Collector must have taken it when she killed Aileth Rawls."

We walk across the room to the door and into a hallway. At the far end I can hear a man and a woman shouting indistinctly. A ticking emanates from somewhere.

On a whim, I peer beneath the cloth on a table in the hallway and see a blonde girl huddled underneath. She clutches a watch to her ear. Somehow, I know the ticking comforts her, distracts her from the yelling down the hall. Distracts her from pain and fear.

Tick. Tock.

28

---·---

THE COLLECTOR

*T*he magic calls to me, sings to me. What does it say? It whispers, so I can hardly hear what it says.

I am not sure when I first heard its call, but I believe it was around the same time I first touched magic, at age five. It has only grown stronger ever since.

Oh, how I want to let it consume me. Let it fill me, flood me, overtake me. But that would be unwise.

Or would it? Magic is natural, it is sentient. Surely it knows best?

So, I let it in enough to comfort me when I need it. I used to hold my dear father's golden watch to my ear when my mother was finished berating me—the ticking soothed me. Now I let in the magic to create a ticking sound within my mind.

I like to share the sound, to hopefully comfort others. Sharing is important to me, particularly since I had little as a child. No toys, no friends, no affection. My family had some money, so we never starved for food or shelter. But I did starve: for love, for a childhood, for connection. So, I sought it from my peers; I wanted them to share with me their childhoods, their experiences, and so forth.

The only thing they need not share was magic. I was never supposed to use magic, being a girl at the beginning of the nineteenth century, but its *call overpowered any fear I had, and I cannot be more grateful for that. The magic allowed me to help others share, first tiny things in childhood, then bigger things. Like memories. Experiences.*

The ocean. The ocean must be shared. It is too much for one person, one people. Even in death. Much like magic, the ocean calls to me. But in a different way. A sinister way that speaks of the inexorable. This is a call I strive to ignore, to avoid. The ocean must be shared, but it is brutal, evil in its indifference. It must not be trusted. It must not be loved. It can and should be utilized, but nothing more. Nothing less.

But I have done enough sharing. Now it is time to be alone with my collection.

29

THE KEEPER

I am lost. So lost. Swamped in the Collector's soul.

I can barely keep afloat.

The Exorcist pursues me through the Collector's memories and thoughts, so I cannot linger, but the emotions and thoughts cling to me as I dash through, and there are so many similar recollections that the themes stick.

Crusader through-and-through, I can tell. Not just from her porcelain skin, white clothes, and fragments of the island that I recognize, but the hatred and entitlement. Only colonizers would have such sentiments. She takes and hates, though for her the taking becomes less physical over time. She hates herself, but she blames others. So she takes from them to transform herself.

Why am I here? I think I know. The Collector wants me for something. Something that requires me to be alive. But she couldn't find me like the Exorcist could. When he became a threat to my soul, she broke into his realm with her own soul to protect me. And entrap me.

I think I am losing the Exorcist.

I race through a door—into my parents' kitchen.

A young, long-haired version of me kneels on a chair at the kitchen table, trying to knead dough.

My mother stands behind me, a smile on her lovely face. "Try this, Thane," she suggests, leaning down and guiding my hands.

"Mother?" I whisper. Tears well in my eyes. I have no memory of this. Is it real? Is it simply a projection of what I want to remember?

I take one step, two, closer, then more until I am standing next to myself and my mother. I reach out to touch her shoulder—

Everything vanishes.

A small doorless room with black walls forms around me. A throne the color of coal sits against one wall.

Chills race down my spine; I have read descriptions of this space, seen it in my dreams.

This is the Tomb.

I jump as part of the wall opposite the throne pushes inward and vanishes, forming a doorway. A slender white woman enters and glides over to the throne. Her manner is eerily familiar—this is the Collector, before Naida. She seats herself, tosses her light hair over her shoulder, leans back in the throne. Glowing golden chains form and wrap around the Collector's head and limbs, binding her to the chair. Their light begins to pulse softly.

Something tells me what is happening now: the Collector's soul is being removed from her body and transferred into the Tomb, which as it stands now, is inanimate and without a power source. Her soul is becoming the Tomb's so that it may become alive and fully functional.

When the transfer is complete, the Collector's old body is listless. The chains disappear, leaving her to slump in the throne. The Tomb moves location, and the body fades out of sight, left behind.

Why? Why not disintegrate the body like that of the Beggars? The memory gives me no answer.

Years pass. I sense that, but I cannot tell how many. Then the door opens once more.

Naida steps in, awe on her grinning face.

"Naida, do not go in there!" my own voice warns from behind her.

As in my own memory, she ignores me.

The door shuts behind her.

Naida whirls around.

My heart is in my throat as I watch her frantically pound on the wall.

Her hands glow with fruitless power. "Thane!" she cries. She swears. I had forgotten how dirty her mouth was. Her fists slide from the wall. She turns in place, examining her bleak surroundings.

For a moment, the anemic light in the room brightens. "*Naida...*" the Tomb whispers.

She stiffens. I can see the fire still in her eyes, burning, fighting, but to no avail—Naida marches toward the throne. Magic sparks uselessly around her fingers.

"*I only want to share with you, Naida,*" the Collector murmurs.

My touch flooded the Tomb with the energy it needed to move after the Collector's soul vacated it for Naida's body. She moved on to my family—both in the past and present.

When she finds them, preparing for dinner, I walk away, unable to watch. Once was too much for me.

The Collector believed she only wanted to share, but she wanted to take. To possess. No one who wants to share turns people into Beggars.

Before I can reach a doorknob, a *thunk* shakes the door. Fragments of wood fly past me.

I recoil in time to see a curved blade withdraw from the newly formed hole in the door and swing forward again to widen the gap.

I run. Run past my dying family, past the Collector, down the hallway. I burst through the next door I see, then the next, then the next. When I come across a locked door, I waste no time searching for the next unlocked one.

The seventh or eighth door I dash through opens into a vast cylindrical room. I am on a walkway ringing the edge about a third of the way up. No, it is not any floor below me, but water, black and still. There are no other doors.

Where do I go? *Down.*

I swallow.

I do not have time to deliberate, so I clamber over the railing.

As I brace myself to jump, a hand grips the back of my jacket.

My heart jerks in my chest when the Exorcist whispers in my ear, "Hello, Thane. That was quite a chase, wasn't it?"

My body takes over for me. My elbow snaps back into the Exorcist's face.

His head jerks back with a *crack*. His grip on my jacket weakens but holds.

I topple off the edge of the walkway.

The Exorcist, still grasping me and too stunned to right himself, tumbles over the railing.

Together we fall. I straighten myself, feet toward the water. The Exorcist does not. We slam into the water. Bubbles rise around us, and through them, I see the Exorcist sinking.

I swim past him, deeper into the water.

A hand grips my leg.

I kick, miss.

One hand still grasping my leg, his other grabs my jacket and pulls me close.

We surface, gasping.

I reach over my shoulder for his bloodied face, magic surging into my hand. When it contacts the Exorcist's face, the spell forces him to release me. I grip his hair and pull him down into the water.

He flails and strikes me as I turn toward him.

I shove at his chest, using magic to send him flying back in the water with much more force than I could on my own. I waste no time diving back underwater and swimming downward as hard as I can.

Pain slices across my back.

Water goes up my nose and down my throat as I reflexively gasp.

The sickle slices me again.

I twist and block the next blow. My lungs burn. I grip the Exorcist's hand and disarm him.

The sickle sinks down into darkness.

The Exorcist struggles against my grip, but I do not release him.

My head breaks the surface again. I place my hand over the Exorcist's face, try to prevent him from surfacing as well.

We roll to the side.

The Exorcist flails and hits me, his blows gradually weakening. It becomes easier to hold him down, even as I yearn for air. After an eternity that only lasts seconds, he stills.

I do not release him.

Instead, I sink with him, and when he is gone, I close my eyes and let myself descend further.

My face lies against something coarse and warm. My body is washed in waves of cool water. I open my eyes, and my heart sinks.

I have washed onto sand, which my face rests upon now.

What I hear falls into place: the low roaring and hissing are that of breaking waves. They are almost loud enough to drown out the infernal ticking.

Drown.

Am I dead? Did I drown, or simply move on to the next part of the Collector's mind?

Why do the waves break so evenly, so consistently, almost like clockwork?

My breath hitches in my chest. I force myself to my feet to look at my surroundings.

I stand on a narrow sandbar that stretches beyond my eyesight in two directions. Rhythmic, steady waves bite from the other directions. A bright blue yet sunless sky hovers above me.

An immense pressure crashes down upon me, choking me—*deep hells, I am dead*. These waves will eat away at the sand until they drag me into the water, where I will then be pulled to my eternal fate. No matter how long I try to avoid it, the ocean and the billions within it will have their way.

Barely able to breathe, I run. Air rasps in my throat but barely makes it farther in. Still, I run. Left foot, right, left foot, right, as if I can outrun the destiny that was my own doing.

At some point, I collapse to my knees and bury my face in my hands. My empty chest heaves with strained sobs. I can't, I can't, I can't do this. I should have let the Exorcist destroy my soul, why did I run? Why did I *kill* him?

Then I hear the most beautiful voice in the world.

30

TESS

"Keeper?"

He kneels in the sand, shuddering, face in hands. At my voice, he raises his head to show the face of a broken, hopeless man. "Teresa?" His voice is hollow, it cracks.

I kneel before him, take his tear-dampened hands. "I'm here. Keeper, we need to go. The Collector and the Exorcist are coming for us."

From far away, he shakes his head. "The Exorcist is dead. Just leave me here, Tess. The ocean will take me soon enough."

I am both relieved (about the Exorcist) and frustrated (I think it's clear why). *This isn't real, you absolute knick-knack!* I want to scream, but I bite back the words. Instead, I say, "This isn't your ocean, Keeper. This is just the Collector. And she, incidentally, is very much alive, and the Aivar says she knows you're here."

The Keeper still does not break out of his daze. "He is dead," he breathes.

The Aivar leans in. "Teresa, use his name. We do not have time for this."

"Are you sure we shouldn't save it?"

"If we save it, we won't have another time to use it!"

She's right. I take a deep breath, look the Keeper in the eye, and search for that ring, that connection, he described to me before. I try to shove down the memory of me failing at this previously. "Thane. You need to come with us."

Slowly his gaze comes into focus. "Yes. Okay."

Relieved, I help him to his feet and lead him over to the door the Aivar and I had come through.

It's locked.

I curse and turn to her. "Suggestions?"

She sniffs the air and bounds past the door. "This way."

The Keeper and I chase after her. Thankfully, the sand is relatively hard packed beneath our feet, so it is not as difficult to run as it might be otherwise.

A door appears in the distance. As we approach it, a little girl appears as well. Perhaps seven, with blonde curls and a white dress (*the girl under the hall table?*), she stands by the door, facing the ocean to our left.

The Keeper stops when we are near.

"What are you doing?" I hiss. "We need to go!"

He pays me no attention. "What is your name? Are you lost?"

What does he *think*, that she's lost in here like we are?

I stride to the door, open it. *Thank goodness it's unlocked.* "Keeper?"

He hasn't followed me. He still gazes at the girl, imploring her to step away from the ocean.

She doesn't seem to hear him. Heedless of his warnings and be-seeching, she steps into the water. The waves surge around her legs as if magnetically drawn to her skin and bones. Higher and higher they swell. Only when the waters reach her chest does she turn to him, her eyes wide (with fear? I'm not so sure). "Help me."

And the water takes her.

"*No!*" the Keeper screams. He lunges forward, but the girl is gone.

I dive after him, grab his arm before he can plunge in for her. "She wasn't real, okay? We need to *go*."

He just stares at me, uncomprehending.

"*Thane.* I love you. I don't want the Collector to hurt you." The words slip thoughtlessly from my mouth. My eyes widen in shock, but there is no time to contemplate what I just said.

I see something *click* inside him. He places a hand over mine, swallows, nods. "Let's go, then."

With an impatient growl, the Aivar follows us through the door. We race through more rooms of memories, refusing to linger. Eventually we enter a cylindrical room with a ceiling high above. Below the walkway we stand on is a swath of still, dark water.

The Keeper backs away from the walkway's edge. "No. No. I cannot go in there again." He turns back to the door and jerks at the handle. It's locked.

"Thane, swimming down through the water is the only way out," the Aivar growls. "We are almost there."

The Keeper turns and presses his back against the door. His eyes are huge, his lips pressed tightly together. "The water—I can't. I k—" He swallows, hard. "The Exorcist died in there."

"You won't die," I reassure him, trying to sound calmer than I feel. "It's just another sort of doorway."

He stares at me. "I think I died too, Tess. That's why I ended up at the ocean."

I take his hand. "You didn't die. And this time you have me. It'll turn out different, I promise."

The Aivar, evidently taking this as a sign that we are ready to go, leaps over the railing and greets the water with a loud splash.

The Keeper and I clamber over the railing and pause there on the ledge.

"Okay?" I say. "Let's jump on three." I squeeze his hand; I need it as much as he does.

He nods nervously.

"Okay. One, two, th—" My last word ends in a shriek as someone grabs my braid, nearly ripping it off. "Keeper!"

He twists on the ledge, slipping off and pulling me with him. As he turns, he swings his free hand around. A bubble of light swells from his palm, growing until it bursts into a stream of power. It sails behind my head.

The grip on my hair falls away.

I plummet with the Keeper and twist to see the Collector with her hands over her face.

Then I hit the water. The impact drives the air out of my lungs and shoves the Keeper and I apart. I try to inhale, but water rushes in. I close my mouth and flail for the surface. My head breaks free of the water, leaving me spitting liquid and gasping for air.

Above me, the Collector lowers her hands and points at me. A streak of light flashes from her finger toward me.

Something bursts out of the water before me: the Aivar.

The light strikes her square in the shoulder. She howls, "*Go*, Teresa!"

Another light flashes above me. I take a deep breath and plunge into the water. I stroke downward as strongly as I can. My lungs and muscles begin to burn. My eyes, too, as the freshwater turns to salt. *I can't make it.* No sooner does the thought enter my head than I see a dim light ahead. I feel a trickle of relief at the sight. *You got it, Tess. Almost there.*

My head breaks the surface. My chest heaving, I take a moment to just breathe.

A wave catches me from behind, tossing me forward and under.

Surprised and panicked, I thrash for a moment before finding the surface once more. At the next wave, I am more prepared, and swim with it. I can see trees ahead looking down upon the water from clifftops.

Soon my feet touch ground and I hurry toward the rocky beach before me.

My head swims as much as my body just had: did the Collector kill the canine Aivar?

"Keeper?" I cry. I stagger out of the waves and finally spot him, sitting farther down the beach.

Then I notice the blood.

Alarm pulses with my heart. I race toward him.

Blood soaks through his sodden clothes all over his body, the only areas free of it his head and neck. In most places, the stains are a dilute pink, but his left hand and forearm are drenched in thick, dripping crimson.

He sits, shuddering, hyperventilating, staring wide-eyed at himself. He doesn't respond when I say his name but does recoil at my touch.

"Let me look," I say as soothingly as I can. "We need to stop the bleeding."

The Keeper flinches as I touch him again but allows me to peel back the sleeves of his jacket and shirt.

I want to throw up at what I see. The little experience I have of nursing through shadowing did not prepare me for the bloody mess of his arm. Swallowing back horror and nausea, I carefully replace his sleeve and pull off my cardigan. I wrap it tightly around his forearm. "That'll hold. Come on. You'll be fine when you wake up." (I hope.)

I help him up and lead him across the beach to a path up a cliff face. *Are we going the right direction? Where is the Aivar to guide us?*

Atop the cliff, grand old houses loom among trees and grasses. I take Thane past them to a street lined with smaller homes, my heart unsure but my feet rushing us along.

The Keeper stops before a pale blue house with white trim. "This one," he says faintly.

I open the front door, and we cross into the same small, dark room the Aivar and I began in.

"How do we get out?" I ask.

Next thing I know, I am lying on the glass-and-metal floor of the ISERE's atrium. I sit up. My clothes are dry, my cardigan on and blood-free. I look up for the Keeper.

He stirs at my feet, slowly at first, then quickly. His eyes open with a frenzied look to them. He shoots into a sitting position, running his hands over his body. He tears at his clothes to look at his unbroken skin.

When he gets to his left arm, I gasp; I thought perhaps it was some spell from the Collector that had cut his skin open in that other plane of reality, but I realize now it had cut open old, very real wounds. Railroad track scars weave across the inside of his left forearm, looping around on each other where skin had been grafted back onto the area. Grafted on after being sliced off.

The Keeper clutches his arm to his chest with a sob. He turns away from me to cry.

31

THE KEEPER

The blackened tattoo on my collarbone bores a hole through my chest, one I do not know how to fill. At the same time, it is heavy. So heavy. I want to sink into the water, but I do not want to die. I do not believe that I do.

I sit in the shallow water at the edge of the ocean, rain pouring down on my head and shoulders, waves pulling at my feet. My knees are drawn up to my chest, my eyes closed. Quietly I cry.

I have killed a man.

Now I must kill the Collector. There is no other way out.

"I can't do this," I whisper to the ocean, to my ancestors.

There is no way out.

32

— • —

TESS

Thane wanted me to leave him alone. He didn't tell me outright but disappeared outside and locked me in the ISERE.

I managed to turn the mirror above the console into a screen that displayed him sitting in the shallows of the ocean. I watched for only a minute, as it was so intensely personal and private that I couldn't keep watching. So I turned it off and waited on a bench in the atrium.

The bear Aivar appeared soon after, having sensed his kin die.

I told him what happened.

He explained to me, as far as he understood it, that we were wandering around the Collector's *soul*. The Collector knew from Aileth Rawls how the Exorcist's realm worked—any soul can go in, which makes it possible to also get out—so she broke into the Exorcist's realm with her own soul. That connection made it possible for the Keeper's soul to enter hers. We simply followed the Keeper's soul.

At some point, despite everything, or perhaps because of everything, I dozed off. I wake to find myself alone.

The ISERE's entrance is unlocked when I check, and the Keeper is nowhere to be found outside. I roam through the garden and part of the library before checking his room, but he seems to be nowhere. I reemerge into the atrium and notice a spotty trail of water on the floor that I must have missed earlier. It seems to have come from the ISERE's entrance and leads down the steps toward the kitchen.

Bemused, I follow it. I enter the kitchen and do a double-take at what I see.

The Keeper lies on his back on the kitchen island counter, his legs dangling over the edge. His clothes and bare feet have pooled water below him. His navy jacket sprawls on the floor in a puddle of water. A bottle of whiskey is clasped loosely in one hand.

He rolls his head over to give me a broad, spacy grin. "Hello, Teresa." He raises the nearly empty bottle of whiskey to his lips and takes a drink.

He's drunk. Great. I stifle a sigh, not too pleased with his coping mechanism.

"Hi," I respond, trying to keep the unhappiness from my voice. I sit at the island by his shoulder.

"Drink?" He extends the bottle to me.

It's cherry flavored. I pull a face at the taste of extra-concentrated cough syrup and hand it back.

As the Keeper takes the bottle back, I see beneath his open collar and notice the brand of the sickle has turned black.

Apparently oblivious to my gaze, the Keeper stares up at the ceiling and sings under his breath, "*Today'll be the day, I believe it when I say, things'll start to go my way...*"

"So, where have you been?" I finally ask. I don't want him to know I had witnessed any amount of his time alone.

"The ocean," he answers idly.

"You go for a swim?"

"No. I was...praying." He stretches out the last word.

"Aren't you cold? Maybe you should change clothes."

His gaze wanders from the ceiling to my face. "Cold water helps." He looks away again, drumming against his stomach the fingers of the hand draped across his body. "It calms my skin."

My left eyebrow shoots up my forehead.

The Keeper sits up, runs his fingers through his drying hair with a grimace. His hand drifts down to scratch at the nape of his neck. With a huff, he clenches his fist and slides off the kitchen island. Whiskey bottle in hand, he walks away. His gait contains a sway that could either be drunkenness or exaggerated leisure. "Have you noticed my persistent scratching?" he calls back without turning.

I hurry after him. "Yeah."

We leave the kitchen and climb the stairs to the atrium.

"It has become a rather insidious habit. It started—" He snorts. "—oh, who knows when it started, but my skin came to itch almost constantly. No one could understand why."

I follow the Keeper into the garden, which is almost entirely dark except for orange lanterns spread evenly along the paths. He meanders toward the trees.

"You were saying?" I prompt.

"Mm? Oh. Yes. Turns out it is psychosomatic." He pauses to drain the last of the whiskey and drops the bottle.

I pick it up.

"Its intensity varies with my anxiety levels."

The path splits, going straight ahead along the top terrace or down to the next. The Keeper leads me down the latter path. The next terrace feels cooler than the first and instead of green leaves, many are yellow or red or orange.

"When I was young, I knew of nothing that could relieve the itching, mainly because we hadn't the slightest idea why it was happening. So I would scratch until I bled and scratch more." He sighs. "Eventually I found a way to temporarily relieve the itching—I started cutting. I used anything I could find to cut." He pulls up his shirt and shows me a nasty, three-inch long scar on his left hip. "This one? I used broken glass. It was awful," he says with some satisfaction. "That is why it has not faded. The ones with knives or razors have gone. Well, most of them.

"But of course, it stopped working so well over time. I needed more cuts, deeper cuts, to stave off the itching. After all the years of cutting, the scars covered nearly every bit of my body."

"Could you not heal them?" I ask cautiously.

The Keeper shakes his head. "Self-inflicted wounds are notoriously difficult to heal."

Neither of us says anything until we reach the third terrace, which is even colder than the last. The plants around us are in their winter states, browning, leafless.

"What happened to your arm?" My voice is soft, tentative. I probably shouldn't be asking...

The Keeper sighs again. "That." His eyes are half-closed. "Two days after I was locked in that room with the woman, I had a...breakdown. The typical cutting did not work. I cut off my own skin."

I close my eyes and shiver. That would certainly explain what I had seen on the beach. "I'm so sorry," I murmur.

I'm not sure he heard me, as he's started humming that song he sang a line of earlier.

He hops down the steps to the fourth level and stumbles.

This level is not a terrace like the others but is simply a circle of land surrounded by the three terraces. The air here is pleasantly warmer than the previous level, and the plants are blooming. It smells like spring. The stream from the top terrace has trickled down through the levels and empties into a pond here before us.

The Keeper begins rolling up his pant legs. He's too drunk to balance, so he plops onto the ground to complete his task.

I sit on a rock at the water's edge, setting the empty bottle next to me.

When he's rolled up his pant legs as far as they can go, the Keeper shoves himself to his feet and staggers into the pond. His shoulders tense, then sag. "That feels amazing." He takes a deep breath, throws his head back. After a time, he sprawls onto a nearby rock, feet dangling in the water, and looks at me. "I kept my hair short because of the shame."

"What do you mean?"

"When I was first conscripted into the army, they shaved our heads. It was a way of erasing our Veqah identities. After my breakdown, I was dishonorably discharged. I kept my hair short for years out of shame."

I think of his shame for not saving all those dimensions before mine. "Is that why your hair is still short?" As soon as the words are out of my mouth, I am certain I crossed a line.

He tosses his head back and is silent for a time. "Teresa, tell me something."

I tense. I don't know why. Do I have anything bad to tell him? Anything to hide? "What?"

"Have you thought any more about what you will do after all of this, if it turns out the way we desire?"

I blink in surprise. "What?"

"Obviously you will return to see your parents again. What else do you want to do?"

"Oh." I clear my throat. "Well, I was thinking…" I trail off. Do I tell him the truth? It may tip him off that I'm queer. But would it even bother him? He didn't seem fazed by Annette and Zazil being partners, and he found out he himself is queer about two days ago without seeming to simmer in self-hatred for it.

I take the plunge. "I was working on an application to study gender and sexuality so I could ultimately work as a counselor or some kind of support personnel for queer people." I pick at my shoelaces.

The Keeper stares at me with huge eyes. "Do you still want to do that?"

I shrug uncomfortably. "I don't know. I haven't thought about it since…"

He nods.

A tear forges its way down my left cheek. Is it from relief that the Keeper didn't outright reject me like Hunter did? Or is it from the pain of not feeling ready to trust Thane entirely, despite my feelings toward him? The last thought threatens to smash me into pieces, glue or no.

I push that aside and watch the Keeper lie on the rock with his eyes shut, trailing one hand in the water beside him. "Keeper?"

"Mm?"

"Do you want to talk about what happened today?"

"Bad things, Teresa. Bad things happened. That is all I would rather say right now." He scratches his face and sighs. Without warning he slides off the rock into the water.

I straighten, alarmed. "Keeper?"

His head pops up again a few seconds later, his dark hair plastered to his face. He must be crouching on the pond's bottom. "Tess, have you tried this?"

"Tried what?"

"Water. It is healing."

"No." I doubt his comment, but I have to admit I'm half-tempted to slither in myself, just for the hell of it.

He stands, backs up a few steps. The water is up to his waist. He holds out his arms. "Come here."

"Why?"

"Because I asked."

"You didn't ask."

"Will you please come into the water?"

I pull off my shoes and socks and slip my bare feet into the cold water. Chills run up my entire body, but I ignore them and stand. Mud rises between my toes. I shudder.

"Come here," the Keeper repeats.

I shuffle forward, trying not to slosh water onto my skirt, but then I give up, because my legs are so much shorter than the Keeper's.

He meets me halfway to wrap me in an embrace. He kisses my forehead and rests his chin on top of my head.

I wrap my arms around his sodden midsection, suddenly not caring that water is seeping through my clothes.

"You said you loved me, Tess," he murmurs.

I did, didn't I? "I meant it," I whisper.

"I mean it when I say I love you too."

33

THE KEEPER

I wake with my throbbing head pressed against the cool floor of my bedroom. The rest of me is also sprawled on the floor, encased in stiff clothes. I groan and try to think.

The memories of last night fall into place, followed by the rest of yesterday. I curl up and try not to cry.

What have I done? I am lucky that I did not try to cut myself. It has been years since that happened, but I have relapsed before. Perhaps Tess found me before I otherwise would have; I had been in the kitchen for some time, after all.

Tess. Shames washes over me. What does she think of me now? How can she still love me?

Eventually I find the strength to pull off my clothes and crawl into bed.

Time passes. The only reason I know that it does is because the ticking still has not disappeared from my head. However, I do not bother to keep count of the seconds. Instead, in the near-comforting darkness of my room, I ponder death. These thoughts drain me. Or rather, something else drains me and pours in these thoughts to fill the resulting void. I ponder the death of the Exorcist, the death of the Collector, and most prominently, my own death.

Sometimes the ocean tells me it can be my freedom, not my demise. Even from here, it calls to me, whispers my name. I want to answer the call, but I do not have the strength.

Perhaps the ocean is lying. After all, I do not deserve freedom. All the horrible choices I have made, all the people who are dead because of me... The deaths of billions are on my shoulders, their blood staining my hands. Yes, I deserve damnation.

I deserve what my penance will bring.

During the little sleep that comes to me, I dream. Sometimes the Collector enters the ISERE to deliver me to my damnation. Other times she takes me to the Tomb to do terrible things to me, things that wake me before they can be inflicted. Sometimes the Exorcist appears.

On occasion, Teresa comes into my room to check on me and bring me food that I do not eat. I believe that at first she thought I was physically ill, because she checked for a fever and asked me my symptoms the first few times she entered. My only symptom is exhaustion. Fatigue too powerful for me to eat or do more than use the toilet. At a few points, my thoughts begin to race and I toss and turn in my bed, but do not have the will to do more. Those times are soon swallowed by unadulterated despair.

Damien's last words echo through my head: *"Everything won't be all right, will it?"*

One day Tess bustles in and begins rifling through my armoire.

I want to ask what she is doing, but I also do not want to.

She throws a pair of pants and a shirt onto my bed. "I want you to do two things for me, Magic Man: put on these clothes, and come on a short walk with me."

I would rather not. Even if I could.

At my lack of a response, she puts her hands on her hips. "I'm worried about you. It's been six days since you've left your room. You don't have to talk to me about what's going on, but I want you to do this for me."

Guilt sparks in my chest but is quickly extinguished by the malaise. "Tess, I can't," I sigh.

"Look." Tess sits on the edge of my mattress. "I don't know exactly what you're going through, but I know it really sucks. The thing is, you can't let it consume you like this. Terrible things happen, and I know you've had more than your fair share of them. But good things happen too, and you're going to miss out."

Maybe I want this to consume me. Maybe I do not care if I miss out on the good things.

Maybe this is not true.

Tess takes a deep breath. "I want to fight this for you, I really do. But I can't. All I can do is be here with you. I can help you if you let me, if you push through this enough for me to take your hand." A tear trickles down her cheek. "You don't deserve to suffer, Thane. But you also can't just wallow in the pain. Trust me, I know it's easier to do that, but sometimes you need to fight just a little."

I sigh through my nose. I have done enough fighting in my life. Then I think back to how I have handled things in the past... I never fought the pain, I fought myself. "Okay," I whisper. "I'll be out in a few minutes."

It is worth it to see Tess smile.

34

— · —

TESS

I am angry. I am ashamed of that anger, because the Keeper can't help being depressed, but *dammit*. He never asked me for help, never told me he was depressed. I had to figure that out, and what to do for him, on my own. And who am I to decide what he needs?

The Keeper emerges from his room sporting finger-combed, greasy hair and the fresh clothes I had picked out. He is unshaven and his eyes are red and puffy. "Where to?" he asks, rather flatly.

"How do you feel about a short walk in the garden?"

He indifferently flicks a hand out to one side.

I take that as a, "*Sounds great, Tess!*" and walk with him up the spiral staircase. I don't really know what to say. *So ask, I guess? Genius.* "Do you want me to talk?"

"No."

That makes that easy, I suppose.

The sky in the garden is cloudy but not dark. A breeze ruffles our hair and clothes.

The Keeper wanders off to the left. He doesn't make it far before he lies prone in the grass, arms stretched out to either side.

I join him there on the ground, mirroring his pose. Our fingertips nearly touch. Our eyes meet. I fight the bizarre urge to giggle. We stay like that for a long time, listening to the wind and the birds.

"Tess."

"Thane?" I love being able to say his name.

"Can you promise me...you will not hate me if I tell you what happened?"

My eyebrows twitch upward in surprise. "Of course. I promise."

"I..." He swallows. "I killed the Exorcist."

I look at him levelly. I had wondered in the back of my mind how this Exorcist had died but had tried not to dwell on it. (Did I not want to view Thane as a killer?) "Okay." I choose my words carefully. "Why you did it is understandable. I know it's hurting you; just remember it was self-defense."

Tears spring into his eyes. "That's it, Tess. It reached the line between self-defense and...and murder. I weakened him, and maybe could have gotten away, but...something came over me. I drowned him, Tess. I pushed him down and held him under the surface until he died. I murdered him." A tear pools in the corner of his eye before spilling over the bridge of his nose.

"Keeper, I...I don't know what to say." What am I supposed to say? What *can* I say? That my heart breaks for him? "I don't hate you. I just don't know what to say."

He screws his eyes shut. His mouth twists as more tears fall from his eyes.

I place my hand over his. "He wanted to kill you, Thane. He would have."

He heaves a gasping sob. "I took a life that wasn't mine to take. There had to have been another way. There always has been."

I don't know what else to do but squeeze his hand.

Next door to the kitchen is a living room complete with a sectional and a fifty-five inch TV. I take the Keeper there when he seems convinced that I don't hold against him what he did to the Exorcist.

"Lie down there," I instruct him, and throw a blanket over him when he does. I settle down next to him, pull him into my side. "We are going to watch *Bob's Burgers,* because if the essence of this show could be turned into a pill, it would make the best possible treatment for depression. It has helped me through many a tough time and only gets better the more you watch it."

"I suppose I can give it a chance." Is he joking? I decide to be cautiously optimistic (yes, I know that people who are depressed can also joke).

We start with season one, episode one, and progress from there. By the time we get to episode three, the Keeper's breathing has deepened and steadied.

I stroke his hair and let him sleep.

35

THE KEEPER

To try to retain the fleeting peace I felt when asleep next to Tess, I think of Damien.

Damien lived in a small house with his grandmother, Midde.

Midde was a hunched old woman with long gray hair held back from her dark face by a thick band. She often wore a green sash around her waist and always bore many rings on her thin fingers.

Upon realizing that she and Damien were Veqah, my legs trembled with relief and something else. I had not been around my people in years at that point. Since my family was killed. The thought of my family only reminded me of my dimension's fate, and the fate of my second dimension. All the people I knew, all the faces I had seen—gone. Why? What was wrong with the multiverse?

I collapsed.

Damien picked me up as though I weighed nothing. He carried me to a bed, where he settled me down. He clasped my hand in his. "There, love. Everything will be all right."

He used the word for love of a caretaker.

Damien was slumbering beside me when I woke for the first time in his home. His hand rested on my shoulder, draining away the energy of the interdimensional barrier.

I watched his beautiful face for a time, a deep sadness yawning inside me. This face, this face, would surely not last another five years. My eyes burned with tears. I needed to do something to stave them off. I sat up and swung my legs off the bed. When I put my weight on them, they instantly crumpled. I sobbed.

Damien awoke and came to my side. "Come back to bed. You still need to heal."

A wild desperation seized me. I gripped his shirt. "No, I can't! You are in danger, this universe is in danger, something is set to destroy it!"

"There is nothing you can do about it in your state," he said patiently, trying to marshal me into bed.

"You do not believe me." I had so hoped he would. It broke my heart that he did not.

"I do. I believe you," he said earnestly, kindly. "How long do we have?"

I swallowed. "Possibly a couple of years. I am not certain."

"Then we have time." He tugged on my elbow. "You can rest and recover first. Then you can do what you need to do. Everything will be all right."

I don't deserve this. This compassion. This mercy. Tears rushed down my cheeks. "I don't know what to do," I cried. "I don't know how to save the multiverse. I couldn't even save my family."

Damien pulled me in close.

For a moment I huddled against him, but then I straightened to look him in the eye. I took his face in my hands. "Just promise me—if you see someone with golden eyes who begs, please stay away from them. Do not touch them."

He held me tighter. "I promise."

My thoughts shift to the following days, when Damien tried to heal me. It should have felt warm and soothing, but it felt raw and burning. The magic settled on me and in me but would not be absorbed. My body, so injured by the energy from the interdimensional barrier, rejected magic.

So I had to heal without magic. Midde gave me medicines, but they only helped so much. As a result, progress was slow. It was especially so since, in the beginning, I had no desire to recuperate. I saw no point to it, since this universe would end in time, and I could do nothing about it.

Damien spoke to me a lot in my recovery. His words took my mind off my preoccupations. He gave me far lighter things to ponder, things that reminded me of the worth of living.

As I began to recover my will to live, I began to help Midde in the garden. Essentially every home had one, since the larger communal fields had been leveled for mining operations and to accommodate population growth and roads.

"You were lucky it was Damien who found you," Midde told me one day as we weeded the garden. "Many others on the island are repelled by anything to do with other universes. Had anyone else seen you below that rift, and had you told anyone else where you are from, you might be dead by now."

I did not betray the sinking feeling that formed in my stomach at the thought. "Odd. In my dimension, people were readying to explore other universes, and yet things are much the same here otherwise."

Damien made his way up the walk. "Hello, Grandmother, *manne.*"

Something constricted in my chest at his words, though not unpleasantly. It was the first time he had referred to me as a familial love.

In the months after Damien and I had first begun expressing our familial love, that love developed. Grew.

One day when we were home, he showed me a dance he learned at a ceremony a few months before we met. We started at opposite ends of the room and advanced toward each other as the dance progressed.

My muscles burned with exertion and joy as I moved. A broad smile spread across my face. One last spin and we came together, panting.

Damien's hands came to rest on my waist. "Excellent performance, Thane."

My face burned. "Thank you." I remember an odd feeling swelling in my chest. I suddenly had the overwhelming urge to say...well. Dare I say it?

"You have a strange look on your face," Damien remarked. "Are you all right?"

I opened my mouth to answer, but the words stuck in my throat.

"Thane?"

"Ne...ne amin," I stammered. *I love you.*

Damien grinned. *"Ne amin dan." I love you too.*

Then we were kissing. A few moments later, we pulled apart. We grinned at each other like adolescents who were getting away with something.

Without warning, Damien's hands on my waist seemed to become much heavier, sending repulsion arcing through me at the ideas the heavy sensation brought.

"I don't want sex," I blurted.

A pause. "Now or ever?"

"Possibly not ever."

Another painful silence. "Okay."

"...Okay?"

"As long as I know that you love me, that is enough."

Damien and I became much closer, but still I did not tell him about the other soldiers, or my self-harm.

Until one day, when I was changing clothes for work. Damien wrapped his arms around my shirtless body from behind and kissed my neck.

It was almost as if he did not see my scars.

I turned in his embrace and kissed him back.

Before I could find the fortitude to end the moment, he picked me up and placed me on the bed. He settled over me, his weight firm but gentle. His kisses trailed away from my lips, across my chin, and down my neck to my collarbone. Then he took my left hand, brushed his lips across my knuckles. He paused at the scars on my inner arm.

I froze, expecting to detect disdain or disgust in his gaze. But there was neither. I gasped as Damien caressed the scars, stroked me where no one had touched me since I inflicted those wounds, showing me compassion in a place no one had before. Relief and tentative delight trickled into my heart.

Then he brought the scars to his lips and kissed them softly. Kissed *me* softly. His lips wandered up my arm, tracing across so many of my scars as though they were not something to be repelled by.

Electricity arced outward from his every touch, sending my heart racing. I had had no idea that something like physical touch could feel so intense and wonderful.

Damien continued down my chest, my stomach.

I shuddered as he kissed the knotted scar on my hip, and again with something almost like fear as he kissed me below it. "Stop. Wait," I said with a note of panic before he could touch the waistband of my pants.

To my relief, he listened without hesitation. He slid off me and lay on his side next to me. A spark of concern lit his eyes. "Are you all right?" He placed a hand on my chest.

Could he feel my heart pounding? Could he infer why it did?

"I—I need to tell you about my scars."

Damien smiled sadly. "Thane, I already know. I have seen self-harm scars before."

My eyes burned with tears. He already knew. "This one is—different," I said, gesturing to my left forearm.

Wordlessly he took my left hand, pulled it to his own chest. His gaze did not waver from mine.

"I still did it, but—why—" My voice broke. "Damien, I—" My breath became shallow and quick.

Damien rubbed my shoulder, the concern in his eyes growing stronger.

I tried to tell him through the gasps. "The other soldiers—when I was in the army—they—"

"Take some deep breaths, Thane. You don't have to explain any-thing."

"I want to. I'm just afraid."

He responded with words I didn't expect: "I am sorry."

Somehow, for some reason, my breath evened out. "I love you." *Please do not love me less for this.* "When I was in the army, the other soldiers noticed I didn't...have certain experiences. So they locked me in a room with a woman who wanted to experience such things with me."

The worry in Damien's gaze sharpened into protectiveness.

I continued, "After trying to warm me up, she initiated. I paralyzed her with a spell and retreated across the room. We both were panick-ing, she because she was told I wanted to participate, and myself...for other reasons. When we realized just how far we had been manipulat-ed, we escaped the room and never saw each other again." I finished the story by telling him about my breakdown and public humiliation.

Damien squeezed my shoulder, seemingly deep in thought. Finally he said, "So you have never wanted sex?"

That *is your response?* The words came so forcefully to my mind that I snapped them out loud.

Damien looked taken aback. "I am sorry. That wasn't—how I meant it," he said weakly. "I'm sorry. I can see how this has affected you, and I can begin to understand why; I would have panicked too had I been in that situation."

The fury ebbed into weary half-relief. "Do you believe me when I say it does not mean that I love you less than I ever could?"

"I believe you," he murmured. "I love you."

Tears welled in my eyes. I drank in his face for as long as I could. Then: "I have to go," I whispered.

After I left the house, I flipped up the collar of my jacket even though the wind was not strong. I wished I could have stayed in those moments forever, reciprocated Damien's expressions of love, but that was impossible.

The last night I can remember before Damien died was a warm spring night. The sky was clear, the breeze fresh.

Damien and I lay side by side in the small bit of yard that was occupied by grass instead of garden, not quite touching. It was dark and late, so no one was likely to see us, but we did not want to risk physical intimacy of any sort.

I lay there wondering about the other planets above me. If there was sentient life there, too. I asked Damien what he thought.

"If we're here, I suppose there's a decent chance there's someone else out there."

I agreed. "Do you think they would affect the multiverse like we do?"

"Why wouldn't they?"

"Do you think they would be like humans?"

"What do you mean?"

"As horrible." Misha, the other soldiers. The Crusaders. "And as wonderful." Adeka. My family. Midde. Damien.

He propped himself up on an elbow and gazed down at me, his loose hair brushing the ground. "What's going on in your mind?"

I smiled at him. "The usual. A little bit of everything."

"I think you're a little sad."

I was and could not identify why. Could it have been because I was still grieving Midde, who had died a few months earlier? Could it have been for no reason at all? "How did you know?"

He reached out as if to touch my face but withdrew. "You seem weighed down. I don't know how to explain it."

I said nothing.

We turned back to the sky. Damien settled onto his back again, his hand brushing against mine as he did so.

We lay there in silence for a long time.

"Do you feel like we are being watched?" he asked after a time.

I laughed nervously. "Oh, I thought I was the only one."

We went inside, to our bedroom. Damien stretched out on the bed, and I stood nearby, unbuttoning my shirt to prepare to get into bed.

Before I could remove the shirt, Damien sat up. He reached out and placed his hands on my bare waist, then ran his thumb over the rough scar on my hip. The next thing I knew he was caressing my other scars too, his fingers dancing lightly over my skin.

I did not know what to feel or do, so I just stood there.

Damien's hands came to rest on my hips. "May I ask you a personal question?"

I licked my lips. *I might not answer,* I wanted to say. "Yes," I whispered.

"Why did you start cutting?"

I pressed my lips together. That was something I had not thought about in a long time. I sat next to Damien. "I was aged fourteen. At school, students were discussing romantic feelings. With the way they were describing them, I could tell that I had never felt such emotions. I made the mistake of saying this. They started calling me things like 'hollow' and 'empty' and 'heartless' and worse. I became so embarrassed and anxious and afraid that I would never feel such things that it became overwhelming; I could not handle it. I had already been so itchy before, and with this, the scratching would not suffice. I broke my skin scratching, and that gave me the idea to use a knife. So at the end of the day, I went to the kitchen and took one of the knives and cut myself once. The relief was instantaneous but not complete. So I cut myself two more times, and the itch disappeared entirely." I shook my head. "I could not believe it. I did not feel nearly so bad about what the others had said to me. So every time I had an itch, I cut myself. More and deeper as time passed, because it worked less each time." I looked at the floor. "I started on my legs, because it was easiest to hide, but then I moved on to my torso, and then my arms. I have not worn anything but long sleeves and pants since. Neither have I needed to cut for a long time, but I am afraid of going back to that place."

Damien kissed the hollow at the base of my neck and rested his head on my shoulder.

We said nothing more.

"Everything won't be all right, will it?"

36

— ⋅ —

TESS

My parents have practically been blowing up my phone; I haven't been calling or texting like I had been before the Collector and the Keeper came to our universe. I haven't been calling or texting at all, in fact.

But I have been reading their texts and listening to their voicemails.

"How are things? We know you're in a difficult time right now—we just want to support you. All you have to do is tell us how to do that. We love you."

"We haven't heard from you in a while, just wanted to check in again. We're worried. Ada's parents have asked if we've heard from her; they haven't, we haven't, so they're getting worried too."

"Marsha at the bookstore reached out to me. She said you haven't been coming to work or even calling out. Tess, please. I know this is a rough time right now, but please just send a text to let us know you're okay."

"Tess. We've reached out to all your friends whose contact info we have. Please. Just...just let us know you're okay. I even texted Hunter. Please. We just want to hear your voice again. We just want to know you're safe."

"We didn't know what else to do. We called the police. We reported you and Ada as missing. We love you. Please call back."

I cry every time I hear the increasing desperation in my parents' voices.

I've never felt so alone.

Then one day, I crack. I call my mom.

"Tess?" Even through just my name, I can hear the tears and hope and terror in her voice.

"Mom, I'm sorry. I can explain. I mean. Maybe. I'm sorry. But I'm—" My voice cracks as I lie. "I'm safe."

I don't think I've ever heard her sob like this. Not even when her parents died in a car wreck ten years ago.

"Where are you?" she asks when her sobs subside. "I need to see you. Please."

I open my bedroom door a crack to check that the Keeper isn't standing outside listening. (He's probably still in his depression nest.) "I can't come home right now. I'm safe, I just can't come home now. I'm in Charlotte, North Carolina. Can you meet me here? I'll explain everything when I see you." (Will I tell the truth? I have no idea.)

"Yes." Her relief is palpable, even over the phone. "We'll be there ASAP. Is Ada with you?"

I hesitate. "No. Please don't tell people you're meeting me, though."

Further fear and worry leaks over the connection. "Okay. Your dad and I will be there by the end of the day. We'll keep you updated."

"Okay. Thank you. I'm sorry. I love you. Bye."

And I try to decide what to tell them.

About six hours later, my parents arrive in Charlotte and pull into the parking lot of the random park I'd chosen. I huddle in my coat, frozen more by anxiety than the cold.

Once my parents have stepped out of the car, though, my paralysis breaks, and I run to them, tears already spilling down my cheeks.

They greet me with open arms—more than I deserve for what I did to them, but I welcome their embraces regardless.

"What happened?" my father asks, pulling away just enough to look me in the eyes. My father, Asher. One of the smartest people I know. One of the best, too. I can trust him with pretty much anything and receive no judgment; instead, I can expect sound advice every time I ask for it.

"It's—it's hard to explain," I manage. "I don't even know if you'll believe me."

"Try us," my mother says firmly. My mother, Maureen. Undoubtedly the most badass woman—no, *person*—I have ever met. In high school, she played six sports a year, including wrestling and track and field (where she competed in nearly every event, from the shotput to the hundred-meter dash, and was good at them all) and still managed to excel in all her classes. After graduating as valedictorian, she joined the Coast Guard for several years before returning to Ohio to be near family. Ever since then, she's worked as a mechanic. She's taught me just about everything I know, including self-defense.

I bite my lip. Wipe away my tears. "There's a picnic table over here. Let's sit down."

When they are seated across from me, I begin. "I'm with a friend. You haven't met him. His name is Thane. He's...looking out for me."

My father's brow crinkles.

"What I mean is, I'm trying to help people." A universe of people. A *multi*verse of people. "He's making sure I can do this. I disappeared on you because I'm trying to—to—keep you safe."

I can see my father clicking together puzzle pieces in his mind, though he has far from the whole puzzle. "Elaborate, please," is all he says.

I exhale through my nose, reluctant to go into details. "Someone is...trying to stop me from doing what I'm trying to do. She's...sort of...after me."

My mom stiffens. "What do you mean, after you?" Her voice is tense, she is ready to fight.

I've never seen such an inscrutable expression on my dad's face.

"She..." Hell, I'm going for it. "She wants my soul."

My parents only stare at me in disbelief.

I fight the urge to retreat into my coat again, to pull the hood over my face and disappear.

"Where's Ada?" my father asks before I can muster the words to explain.

Further tears prick my eyes. "The person who's after me killed her." The words wheel back around and punch me in the gut; I realize this is my first verbal acknowledgment that Ada is *dead*.

My parents are horrified.

"You mean your *life* is in danger?" my mom exclaims.

I nod reluctantly. "But more than that, a *lot* of other people are in danger. An inconceivable amount. And I can save them. I mean, that's what I'm trying to do."

My mom reaches out and rests her fingertips on my sleeve. "Tess, this isn't your responsibility. Come home. Please. Let the police handle it. Or someone, *any*one else."

"Thane can't do it alone."

"Please don't think you have to play hero, Teresa," my father tells me.

I meet his gaze squarely. "I'm not playing hero, Dad. I'm doing what needs to be done, and what no one else knows to do."

"What do you mean?"

"I mean, how many people in the world know about the multiverse and how it's in danger?"

They exchange glances.

"Tess," my mother says gently, "come home, and everything will turn out all right."

My throat tightens at the expression on her face. "I'll come home soon. I promise. Just a few more days."

"No, Tess," my father replies. "I think you need to be home right now."

An errant tear escapes me. "I'm sorry, but no. Not yet." I stand and step clear of the bench.

"Tess, *please*."

My blood freezes.

That tone.

I recognize that tone.

Slowly I meet my parents' eyes.

Gold. Lifeless. Not theirs.

"Tess?" My dad places his hands against his temple, as though he has a headache. "Please come home." His voice is so plaintive, so vulnerable. "I need you. I—I need you—to—to please get it out of my head."

"Please help," my mom groans. She cries out and touches her head with one hand while searching for me with the other. "Oh, it hurts."

I can't move. I can't even tremble. I want to reach toward her. But my feet are welded to the earth, my arms to my sides.

My father stands shakily, trips as he tries to leave the table. Then he screams. "It's ripping me apart!" he wails. "Get it out, get it *out*, *getitoutgeti*—" He drops to his knees, shrieking, clawing at his face and scalp. Pink streaks form along his skin, streaks that well a moment later with crimson blood.

Slowly, dreadfully, I shift my gaze to the white form that has appeared behind him.

The Collector stares at me impassively. Raises her hand. Clenches her fist.

My mother screams in agony.

Then my parents dissolve.

First their limbs crumble, their heads, and when their torsos collapse to the ground, those too break apart into dust.

When my parents are disintegrated entirely, I can only lock gazes with the Collector; I think her stare is all that holding me upright.

She unfolds her hand. Beckons.

My feet move. I don't know how, I can't remember how to walk, but my feet lead me toward the Collector.

37

THE KEEPER

My hand grips the Collector's shoulder. When she whips around to identify the owner of the hand, it becomes a fist and strikes her chin, snapping her head back the other way.

"Leave—Tess—a—*lone*," I snarl, each syllable punctuated by the *crack* of a magic blocker snapping around a limb. I slam the bound Collector to the earth.

She stares up at me dispassionately.

I crouch next to her and pull the silver ring off her left hand. I pocket the piece of the Master Key. Then I pause and meet the Collector's gaze.

Kill her.

But looking into those gray eyes, I don't think I can.

"Naida," I whisper. I do not know what brings me to say it, yet I say it.

There is no flicker of recognition. No love. No softness. No mercy. Instead, her lips part. "*Thane.*"

I stiffen as the magic freezes my bones, my blood, my brain. The steel grip of my name is impervious to my terror, to my silent screams, to my despair. My instincts want to fight, but I don't believe I have the strength.

Tears trickle down my cheeks as the Collector reaches for my hands and pulls them out between us.

I try to fight. Or maybe I do not. Some part of me pounds its hands against the bindings, but how hard is it trying?

Almost gingerly the Collector taps each of my rings once with a long forefinger. After seven taps, she returns to the ISERE's key. Her finger hovers over it for a moment before making a turning motion with it; her entire hand rotates until her palm faces upward, waiting.

I want to scream but can't. Won't? Don't. All I can do is betray the ISERE and hand the Collector the ruby-studded key.

After her fingers curl around the item, the Collector points at me, then at Tess. Then at herself.

"No," I whisper.

Inexorably, I turn.

38

TESS

I stopped being pulled toward the Collector when the Keeper struck her, but now he approaches me, eyes hollow, cheeks traced with tears.

I back away as slowly as he nears. "Keeper? Thane?"

He looks so weary. So resigned. So dangerous.

"*Thane.* Thane, you can fight her."

No answer.

Behind him, the Collector's mouth moves soundlessly, and the glowing bands around her limbs fade away.

"Please, Thane, I don't want her to take me." My voice trembles, nearly breaks. "Don't let her do anything to me." I turn my face to the sky. "Someone please help me," I beg the universe.

A roar answers my plea.

A black bear the size of a sedan bursts from the side of a tree and barrels into the Collector: the last Aivar.

He grips the Collector's neck in his jaws and tears at her body with his claws.

The Keeper collapses like a marionette whose strings have just been severed. "Teresa," he gasps.

"*Help* him, Thane!" I cry.

The Collector snaps her fingers, and the sound of a shotgun blast goes off.

The Aivar is hurled into the picnic table. He vanishes. A fraction of a second later, he reappears behind his adversary, jaws wide. His teeth clamp down on the Collector's head.

The Keeper cries out. "Naida!"

The Collector, unfazed, grips the bear's jaws and pries them open with a strength that should not be possible with those thin arms.

I watch in horror as flames flare up from the Collector's hands and race across the Aivar's face and neck.

The Keeper's hand grips my arm and hauls me away.

At his touch, I scream. And I don't stop screaming.

I don't know when my screams turned to sobs, but after some time, I come back to myself, my throat sore, my chest aching like nothing else, my cheeks and even my shirt sodden with tears.

The Keeper sits on the atrium bench opposite me, his elbows on his knees, fingers wound together and pressing against his lips. He doesn't say a word to me; I don't think he has said anything since we returned to the ISERE.

Not that it matters.

I killed my parents.

That's all that matters.

I killed my parents.

Now I can fully understand why the Keeper carries so much guilt and agony about failing to save everyone he has ever met.

I'm now carrying some of that weight too.

"How do you survive this?" I ask him.

He stirs. "I did not have much choice. I wanted to live, so I did." He pauses. "I could not, cannot, undo the things I have done, nor do the things I have not done. I have shifted my grip many times over the years to carry that knowledge. I wanted to live, so I lived. I moved forward while holding the weight of my decisions." Another pause. "I am sorry I do not have as much guidance as I should. All I believe I can do is support you and acknowledge how much it must hurt."

Fresh tears hurry down my face. "God, I didn't think I could hurt this much." I bury my face in my hands. "I'm sorry, I just feel so stupid and terrible and weak."

Hands rest on my shoulders as the Keeper kneels before me. "You are neither stupid nor terrible. And never feel weak for being strong enough to love."

39

THE KEEPER

The absence of the key to the ISERE is, itself, a weight on my hand, on my soul. Other than that, I am numb. Emotionally and physically. In fact, I feel like my mind and soul are not quite aligned with my body.

I float on my back in the cold water of the pond, staring up at the dark sky, and thinking about when my father gave me my own copy of the key.

I cannot remember just how old I was, but I am sure it was before my sister was born. My parents had made a breakthrough with the ISERE and were hopeful for funding for a mission. The funding ultimately fell through, but he gave me the key before that happened.

He found me drawing outside. His hands were behind his back. I remember he was smiling. Perhaps he was not, but I like to imagine that he was.

"Thane," he said, "there is something I want you to have." He held out the Decomis by the chain.

I can still see the way it shone in the sunlight, spinning lazily and glinting.

"It is called the Decomis. It is a device that communicates with our machine that I will be traveling in. You can use it to see where I am and even send messages to the machine that I can read and reply to." Since then, I have discovered more capabilities, including its ability to translate almost any language.

I took it and marveled. The chain was light but sturdy, the device itself the size of my palm. Engraved on one side of the case were the words "Life Awaits."

"Look inside," my father urged. "There's something else."

I opened the device, a small *click* preceding the reveal of the key to the friend I have known the longest.

"Don't tell your mother. I just wanted you to be able to explore the ISERE before we leave on a mission."

I could not have treasured the gifts enough.

Without real thought, I replay the memory over and over again until it blurs into the haze that comprises the rest of my mind. I close my eyes and try to focus on the cold of the water around me, try to truly feel it. However, my mind keeps slipping away and settling back into the haze. I give up. When the numbness from my fingers and toes spreads to my hands and feet, I emerge, uncured, from the water. I dry myself off, don my clothes, and walk up the trail. At the top I pause to feel the warm air on my chilled skin.

It does nothing to burn off the fog inside me. So I continue.

A cold breeze sweeps through the dim atrium; Tess sits in the open doorway, her feet dangling out into empty air.

I join her.

"Are you ever afraid of falling?" she asks.

"The ISERE would stop any fall before long."

"Have you fallen before?"

"No," I say truthfully. I pull my felt-tip pen out of my pocket and drop it between my knees.

It descends into the night for a few seconds but bounces back up and directly into my waiting hands.

Despite everything, I think she looks a little impressed. "That's a cool feature. Was it programmed like that? Who would expect the ISERE would spend time this high in the air with the door open?"

"I believe the ISERE may have learned to do it."

"Really? How?"

I flick a hand outward. "She is not a mere machine. There is more to her than you might think."

She cocks her head at me. "You speak of the ISERE like she's a friend of yours."

I half-smile. "She is. She has been here for me throughout everything. She even taught me how to repair her when needed." I feel a twinge of shame. "I did lose her for a while, though, many years ago."

"What happened?"

"I told you that I was thrown from the ISERE when crossing from my second to my third dimension, yes?"

She nods.

"Well, I was too injured to search for her after, so some Developers found her. They tried to break in but studied her in every way they could when they didn't succeed. I found this out because I had no legal identity; the government learned of me and decided to force me to study dangerous anomalies under the same scientists that found the ISERE. They threatened to expose that I was from a different universe, which was a terrifying concept to those on that version of the island." I recall being so afraid of facing the job, the world, that I hid under the bed covers. Damien joined me there and held me, told me everything would be all right. I was sure it would not be, but his words were reassuring nonetheless.

"I worked for those scientists for a long time, collecting data on rifts and anomalies in the field, while the ISERE waited in the lab to be freed from her bonds."

One day I was studying a rift with my research partner, Nazden, when a Beggar approached us. Under my orders, Nazden and I both created a magical barrier around ourselves to prevent the Beggar from touching us. But I learned much later that people also become Beggars from mere proximity to the Collector. And the Collector was there. That was the first time I had seen her in years. By then, she had bleached Naida's hair and skin to the trademark cold white. The sight sent a wave of icy terror crashing over me that still echoes to this day whenever I see the Collector.

That was the second time I felt the claws of the Collector scrape against my soul, the first being the day the Collector first possessed Naida's body and the two fought over my soul. That was the day I somehow reversed the spell and saw into the Collector's own soul. The only reason Nazden and I escaped intact was because of our barrier spells. Even now, I get chills thinking of it.

Tess breaks me out of my thoughts. "How did you get her back?"

Who? Nazden? Naida? Then I recall what I had been saying. "Ah. When Damien died, I stopped caring about consequences. I had no reason to stay anymore, no reason to fear the repercussions of walking up to the ISERE and unlocking her. So I went to the lab and did just that."

Tess's eyes brim with tears. She takes my hand. "I'm glad you could get her back."

I'm glad you could get someone *you lost back.* The words I believe she wants to say hover between us, unspoken by either.

I am nearly asleep when I recall that I took the final piece of the Key from the Collector. I roll out of bed and run to the console, where I have stored the other pieces.

All five pieces united in my hand now emit a low hum, barely perceptible over the soft pulsing of the ISERE's heart. I set them on the console and play with them, pushing them closer together and pulling them apart, listening to the sound shift. The closer they all are, the louder the hum. When I get bored with that, I don them, placing one on each finger of my left hand, as there are no fingers with multiple rings already on that hand. Each ring adjusts to fit my fingers.

I put on the last ring. Silvery wires shoot out from each ring and connect in the center of my palm and the back of my hand. When the wires are taut, sheets of metal unfold out of the ring, as if the jewelry is comprised of much more material than it appears to have. The metal follows the lines of the wires to form a gauntlet.

I flex my hand. The metal is light and pliant. I pull off a ring. The material retracts until I am left with only rings on my hand. I replace the ring and the gauntlet returns.

Now how do I destroy this? I know I should not yet, because healing the multiverse is part of my penance.

Speaking of, when should I try to heal it?

There is only one day I would be powerful enough to do that.

And that day is coming only after two more nights.

40

— · —

TESS

The next day, the Keeper pulls me aside.

He looks better than he has over the last several days, with his hair washed and neatly combed and his clothes clean and unwrinkled. Still, I worry. But I sense that he doesn't want me to say anything about that right now, so I listen instead.

"Teresa, there is something I learned while...in the Collector's soul...that I have not yet told you. And it involves you."

My gaze sharpens with nerves. Could what he learned be what I have been planning on telling him?

"I found out more of the reason the Collector wants your soul."

His words do not ease my anxiety—instead they ratchet it up.

"I thought you might want to know," he says, "but I could be wrong, judging from your expression."

What does my expression look like? Hastily I try to smooth it out. "No. Tell me. Please."

His voice is slow as he picks out the words. "She wants you for the traits that reflect and contrast hers."

"Oh, I would *love* to hear how we're so similar," I say, the sentiment slipping glibly from my lips.

The Keeper looks uncomfortable.

"That was only partly sarcastic. Continue."

He hesitates but makes his way onward. "Your...intimidating qualities, boldness, propensity to anger, and...your...occasional abrasive-
ness seem to be things that the Collector sees in you both. Simultaneously, your ultimate kindness and capacity to love contrast her...lack
thereof."

I almost want to laugh; I actively consider crying. To prevent either,
I press my lips into a thin line. I'm not sure anyone—neither a person
like the Keeper nor someone like the Collector—has ever been so
honest and straightforward about my personality. And that's hitting
me hard. "Are those your descriptions, or the Collector's?" I ask in a
small voice.

"Tess, none of that makes you a bad person," the Keeper says softly.

I sniff. "Well, that may be easy for you to say, but the Collector
doesn't want you for personality traits that complement hers."

"I will repeat what I last said ad nauseam, if necessary."

I look down at the floor. I'm not sure whether to believe him. "Do
you believe that?"

"Of course!" he exclaims, voice tinged with something like concern.

The last words I heard from Hunter ring in my head. Well, there's
no time like the present to learn whether a person you love *actually*
thinks you're better than someone they hate.

I take a deep breath. My gaze shifts to the Keeper's ear and my hands
come together to wring each other. "Keeper, there's something I want
you to know."

"What is it?" The concern has not left his voice.

"I'm, uh, I'm bisexual."

"Ah. Okay."

I flick the briefest of glances at his face, but his expression is inscrutable. My heart sinks, starts to fracture again.

Perhaps my face reflects this, because he hurriedly adds, "This does not change my feelings toward you."

Relief trickles into my heart. I try to smile, but I suspect it appears as more of a grimace.

"Thank you for trusting me."

I nod as tears threaten. "I just wanted you to know," I reiterate, still without looking him in the eye.

"How did you learn?" he asks.

"There's this TV show. *The X Files.* My parents turned me onto it. I, uh, kind of fell in love with both main characters." A note of sadness swells inside me at the fact that I would never be able to share this with my parents. After Hunter's reaction, I had been so afraid... And, well, I thought we had many more years together.

"Tess," he says hesitantly. "Would you mind if I confided in you as well?"

I wipe away a tear. "Not at all. Especially when we're practically in the confession booth together already, right?" I give the world's weakest chuckle.

He looks confused.

"Sorry," I tell him. "What's going on?"

Thane flicks both his hands once, less in his horizontal, *I don't know* way and more in a vertical, agitated way I haven't seen before. "I am not sure how to tell you this, as I am honestly not sure if I have ever said it aloud..." He trails off.

Without thinking, I reach out and touch his arm just above the elbow. *I'm here.*

He looks down at my hand. It seems to strengthen his resolve, as he flexes his fingers and picks up where he left off. "Teresa. Tess. I know you are already aware that I have struggled with depression. However, there is more to...me...than that. Have you ever heard of cyclothymic disorder?"

"Yeah, I think so," I reply. "It's related to bipolar, right?"

The Keeper nods, flexing his fingers more. "I have cyclothymia. And...autism as well."

To the surprise of both of us, I smile. "I can see that." I squeeze his arm gently.

Something like shock writes itself across Thane's face. "Did—did you *know*?"

I shake my head, drop my hand. "No. It just doesn't surprise me, is all." At his bewilderment, I elaborate. "Come on, Magic Man. Until now, I didn't put any thought into it beyond '*That's Thane*' but you over-explaining things when people would prefer you not to in that moment, eye contact that can seem forced, and what I assume is near-constant stimming with your hands?"

"I— And you're...fine with this?"

"Of course. It's you. It's Thane."

Then, to my surprise, he pulls me into an embrace. "We will make it through this," he whispers in my ear. "Life awaits."

I can feel him trembling against me.

41

— · —

THE KEEPER

Tess crosses her arms. "You want to do *what* on your own?" She shakes her head with an incredulous laugh. "There's no way you can stop her on your own. Even if you *can* plunge the knife."

I cross my arms as well, frowning at her. "The kindling moon is in a few hours. I do not have time to argue; she will surely try to destroy as much of the multiverse as she can tonight. You are staying in the ISERE. Where you will be *safe*." As safe as someone can be when the person pursuing her has the key to the former's place of refuge.

"Why do you care about my safety all of a sudden?"

"It is not sudden!" I protest. "There is more at stake for you now than ever before. The Collector *will* make a move to take you any time now, and I do not want to lose you, especially when we are *so close!*"

"How can you do this all on your own? The Collector still wants you for something if the ISERE's key wasn't all she wanted. I mean, she practically *let* us run away with the last piece of the Master Key!" Tess cries. "I'm scared for you, Thane!"

"And I am scared for *you*!" Do I remind her that there are no more Aivar to protect her?

"*Dammit,* Thane, she stole the key to the ISERE! I don't *care* that you said she technically stole it, and I don't *care* that any key may not trust her because of it—*I'm not letting you go alone*!"

Before I can respond, the lights go out, the engine dies.

This snaps me out of my thoughts. "No, no, no, no," I mutter. I summon a light. My hands fumble over the console. "What is wrong, what is *wrong*?" I run for the engine room.

Tess chases after me. "What's going on?"

"I don't know!"

The power is entirely out; the emergency lights are not even on. This is bad. This is very bad. Something must have drained the ISERE of all its power.

Horror floods my stomach. I put the pieces together.

Too late.

Behind me, Teresa cries out.

I whip around to see the Collector gripping Tess by the arms.

In the next breath, they are gone.

42

TESS

I stand in a field. The trimmed grass is vivid green, the clean air warm on my skin. I squint from the bright sunlight and try to figure out where I am.

"Tess!"

My heart skips a beat. Ada's voice. I turn.

At a picnic table just a few yards away, Ada sits with my parents. *They're alive! They're here!* A rush of joy floods me. It washes away the glue holding me together to reveal a new, intact self.

"Come *here*!" Ada says with a laugh.

My legs unlock. Slowly I approach the table and seat myself next to Ada, across from my mother.

"Something wrong?" my dad asks teasingly.

"I don't think we're dangerous," adds my mom.

Tears spring into my eyes. I thought I'd missed their voices before, but boy was I wrong. (How can I miss something when it's here? Yet I do.) "N-nothing's wrong," I choke out. *Just happy.*

I blink, and someone is standing behind my parents: a blonde woman with a pixie cut. I blink, and she's gone. Gone from sight, gone from my thoughts.

Ada waves her hand in front of my face. "A little out of it today, huh?" she jokes.

I turn to her, to that face I've missed so much, and I can't look away. I drink her in like she's freshwater and I've been stranded in a desert.

"What?" she giggles. "Don't look at me like that, we've seen each other recently."

"It doesn't feel recent," I murmur. Besides, 'recent' doesn't matter because they were gone, gone forever.

So I thought.

Is this real?

I pinch myself. It hurts. My grin nearly hurts too, spreading across my face so fast and so wide.

This is real. Or perhaps it is a spell, but god, it feels so *right*, so vivid and wonderful. It is real enough.

43

THE KEEPER

I cannot fix the engine. I have tried all I know, but I cannot fix the engine.

I slide down a wall, flicking my hands till the joints ache, failing to fight back tears. My shoulders tremble with the knowledge that *I cannot save Tess.*

I cannot even fix an engine.

"What do I *do*?" I sob aloud.

Stop pitying yourself. The words are so clear it is as though Tess is standing right next to me.

My hands still, my breathing evens out, my tears stop coming. Immediately I have heeded the words. Stopped pitying myself.

I can do something. There must be an option, but what is it? The ISERE is not one. The kindling moon is less than an hour away, and I am on the other side of the world from where it will happen, so flying is not an option either, not on an airplane, nor magically. That leaves...

Dread swims in my chest.

Traveling. Magically Traveling.

I wring my hands. "I cannot do that," I whisper.

Or...I could not. Perhaps it is time to try again.

For Tess.

For Tess.

I close my eyes. Take a deep breath. Let the magic flow.

I do not recognize my home. Am I in the wrong place? There is no beach, there are no boulders, no trees. Just...ivy. Ivy everywhere.

The ocean at my back, I step forward. I try to tread between fronds of ivy, but the growth is too thick. *Sorry*, I think to it, and gingerly walk forward. As I walk, an idea generated upon seeing the ivy falls into place.

I feel hope.

The Tomb is ahead of me, at the base of the cliffs. It too is drowning in ivy, with only the space for the door clear.

I approach and place my hand against the cool side of the Tomb. All it takes to open it this time is a simple unlocking spell. Unease wells inside me; it should not be this easy. Nevertheless, I enter.

A familiar woman lies on the floor before me. Rhys, no longer in the throne, her soul done being subsumed. Does this mean it is too late to save her? I finger the ring on my left third finger. I failed.

Thick grief threatens to wash me away.

The black throne stands across from me. Another woman sits in it, eyes closed.

Tess.

She is seated rigidly, as if strapped into the throne. Her skin looks gray under the ashen lighting of the Tomb. The ring the Collector stole—the key to the ISERE—has been placed on her left middle finger.

"Tess?" Even my soft voice is so loud in the silence. Gently I touch her face.

She does not stir.

I activate the communication spell between our rings in an effort to have her hear me. "Tess," I murmur, "I am sorry for letting this happen. I am here. Stay strong. Stay brave." Reluctantly I drop my hand and turn to find a door. I run my hands over the smooth walls, magic sparking from my fingertips. Soon I find it, off to Tess's left. It opens just as easily as the main entrance.

My unease blooms into dread. I step into a black hallway lined with ebony doors. After some hesitation, I decide against opening any of them and instead set off down the hall; I have pored over the IDEM schematics before and am sure this is the way to the engine room. The only sound is my footsteps as I trace the path there.

I find myself surprised when I find a door much like that of the ISERE's engine room door exactly where I expected it. I open the door.

There is no engine. There is only a rift, massive and flickering.

"What—?" I step into the room to investigate, despite thinking that this is not really the engine room, the engine must be elsewhere. I have little time, but I approach the rift and touch it with the hand that bears the Key. I had planned to face the Collector after disabling the Tomb and before healing the multiverse, but perhaps I can heal this rift first, huge as it is.

That's when I feel the chains and the conduits. The rift is tethered to the room and being drained of its energy. The conduits carry the rift's energy throughout the rest of the Tomb to power it.

The rift *is* the engine.

"No wonder you are so wounded, my dear," I murmur to the multiverse. Anxiously I glance over my shoulder before setting to work mending the rift. The first step to doing so is disconnecting it from the Tomb. It is hard work and takes all my focus. Sweat soon rolls down my face, my muscles soon tremble.

There comes a sort of *click*, and I believe for a moment that I have freed the rift from the grip of the Tomb. Then I feel a *pull* that strengthens with each passing second. Terror wells up inside me, and I try to withdraw—but my hand is fused to the rift.

Magic flows through me into the rift, forming a spell against my volition. A spell to destroy the multiverse.

The Collector didn't want to risk herself to reach her end, so she is using me. Forcing me to use the Key to destroy the multiverse.

44

— · —

TESS

Rhys appears, I look at her, blink, she's gone, and I forget she was ever there. It's impossible to know how many times this happens. I only remember that it *has* happened when she whispers my name in my ear.

"*Teresa!*"

I freeze.

"Tess, something wrong?" my mom asks.

I don't answer, just turn to see Rhys standing beside me.

"This is a trap!" she hisses urgently.

I glance over my shoulder at my family, who smile at me.

"A trap? It can't be." I mean, it's my *family*.

"The Collector wants to keep you here while she subsumes your soul. We need to go."

"Tess, who is this?" Ada asks. "What is she talking about?"

"I don't know," I tell her. Do I believe that? "I don't know."

"Teresa," Rhys says. "*Remember. Please.* Your family is gone. The multiverse is under threat. It's about to *go.*"

Fuck the multiverse, I think half-heartedly.

"This is the end. Of you. Of everything."

"I might as well enjoy myself while I die, right?" I say. *While we all die.* But my heart sinks.

Rhys leans in close, grips my arm. "I have a plan."

I swallow. Nod. Stand.

"Tess, wait." Ada grabs my shirt. "Don't go," she pleads.

"I'll be back," I answer in a thickening voice.

"There is no coming back to this, Tess," my father says sadly.

I blink back tears. "You're not real," I choke out. "But I love you."

And I turn my back on my family.

Only Rhys was not quite trapped like the rest of us, thanks to the Keeper and his spell.

"I think I've found the others, but I need your help," Rhys tells me as we hurry away from my family.

"What do you need me to do?"

"Help me convince them to fight the Collector. Together, I think we can weaken her."

She informs me of a Veqah proverb the Keeper once told her in passing about tools bringing down what they built. "It made me think that we can do it."

I don't quite see how, but I can't think of anything better to try, so I don't say anything.

We dash down indistinguishable black corridors, all lined with identical black doors. Rhys slows when we are somewhere deep in the Tomb. She opens a door on the left.

Snow blows into the corridor. Delighted laughter erupts from within.

Rhys beckons for me to follow as she crosses the threshold.

We emerge onto a snowy field. The air is frigid against my skin. In the center of the field there are two snow forts about fifteen yards apart. Two people huddle behind each fort, then pop up to lob snowballs at the enemy. One projectile connects with the face of a girl before she can hide behind her fort once more. A victorious whoop sounds from the person who launched it.

Rhys points to the girl who has been struck, and it is then that I notice something strange about her. There is an image of another person superimposed upon her. A pale woman with hair the same color as the snow.

"What's her name?"

"Amelia, I think."

A shout confirms Rhys's suspicion. "Come on, Amelia, stop sulking!" her battle partner cries. "I need your help!"

Rhys and I approach Amelia. Rhys calls her name, but Amelia pays the Australian no attention.

We have no time to waste. I scoop up some snow, shape it into a ball, and hurl it at Amelia.

It smacks her directly in the face. The superimposed image of the Collector vanishes. Amelia straightens, looks around, wipes the ice crystals off her face.

"Hey-oh," I say with a wave. "Can you see us?"

Her eyes widen, her lips part. "Who—what—?"

"I'm Tess, this is Rhys, and this—" I gesture to the snowball fight. "—isn't real."

"Amelia?" her partner asks. "What's going on?"

Amelia looks between all three of us. "I think I'm hallucinating," she murmurs.

"I wish," I snort. Then I wince; it hadn't exactly been easy for me, so I should be more sympathetic.

"Think about it, Amelia," Rhys interjects. "Your life isn't progressing, is it? There are no bad times either. You're just existing in the good times. That's not right."

The image of the Collector begins to flicker over Amelia's face.

"No!" I cry. "You're not safe!" I fling more snow at her. "Remember the Collector? The woman in white?" (Did she look the same all those years ago?)

To my relief, the flickering slows, so I continue. "She's taking your memories so they're no longer yours. She's trapped you in the good times so you don't fight back."

"Please, come with us," Rhys implores. "Reclaim your memories."

The image of the Collector fades. Tears streak Amelia's cheeks. "I didn't want to believe anything was wrong," she whispers.

My heart aches for her.

"I understand," Rhys says gently. "I really do."

"Will you help us reclaim your memories?" I ask, trying to echo the softness in Rhys's tone.

Amelia looks at her family. "I don't know if I can leave this. Even if it's not real."

Rhys crouches next to her. "I think it's time you joined the real versions of those who loved you. The versions who have missed you all these years."

Amelia turns to the girl next to her. "You don't love me?"

The other girl blinks in surprise. "Of course I do. What makes you think I don't?"

Amelia cuts her gaze between Rhys and me. "Did this happen to you too?"

Tears well in my eyes as I think of walking away from my own family. "Yeah."

"She's tried to take my memories of my son away from me," Rhys says.

Amelia looks at the ground, back to Rhys. "How do we reclaim ourselves?"

45

— · —

THE KEEPER

I slump to the floor, breath fast and tight with terror as I try to pull away from the rift to no avail. I groan, try to gather enough magic to perform a spell, but only a weak trickle diverts from the river pouring through me.

A small sound makes me open my eyes. White fills the corner of my vision. I turn my head toward it.

The Collector.

46

TESS

The next two women are named Meredith and Bianca. They are about as difficult as Amelia to reach. Rhys, however, is most worried about Naida, as she has been trapped for the longest by far.

We enter a room filled with a forest in full summer foliage. The trees are old, thick, and immensely tall.

At first, I don't see anyone, just trees and undergrowth and paths. Then I hear a voice from up above.

"Thane!"

I jump and look up. *Thane's here?*

He is, but not in the capacity I first thought. A pre-adolescent, long-haired version of him sits perched among the branches of a near-by tree. He gazes toward the ground, a faraway expression on his face.

"Thane, come up higher. The branches are still sturdy," a girl calls from the same tree. Her bright red hair glints in the snatches of sunlight that peer through the leaves, even through the image of the Collector superimposed upon her.

Thane starts and climbs up after her.

"Naida!" Rhys yells.

The girl ignores her, scampers up to a higher branch.

"Be careful," warns Thane as he approaches her.

"I *am*!"

"You never are, Naida."

Rhys yells for Naida once more and is ignored yet again. She turns to me in frustration. "No snowballs this time."

I look up, set my jaw. "No, but I can climb the tree." Without waiting for a response, I walk over to the tree and haul myself onto a low branch.

Rhys protests (she doesn't say my weight might be too much, maybe a thinner person should try, but I'm sure she thinks it).

I wave her off. Not only am I stubborn and spiteful at the imagined comments, I really think I can make it.

I pick my way up the branches, wishing I could scurry up them like Thane and Naida. Nonetheless, I eventually find myself on the branch next to Naida's while she is perched next to the trunk, gazing out into the foliage.

Thane is a couple branches below us.

I am tempted to break off a stick and throw it at him, but instead I throw it at Naida.

She frowns and brushes her skin where it hits.

"Naida," I say loudly.

She goes back to observing the foliage.

My heart sinks. This isn't going to work.

"Naida," I repeat. "Thane misses you. He still thinks he can save you. But I think you have to save yourself. Can you hear me?"

She seems to at first, turning toward me with some confusion, but when I stop, her bewildered expression disappears, and she turns away once more.

What caught her attention? Was it the mention of Thane?

I suppose it was, and start telling her all I know about Thane, starting from after his home dimension was destroyed. I tell her about the people he met and loved since then. I tell her how I see him and what he has done for me and how he must have changed and stayed the same.

I am so wrapped up in talking about him that I barely notice when she turns back to me and begins *listening* with great interest.

When I am done, she whispers, "How do you know all this? Thane is right there. He is aged twelve years, certainly not how old? One hundred twenty-four?"

"I think you know as well as I do that that isn't the real Thane," I reply sympathetically. "The real Thane is trying to save us both from this illusion."

"How do I know you are not the illusion?"

I tell her what Rhys told Amelia, about living only in the good times and never aging, never progressing in life like we should. "The illusion is that Thane was never broken, either. Do you remember that?"

Naida's face falls with deep sadness. "Yes. Now I do."

"Come with me, Naida. Please." I make my voice as gentle as I can. "So you can see the real Thane again." I doubt that it is possible, but I want it to be. For them both.

She presses her lips into a thin line. "Very well."

We are climbing down the tree when I remember something. "Naida, what is the Collector's name? Do you know it?"

47

THE KEEPER

Looking the Collector in the face, I am swept back to the branches of one of the trees Naida and I climbed as children. Naida herself gazes at me with great sadness and focus. She opens her lips.

Four words.

Her.

I am next to the rift again, but I can hear Naida's voice.

Name.

The Collector looms above me, head cocked.

Is.

Watching me drain away.

I open my lips.

"*Aileth.*"

48

TESS

Naida and Meredith are the only two of the six of us who can use magic, but Rhys believes it is enough.

At the base of Naida's tree, we stand in a circle and link hands.

"Focus on the Collector," Naida advises, "with all your mind. Meredith and I need you to do this while we work the spell to weaken her."

I lick my lips. And focus.

49

THE KEEPER

Her eyes widen, her lips part in the most emotion I have seen on that face in over one hundred years.

"*Aileth*," I repeat. "Free me."

I do not expect it to work, but the Collector raises her hand and casts the spell to release me from the rift.

The moment I am free, I snap my hand outward and release a magic blocking spell.

The Collector deflects it into the ground. With her other hand she unleashes a spell in my direction.

I roll forward and onto my feet. As I rise to my full height, another magic blocking spell erupts from my fingers. I grasp the Collector's right wrist and seal the spell.

But her other hand is still free. It strikes me in the head with a force that does not seem possible.

I crumple, my head splintering and spinning. Anguish rises in my throat. *I can't do it.*

The Collector looms over me. Her left hand reaches for her opposite wrist to free it.

Not knowing what else to do, I gasp, "Aileth, freeze."

She hesitates but does not stop. Instead she moves her hand toward me, magic shimmering around her fingers.

Vision still lurching, I lunge for her hand. One of my hands misses, but the other brushes against her cool skin. The shock of undirected magic that bursts from my fingers sends her staggering backwards. It buys me enough time to clamber to my feet and construct another magic blocking spell.

Something about her is off—she did not finish me off when she had the chance—it cannot just be the shock of me using her name.

I capitalize on it. I snatch her free wrist and slap the spell around it. Without pausing, I build yet more magic blocking spells and slam them around her neck and legs. Then I pin her against the wall. Words I have been waiting to say since being lost in her soul tumble from my lips. "You think that what other people have belongs to you. You believe that other *people* belong to you! Now you will have all that you deserve—*nothing but yourself.*" I press one palm against her forehead and the other against her sternum. "This is for Naida; for my mother and father; for my sister; for Adeka, for Damien, for Rhys; for everyone I have ever known, and for those I never knew," I whisper as I begin the spell. "You took them away from their lives, and now I can take magic away from you."

Doing so should not be possible. Yet it is. I learned it from the copper ring the ivy girl gave me.

I can barely construct the spell. The pieces resist my pulling them together, making my lips tremble as I speak the words, my hands waver as I sketch the glyphs, my mind crumple as I attempt to hold everything together.

But in the back of my mind, I cling to Tess. To her family. To the Aivar. To an inexhaustible list.

I feel the energy shimmering within and around the Collector. I feel it fade and fade. I feel it vanish.

Taking away her magic ends the spells she has running, including the ones holding Rhys, Tess, Naida, and the others hostage.

It also ends the spell tying her to Naida's body. I know it when the ticking stops and the rope in my mind breaks.

"No," I whisper as her body goes limp against me. "No, I didn't want to kill you! No, wake up!"

But it is too late. Aileth is gone.

I lower her to the ground. I brush her hair from her face and painfully turn away.

With the spell to force me to destroy the multiverse gone, I am safe to heal the rift. Safe to try, at least. And I have limited time, while the kindling moon remains.

I feel a twinge of apprehension, but it is swallowed by my pain.

I killed the Collector. I killed Aileth Rawls.

I turn to the rift and with the power of the kindling moon undulating within me, I heal the multiverse as best I can. The energy surges through me but does not overwhelm me. It is almost as though the multiverse knows I am here to help. Or perhaps it is the power of the Key bringing it under control. Either way, I do not even have the strength to be grateful, let alone fight the multiverse. Fight to survive.

When I am done, I turn back to Naida's body and collapse next to her. My head throbs. My body trembles. "Naida," I whisper. "Oh, Naida. Forgive me. I am so, so sorry." A hot tear trickles down my cheek.

I had intended to keep Naida from her own body by allowing the Collector to live. Then I had hoped that with Aileth gone, Naida might return to her body. But she has not.

50

— · —

TESS

When I wake, I find myself on the throne, the key to the ISERE on my hand and a corporeal Rhys lying motionless at my feet. My brain is muddled; I don't know what to make of this situation.

Eventually I form a thought: *Are we safe?*

The Keeper is huddled near the entryway.

I tense when I see the Collector in his arms.

But she is unmoving. And the Keeper is...crying?

Cautiously I stand and approach, my heart in my throat. *Keeper?* My lips form the word, but no sound escapes.

The Keeper's shoulders quake with sobs as he cradles the Collector's head against his chest. No, I realize, his friend's head. Naida's.

"*Tell him I forgive him.*"

"*Yes. I forgive him too. Let him know.*"

Reluctant to disturb him, I stand awkwardly off to the side.

Eventually the Keeper holds his hand before his face. The hand bears a silvery gauntlet. He removes the rings of the gauntlet one by one. Trance-like, he rises and sets the Key on the throne before taking Naida's still body back into his arms. He walks out of the Tomb and across the ivy-coated beach to the ocean. He steps into the water and continues in until the waves are rolling in over his waist.

I hurry after him into the ocean, afraid he may drown himself.

"May the waters carry you to your next journey." His voice is distant and thick. "May you find peace and rest in every destination, future and past. May you find the oceans calm and empty. Love and amity be with you." Tenderly, reluctantly, he lowers Naida into the waves.

Her body sinks beneath the water without another sign.

Still in some sort of trance, the Keeper turns back to the beach and returns to shore.

I remain standing in the ocean, unable to think or decide what to do.

After a long time, the Keeper reemerges from the Tomb, Rhys's body in his arms. He returns to the water and performs the same ritual for her. Afterward, he trudges back to shore.

I follow this time. "Keeper?" I murmur when we are back on the beach.

He does not respond, only removes a copper ring from his left pinky. For a moment he stares at it with such pain and resignation that I myself can feel it. Then he takes it and breaks it into two thinner rings. He places one ring in each palm and curls his fingers around them. When he unfurls his fingers, the rings have crumbled to dust that blows away in the wind. "No more magic," he mumbles vacantly.

Shock washes over me. "Keeper," I breathe. I place my hands on his arms. "I'm so sorry."

At those words, his breath hitches and tears well in his eyes. "Don't," he chokes. "Don't call me that, don't say you are sorry. I failed. I could not save them."

"Thane..."

He presses his quivering lip together, stares over my head. "I cannot even tell them I am sorry."

"*Tell him I forgive him.*"

"*Yes. I forgive him too. Let him know.*"

"Thane." I take his face in my hands, kiss one cheek. "Naida forgives you." I kiss his other cheek. "Rhys too. They *forgive you.*" I remember vaguely, distantly, hearing him apologize to me as well. "*I* forgive you. Okay?"

For the first time, he meets my gaze. "Truly?"

My heart breaks: he can't even believe me. "Truly," I affirm.

He takes a shaky breath as fresh tears pour down his cheeks. "Teresa," he says, and wraps me in a tight embrace, burying his face in my neck.

I hold him just as tightly as I try to hold back tears.

This broken man.

After only a few moments, the Keeper's—Thane's—knees buckle. All his weight falls on me.

I hold onto him, struggling to stay upright as I lower us to our knees. "Thane?"

He doesn't respond, but I can feel his breath on my skin.

Nervousness rises in me as I stare over him at the ivy-covered Tomb. How are we supposed to get to the ISERE now?

It is then, as I clutch him, that I see a face in the ivy draped over the Tomb: that of a little girl.

I grip Thane tighter, but she just smiles softly.

"I am not a threat. The two of you have done well. I will send you home."

I blink, and we are back in the ISERE.

Somehow I manage to get Thane into his bed.

I immediately forget the process and collapse onto a bench in the atrium the first chance I get, because I have become oh so tired. The fire in my chest, fueling me through to this point despite my not fully realizing its presence, seems to have burned out.

Seeing my family again—after Aileth Rawls the Collector had murdered them—doused the flame. Or maybe it was the act of leaving them that doused it.

I walked away from my family.

"There is no coming back to this, Tess."

I'm too worn out to cry.

Something in my gut tells me I shouldn't have walked away, that it wasn't worth it, that everything is fucked up now whether or not the Collector is dead. The rational part of my brain reminds me that I made the right choice to step back from the illusion of my family and help Rhys save the fucking multiverse, but *dammit, just a few more minutes would have been fine, they would have been wonderful, actually.*

I hunch my shoulders, close my eyes.

They're gone, they're all really gone, and Thane is passed out in his own loss, and I'm just lying on the bench, cold and alone and filled with ash.

51

THANE

I wake once. Numb. Empty. Missing a sense. I take a blanket and pillow from my bed—*how did I get here?*—and wander down to the engine room door. There, with the comforting, rhythmic pulse of the engine, I lie down and fall back asleep.

The next time I wake, I am less numb, but just as empty. Missing magic just as much.

Am I an abomination? I used the Collector's name against her. And then I killed her. How do I move on from this?

Perhaps Tess was right about how stopping the Collector, no mat-ter the method, would not me an abomination. The seed of doubt Tess planted in my conviction is now a seedling.

I recall Tess telling me that she, Rhys, and Naida forgive me. Per-haps it is time for more forgiveness someday. Self-forgiveness.

Eventually I find the strength to return to my bedroom to shower and change clothes. When I emerge, I feel a little less awful.

I also hear music: a ukulele and Tess's voice. I follow the sounds to the music room, the door of which is open. I lean against the doorframe and listen to the rest of the song, which is about a headrest for one's soul. I think I could use one of those.

Tess only notices my presence when the song ends. She blushes.

"That was beautiful."

She looks down at the wooden instrument. "Thank AWOLNATION. I mean, thank you." She clears her throat. "How are you feeling?" She blushes again. "Sorry. Stupid question."

I flick one hand outward. "I feel..." I sigh. "I feel as though I will finally be able to accept the losses I have endured. To move forward. To forgive myself. Someday." The knowledge weighs heavy on my heart. I will have to learn that moving forward is not letting go of those I have lost.

Tess nods. "I think I feel the same way."

That is all either of us says for a while.

"What happened to the Tomb?" she eventually asks. I can see the beautiful brown of her eyes from here as she gazes at me. "Can anyone else enter it and control it now?"

I shake my head. "I disconnected the Tomb's plane of existence from this dimension's physical component of the Tomb when I brought out Rhys...her body, I mean."

Sympathy and empathy shadow Tess's eyes. "I'm sorry, Thane. I know how much she meant to you."

I twist my mouth, and a ring around my finger. I clear my throat. "You and the others saved my life, didn't you?"

Tess shrugs. "We tried to distract her. Overpower her, I guess. I don't know how much we managed to do. She was—powerful."

I cross to a nearby chair and sit next to her. "But don't you see, Tess? You truly were stronger than the Collector."

"But it wasn't *me*, if that's true. The others were there too. I almost couldn't—didn't do it, but they helped."

"Ah," I say. "As long as all of you were a part of her—belonged to her, as she thought it—she believed your collective strength did not matter."

Tess looks at her ukulele, then at me. "You really think we helped?"

"I know you did."

She smiles a little. "So, Thane. Now that all this is over, what are we going to do?"

I grin; I cannot help it, something about hearing my name in Tess's voice and knowing that there is someone I have not yet lost fills me with such elation, despite everything.

Tess smiles back. "What are you grinning at?"

I want to throw my arms around her, kiss her forehead. "'*We*.'"

Life awaits.

ACKNOWLEDGMENTS

I have a lot of people to thank for supporting me throughout the years this story has been in progress. I won't name you all, but it does not mean I appreciate you any less.

I'll start with the people who have been here the since the beginning. Kate, Mom, Grandma.

Now for some of those who have given support that has been just as meaningful, though I didn't know you at the time this idea was first conceived. All my friends. You mean so much to me.

Of course I must thank each of my beta readers. Your feedback and input have proven invaluable.

Another group I need to thank is the group of people from the local library system's book-writing boot camp; your different perspectives as writers, and not just readers, I deeply appreciate. Honorable mentions to Ann, who advised me on so much of the publishing process; Jean; and Lottie, for connecting me with beta readers.

I also want to thank my editors. My developmental editor and sensitivity reader, Larissa Melo Pienkowski. My copy editor, Rebecca Brewer. My proofreader and formatter, Heather Hudec.

I appreciate anyone who has helped this story come to life.

ABOUT THE AUTHOR

Mallory Spencer, from southeastern Ohio, lives in Wisconsin with her wily cat of many names. Alongside writing books, she writes and produces her own fantasy comedy podcast, *Midnight on Mercy Mountain*.

TRIGGER WARNINGS

Death

Self-harm

Suicidal ideation

Suicide attempt

Queerphobia (specifically, acephobia, arophobia, biphobia)

Violence

www.ingramcontent.com/pod-product-compliance
Lightning Source LLC
Chambersburg PA
CBHW032154190626
46814CB00005BA/1997